W9-CLV-450

Also by Carol O'Brien Blum
Diderot: The Virtue of a Philosopher

Anne's Head

Anne's Head

Carol O'Brien Blum

The Dial Press
New York

ASBURY PARK PUBLIC LIBRARY
ASBURY PARK, NEW JERSEY

Published by
The Dial Press
1 Dag Hammarskjold Plaza
New York, New York 10017

Copyright © 1982 by Carol O'Brien Blum

All rights reserved.

Manufactured in the United States of America
Second Printing
Design by Francesca Belanger

Library of Congress Cataloging in Publication Data

Blum, Carol, 1934–
Anne's head.
I.   Title.
PS3552.L835A83   813'.54   81–9859
ISBN 0–385–27207–3   AACR2

To Martin, Asher, and Agnes
this book is lovingly dedicated

I would like to express my gratitude to Frederick Brown, Anthony Rizzuto, and Bette Weidman for their wonderfully helpful readings of this book in manuscript form. Thanks are also due to the Missouri Historical Society for its cooperation in searching out arcane bits of St. Louis's past for me.

St. Louis,
August 1902

1

JAMES O'BRIEN, painter of saints, madonnas, martyrs, and Stations of the Cross for the interiors of parish churches, not to mention an occasional civic mural of Osage Indians presenting corn to a French settler—he who had never in his career entered an expensive restaurant by the front door—should not have undertaken Tony Faust's Four Seasons.

The thing had gone badly. The aloofly sublime feminine countenances in which Mr. O'Brien specialized, admired by Tony Faust in the nave of St. John Nepomuk, looked implausible on the walls of his dining establishment as they haughtily stared over the blossoms, grapes, leaves, and snowy branches illustrating Spring, Summer, Fall, and Winter. To Mr. Faust their cold glances bespoke repentance and abstinence rather than conviviality and indulgence.

He asked the artist to soften the expressions of the four allegorical maidens, suggested entwining their hair into the foliage as was fashionable in pictures then. Mr. O'Brien expressed reservations about the conjunction of hair and grapes where food was being served.

Again Mr. Faust pondered the pious visages on his walls. He turned back to the artist, a hint of desperation in his voice. "What about if I hire models for you, James, and you do them over? Pat Short is a customer of mine. He can get us girls from the Gayety."

"I could never look at strange women that way, Mr.

Faust," Mr. O'Brien replied dejectedly. "Let me try them once more. I'm sure I can make them more beguiling."

He added color to their cheeks and highlights to their eyes. The results, James thought, were unsatisfactory; the virginal faces now seemed febrile in their sanctity. Mr. Faust toyed with the idea of wallpaper.

One afternoon in late August, as the artist was still laboring, a photograph in the *St. Louis Post-Dispatch* caught the attention of Mr. Faust. "Look, James!" he cried, thrusting the newspaper into Mr. O'Brien's hands. "Aren't these your daughters? Isn't that your Kathleen that I met at the graduation picnic at Tower Grove Park?"

"So it is," Mr. O'Brien answered, surprised. "Mamie and Margaret, too."

They looked at the photograph together. The caption read: THREE LOVELY LADIES TRYING FALL HATS.

"How old are they?" Mr. Faust inquired.

"Oh," Mr. O'Brien replied, "Mamie just had her eighteenth birthday. Margaret is twenty-one, and Kathleen is a year younger."

"Our Seasons, James!" cried Mr. Faust. "All we need now is a fourth as pretty as these!"

"I do have a fourth," James O'Brien replied thoughtfully. "Anne, the oldest of the lot and the finest-looking one, too. Many's the time I've drawn Anne, to please her mother. Mrs. O'Brien thinks she looks like a great lady, and she had me do her likeness in the robes of a queen." He smiled at the recollection and then, suddenly embarrassed, added, "It was only a little joke and did no harm."

The two men stood staring at the graceful profiles in the picture. "Well, what do you say?" Mr. Faust asked. "Are these our Seasons or not?"

"Why," said Mr. O'Brien after a moment's hesitation, "perhaps they might be at that. Annie could make a grand Summertime."

One day the following week James O'Brien put down his brushes and looked about the private dining room of Tony Faust's Restaurant to see the dark heads of Mamie and Margaret and the golden ones of Kathleen and Anne regarding him tranquilly from their respective foliage. For a moment the father and the artist in him fused, producing a shimmering sensation of compounded pride. If Mr. Faust desired charm, surely now he would find it, smiling down on him from all four walls of the room.

What would Mrs. O'Brien say! That thought destroyed his brief euphoria. Mrs. O'Brien would say he had gone mad. Mr. O'Brien slumped on his scaffold, overcome with confusion. He should never have ventured from the chaste saints and continent Indians of his imagination. He could not leave recognizable portraits of his daughters to preside benignly over the drinking clientele of a public house. Nor could he brush out the faces and bolt through the door, as he felt inclined to do.

He decided to attempt disguising them. Working quickly, he changed the titian gold hair of Anne and Kathleen to a pale blondness, he lightened Margaret's and Mamie's hair to brown, he widened mouths and nostrils a bit wildly, and in a last desperate turn around the room before Mr. Faust arrived to take possession, he darkened the four pairs of blue eyes to black.

When Mr. Faust entered the dining room the Four Seasons smiled at him almost seductively, especially the black-eyed blondes, whose unusual coloring lent a faint nuance of perversity that relieved him no end. So pleased was he at not being stuck with a chapel that in addition to the one hundred dollars he had paid Mr. O'Brien he sent around a dozen silver roses to the four daughters the next day, with an invitation to the whole family to attend the opening-night party as his guests.

Kathleen received the flowers at the front door of the

big house on Washington Avenue and excitedly read the
card:

Mr. Tony Faust
requests the pleasure of your company
to celebrate the opening of three new rooms:
The Fountain Plaza
The Mosaic Salon
The Hall of the Four Seasons

Saturday, August 30, at 9:00 P.M.
Broadway at Elm Street

Before Mr. O'Brien descended from his third-floor studio
to dine that evening, the invitation had been accepted and
the young women were deeply engrossed with their
mother in planning the costumes to be worn. Mr. O'Brien
objected that such parties were not for the likes of them at
all; his voice went unheard amid the excited chatter over
voiles, tulles, and moiré silks. He retired dispiritedly to
take his supper alone, as he always did, at a table in the
kitchen. Mrs. O'Brien served him his meal herself before
Vesta, the scrub girl, wheeled the bulk of the food into the
dining room to be distributed to the family. Mr. O'Brien
found the noise and vitality generated by his progeny intolerable; it fatigued him to imagine them all in one place,
much less to experience such a gathering.

In the dining room Mrs. O'Brien presided at the foot of
the table, while Will faced her from the head. The mother
and oldest son were a handsome pair—two large, black-
haired beings whose flesh seemed carved from pink granite. The commandingly stern blue gaze they shared served
them both well. Mrs. O'Brien used it to cow her brood
and Will found it effective in his work. He was a policeman. Between these two pillars of righteousness—mother-

hood and the law—four young women, the Seasons, lined one side of the table, while the "rag-taggle" boys filled up the other. "Rag-taggle," a derisive aunt of Mr. O'Brien's had called them, describing what she saw as an undistinguished litter. The word was flung at the five from time to time as a shoe might be tossed at yowling cats. "Only their mother can tell them apart," she had commented. Mrs. O'Brien, however, did not often bother to do so. After the grand Will and the glorious girls her interest in her offspring had flagged. She saw to the daily needs of the five younger boys, but she seldom invested them with her attention. Each one seemed less impressive than his elders, more freckled and nappy-haired, slighter in all ways. Yet the same acerbic aunt had pointed out differences between them: James, seventeen, was dim; John, sixteen, brash; Owen, fourteen, impertinent; Thomas, thirteen, fey; and Frank, eleven, terrified. All but Frank were working full time; only Will and the girls had been to high school.

The young women, Will, and Mrs. O'Brien enjoyed animated conversations among themselves at supper; the rag-taggle giggled and kicked one another under the table until their commotion irritated a grown-up and they were temporarily silenced.

On the evening Mr. Faust's invitation arrived, the feminine side of the table was pleasurably agitated. The prospect of being seen at a fashionable party stirred the girls' imaginations deeply; they planned how they would enter Tony Faust's Restaurant resplendent, preceded by their parents and escorted by Will. It was a pity that Mr. O'Brien was so slight a figure. It would not, however, spoil the effect; the girls would command all eyes.

As the O'Brien girls left the house five nights later, large hats wobbling slightly on elaborately coiffed heads, their graceful necks seemed almost too fragile to support such beauty. Their gowns, the products of four evenings' feverish cutting, fitting, and sewing, were made of silk muslin, ranging in shades from gold to green. Mr. and Mrs. O'Brien, as always, wore black. The rag-taggle watched in awe. At the last moment Mamie turned and bestowed a kiss on Frank's cheek while Kathleen protested shrilly that she would surely soil her white gloves touching his hair.

Their arrival at the restaurant was less rewarding than they had anticipated. They had to wait as their hired cab inched up Broadway toward the entrance, which was brilliantly illuminated in primary colors by a famous gas fixture Mr. Faust had installed. The late summer heat was oppressive, and the presence of a great many fine carriages subdued the O'Briens further. Mr. O'Brien in particular appeared wan and ill at ease.

When finally it was their turn to alight, they found themselves wedged into a crowd of well-dressed guests who seemed to know one another. Many of the women were strikingly got up—some with real jewels besides. They were ignored in the crush and deafened by the orchestra and the noisy throng as it flowed into the main reception room, where the new fountain splashed champagne that evening.

Mr. Faust himself finally rescued them from the corner to which they had retreated. He led them to a row of chairs in the Hall of the Four Seasons, had them served wine, and expressed his appreciation of the artist and his decorations. James O'Brien managed to slide his chair partially behind a potted palm tree, peered nervously through the fronds, and hoped that no one would notice any resemblance between the ladies on the walls and those on the chairs. Will stood before them, his arms behind his back, admirable in his cutaway. His slightly rocking posture, however, somehow suggested that he was there to keep an eye on the silver.

The girls had all been "out" before. They had attended weddings and birthday parties, parish functions, a concert, several stage plays, and balls given by the Hibernians, the DiAndries, the Knights of Columbus, and the Knights of Father Mathew.

They had, however, never before found themselves in such company as this. Tony Faust's three new rooms were filled with society figures and politicians, with well-known ball players, actresses, and leaders of the underworld; the beau monde of St. Louis had turned out for the occasion in force.

The crowd drifted noisily in and out of the room. To Mr. O'Brien's relief, no one paused to linger before the decorations. Mr. Faust, solicitous, leaned over them for a moment, pointing out celebrities.

"See the bald fellow standing under the electric fan? That's Judge Robertson. And the big one next to him—do you recognize him, James?"

"Isn't that Walter Fletcher from the Cardinals?" Mr. O'Brien asked. "I saw his picture in the paper." But Mr. Faust's gaze had turned toward the staircase at the front of the room, where a group of newly arrived young people were being greeted enthusiastically. A dark-haired man stood laughing on the stairs with a girl on each arm, his white silk scarf still about his throat. His companions' powdered Oriental faces were identical.

"It's Chris Schneider—son of a gun!" Mr. Faust exclaimed. "Wouldn't you know it? He brought the Wong Sisters from the Gayety!" The restaurant owner moved quickly through the crowd and disappeared into the knot of revelers forming around the new arrivals.

"Who did Mr. Faust say that was, Father?" Anne asked,

leaning across her sister to put a hand on Mr. O'Brien's arm.

Before Mr. O'Brien could reply, a pair of gentlemen appeared and asked Anne and Kathleen to dance. Mamie and Margaret soon followed their sisters onto the floor; Mr. O'Brien was so emboldened by the music, the wine, and the general air of bacchanal that he led his wife to the ballroom, grasped her firmly about the waist, and put himself to waltzing her around with all the rest.

Margaret's partner, a perspiring younger son of a beer fortune, attempted a pleasantry. "Say now, Margie. How is it that you don't speak with a brogue?" Margaret stopped dancing abruptly, released his hand, and, looking him squarely in the eye, said, "Come with me, if you please." She made her way through the crowd, her bewildered partner behind her, and, pointing to a chair, said, "You may sit down there." He did as he was bid. Margaret stood, her arms folded across her bosom, looking down upon the hapless young man. "You asked me a question," she said. "I'll answer it with three of my own. First, what gives you the right to interrogate me in that insolent way? Will you answer me that? And for another thing, what makes you think you may call me 'Margie'? My name is Margaret, and to you it's Miss O'Brien. The third question is this: What has ever given you to believe that cultivated persons born in America of Irish descent speak with a brogue? Satisfy me on these points, please." The only reply he offered was a mumbled "I beg your pardon" as he slunk off between the dancers.

Margaret sat down on the chair he had vacated, cheeks flushed, bright blue eyes ablaze, smiling to herself as she repeated in her mind her magnificently constructed rout of the insufferable brewer's son. She was looking forward to recounting it in the carriage on the way home to her admiring family—especially to Kathleen, who could be made to scream with laughter in the most gratifying way. So radiant did Margaret appear, transported in her imagination, that another young man, mistaking her air of good spirits for friendliness, soon led her back on the floor.

Anne, too, had freed herself of a tedious partner; she arranged her features into a rather forbiddingly cold expression, not wishing to be bothered with unwanted invitations to dance. She slipped her way back into the Hall of the Four Seasons and paused in the doorway when she saw Chris Schneider. She watched his elegant figure with fixed eyes as he made a deliberate tour of the decorations high on the walls. Slowly he approached where she was standing and suddenly lowered his gaze to meet hers. "Come, Summertime," he said, the smile gone from his dark face. "This is our waltz." She took his arm without a word. They stepped onto the floor as the orchestra played the opening rhythmic strains of "Mein Lebenslauf ist Lieb und Lust." They danced together for the rest of the evening. While Margaret indignantly dressed down one partner after another, while Kathleen's melting body and languorous eyes enflamed a manufacturer of iron castings, a bookmaker, and two members of the St. Louis Bachelors' Club, while Mamie dreamily contemplated a variety of indistinguishable partners through her myopic blue eyes, while Will whirled a Miss Geraldine Faust about the floor, while Mr. and Mrs. O'Brien retreated to their corner in dignity, Anne was held and moved in the arms of Chris Schneider. He handed her into the cab at the evening's end.

On the way home Margaret regaled the family with her devastating retorts to various gallant sallies that had been addressed to her during the evening. She mimicked the consternation of her partners so drolly that Kathleen was soon screeching and gasping. Even Mrs. O'Brien smiled.

"And who did you dance with, Mamie?" Margaret asked when her own tale had wound down.

"Oh," said Mamie, "some fine fellows."

"But what were their names? What did they look like?"

Mamie leaned her head back against the seat and laughed. "I don't know about names, Margie," she said gently. "And anyway, I couldn't hear what they were saying, it was so noisy and all."

Kathleen began to tremble with indignation. She grasped her sister's arm and exclaimed, "How did you talk to them if you couldn't hear what they were saying?"

"Ah, well," Mamie replied. "I just look up at them and smile when they talk, or else I say yes and laugh. It always seems to please them. Then I don't have to trouble myself listening to their nonsense."

"Mamie," Will said, "do you say yes to everything a fellow asks? What if he wants a kiss?"

"Then I'll get a look at his face as it comes toward me, because otherwise all I see is some collar buttons and a lapel. I'm that blind without my glasses. I don't know whether I waltzed with the Prince of Wales tonight or the King of the Toads!"

The hilarity was so great over Mamie's attitude toward her partners that Mrs. O'Brien had to quiet her children. "You're overwrought, the lot of you," she said. Anne alone sat quietly in a corner of the carriage, staring out the window at the shadowy summertime streets of St. Louis going by.

They entered the house still savoring the party, and when everyone else had finally gone to bed, Will and his mother sat up in the kitchen, talking over a cup of tea. Will, in an expansive mood, told his mother about his work on the recently formed vice detail. He recounted things that could not be discussed before the other members of the family. He liked his mother's astonishment at what went on in the world, and, even better, he liked her outrage.

"There's a fellow, name of Henderson," he told her, "some kind of law professor up in Boston. He recommends, see, that not only the women should be arrested, but them that frequents the women as well. He says there cannot be a criminal commerce where only one of the parties is guilty. He says run in the men too and we'll soon see an end to all the vice. There is talk of a city ordinance, but the men I know say it will come to nothing. Mike Egan says it would do a world of good. For myself now, I can see it in one way, but in another way, for the life of me, I can't see it at all." He watched his mother's face for her reaction.

"It's a fine plan!" she said, to his surprise. "Run them all in, reprobates and hussies alike, but never put them in jail at all, Will—it's a waste of time. Gilly-teen the lot of them like the French do!" They burst out laughing together, Will repeating his mother's words and wiping his eyes with his handkerchief. He repeated his mother's recommendation at Headquarters the following week, where it caused much amusement.

Upstairs everyone was sleeping except Frank, the youngest boy, squeezed in a double bed between Owen and Tom. He had been crying since Vesta had turned out the lights. Owen had tricked him again, promising him the side of the bed in exchange for a penny Frank had found. He handed over the penny, but at bedtime Owen had pushed him into the middle anyway. Now he could not move in either direction without encountering a piece of big brother; he felt stifled with rage. Out of twelve people, thirteen including Vesta, he was the only one who did not have even an edge of bed to call his own. His sisters had two bedrooms, a bathroom, and a hair-dressing alcove with running water all to themselves, to say nothing of their sewing room, which was forbidden to the boys. Will had his own room, while all five younger boys were crammed into one nasty space like animals in a cage. Frank couldn't even find a mirror to water down his wiry hair. He was not allowed into the sewing room, the bathroom mirror was a foot over his head, and if he got caught combing his hair before the one in the foyer he was denounced by his sisters for leaving spots on the glass. And then they mocked him for having hair like an overgrown hedge! And Sister, at school, pulled it hard almost every time she walked down his row.

He soothed himself with his favorite daydream. When he was grown and a world-renowned pugilist, he would have a house of his own. He and his big-bosomed wife would sleep all alone in one large bed while their son, an only child, slept like a prince in his room on the other side of the house. That would be the lot. He could kiss the wife or tickle her whenever he pleased, she would never have a mouth full of pins, nor would she ever push him away and say, "Be off now with your silliness." Comforted, he fell asleep.

2

THE NEXT MORNING at six thirty, when Mrs. O'Brien, Mamie, Margaret, and Will were leaving the house for Mass, they were surprised to see Anne emerge from the bedroom dressed in her best pearl-gray silk dress, missal and beads in hand. Never in anyone's memory had Anne been ready for a Mass before ten thirty, and many was the Sunday she never went to church at all.

"What has possessed you, Anne O'Brien, to bestir yourself at this hour?" her mother asked.

"I woke up early, is all," she said, and not a word more on the walk to St. Francis Xavier. She dreamed through the service. She did not even exchange glances with her sisters when the false chignon Rosie Joyce was wearing in the pew ahead quivered and suddenly toppled back into Mrs. O'Brien's lap. It was not that she was controlling her giggles—she was merely unaware of what had happened before her very eyes. Mamie nudged Margaret, but Margaret put a finger to her lips. They would have a good laugh outside the church when mass was over.

A more diverting spectacle, however, was commanding the attention of the sparse crowd on the steps of the church when the O'Briens came out. A bright red automobile was stopped at the curb, its engine idling noisily.

"What kind is it, Will?" asked Margaret.

"It's a Dion-Bouton," he replied. "The new 'type G' that does thirty miles an hour."

"Look at them gawking like Hoosiers at a fair," said Mrs. O'Brien. "Let us be on our way now."

A man in goggles, britches, and riding boots emerged from the Dion-Bouton. Anne suddenly thrust her missal and beads into her mother's hand and said, "I'll be off now with Chris Schneider, Mother. Don't expect me home until late." She ran down the steps and was handed into the automobile by its driver, who manipulated the steering column levers, eased his vehicle into gear, and sputtered down Lindell Boulevard.

The parishioners of St. Francis Xavier looked inquiringly toward the astonished O'Briens. Mrs. O'Brien, noting their curiosity, turned to her family and said loudly enough to be overheard, "Haven't they a glorious day for their outing! Let us only hope there will be no rain. Come now, I have breakfast to get. Good day, Father Degnan. Good morning to you, Biddie McBride."

Slowly moving to the sidewalk, greeting neighbors and acquaintances, she ushered her flock out of the crowd. A block from the church Mamie started to speak, but her mother silenced her. "Not a word until we're within our own four walls. And have a care to the look on your face," she whispered to her daughter.

In the foyer of her house Mrs. O'Brien closed the front door and abruptly sagged against it. "In the name of God," she whispered, "what has happened to my girl?" They accompanied her into the front room, where she seated herself upon the settee, while Mamie fetched her a glass of cold water. Mr. O'Brien emerged from the kitchen and was told of Anne's sudden flight. He perched gingerly next to his wife, patting her arm, while she drank the water and regained her composure.

"Is Chris Schneider the fellow Anne was taken up with last evening?" she asked.

"That's the one," said Will. "They must have planned to

go off this morning even while the band was still playing last night."

"Do you know him at all, Will?" his mother asked.

"Not at all," he replied.

"The thing I don't understand," said Mamie sadly, "is why she said never a word about it. Why does she have to be so close? She could have just told us that she was going for a ride with Chris Schneider after Mass."

"Who ever heard of going for a ride in an automobile at eight o'clock on a Sunday morning—" Will exclaimed, "and won't be back until late? Where are they riding, to hell and back, I would like to know?"

"Will," said his mother, "do you know this fellow at all?"

"I told you, Mother," he replied, "I do not."

Kathleen emerged from her bedroom, hair tumbling down her face, struggling unsuccessfully to close a robe over her nightdress. "What on earth is this about?" she cried. "Why is Father in the front room? What has happened? Oh, dear God!"

Mrs. O'Brien stood up briskly. "Margaret," she said, "take your sister back to her room and shut her mouth. Mamie, please go to the kitchen and start breakfast. Will, be so kind as to tell your brothers to get dressed quickly or they will be late for eight-thirty Mass. James, let us retire to our room and talk this over."

The day seemed to pass slowly. The boys were given carfare and sent off to the Alexian Brothers to visit patients without family. Frank protested that he wanted to stay in his room and read instead. "Shame on you," his mother scolded, holding open the door for him. "What of the poor sick who have no one?"

The five boys walked up Washington Avenue together until they were out of their mother's sight. Then Jim ducked down Jefferson to find a drink and John hopped a trolley to call on a fast girl he knew. Frank, Owen, and Tom paid a token visit to the Brothers but spent much of the afternoon in the grass at Tower Grove Park.

At home the adults conversed in twos and threes, quietly. Kathleen was heard weeping from upstairs and then laughing loudly. Mrs. O'Brien sighed and said to her husband, "If it was that one I shouldn't have been surprised. But Anne has always kept her head on her shoulders."

Mr. O'Brien looked up from his newspaper with a start, remembering it was Anne's head on the wall at Tony Faust's Restaurant that had brought Chris Schneider to her, but his wife did not seem to be reproaching him. He returned to his newspaper thoughtfully. The name Chris Schneider was somehow familiar to him. Mr. O'Brien had but one recreational pastime—he read the newspapers every day. Not just one, but on occasion as many as half a dozen. He did not read them the way other men did, skimming the headlines and then turning to the sports or the financial pages. He read newspapers the way an assiduous scholar reads an essential text. He began on page one, made his way to page two, and laboriously read every word, including advertisements, until he had finished the last page. Then he put the paper down, considered the day's events, and picked up another from the pile next to his chair in the kitchen. Sometimes he cut items out, carefully dated them, and placed them in a cardboard box marked CLIPPINGS.

His infrequent contributions to family conversations tended to take the form of factual references to the question at hand. Thus, when Will told him how Anne had ridden off in the Dion-Bouton, Mr. O'Brien pointed out that there were 176 automobiles operating in St. Louis that year, of which more than a third were of foreign manufacture. The family considered the information in respectful silence. Mr. O'Brien's children believed that he knew everything about events in St. Louis and, for that matter, happenings throughout the world.

By supper time Anne still had not appeared. When Frank asked where she was, all the adults told him in unison to mind his own affairs. The edgy atmosphere continued through the evening. After the dishes were done, Kathleen and Margaret decided abruptly that the ragtaggle boys' hair was intolerably woolly and that they were to be shorn immediately in the bathroom. Jim refused, saying that since he was earning good wages at the brewery his hair was now his and not theirs and that he would pay for his own haircut at the barber shop. Even Kathleen's enraged wails failed to move him. Owen and Tom crouched in the chifforobe, behind the clothes, hiding the bone scissors and Mamie's eyeglasses. John was nowhere to be found. Frank approached the by now frenzied Kathleen and timidly volunteered to have his hair cut. She agreed, although in principle he was supposed to be attended to last.

Frank enjoyed his sisters' ministrations—their pinning a towel around his neck, looking at him, chiding him, touching his head with their hands, grazing his shoulders with their bodies. Tonight, however, even this pleasant ritual was disturbed by the eruption of a quarrel between the sisters. Mamie fumbled through drawers and cabinets for her bone scissors until Margaret, impatient, reached for the steel sewing shears.

"Margie," Mamie cried. "What are you doing? You know you dasn't cut his hair with iron!"

Margaret turned to Mamie, red-faced. "This is now the twentieth century, Mamie, and in the twentieth century people cut their hair with iron every day and live to tell the tale. You're a worse old washerwoman than Mrs. Mahoney with your bone scissors. You make me tired." She grasped Frank firmly by the forelock and cut it off in one steel stroke. Mamie moaned, bit her lip, and went to cry in her bedroom. Frank closed his eyes and held his breath. Not only was his strength all flowing out from the cut ends, but Margaret was clipping so rapidly that he was fairly suffocated with hair. A sudden noise from the front hall and Margaret stopped cutting, dropped the shears, and ran from the bathroom.

Anne had come home.

Frank took a look at himself in the hand mirror. The left half of his head was cropped close in ill-assorted tufts, while the right half was still sticking up inches above his scalp. He supposed Margaret would come back and even things up. He was certain to be criticized if he went downstairs as he was. He settled back onto the high stool to wait.

Anne stood in the foyer, unpinning her hat before the cheval glass.

"Anne," said Mrs. O'Brien, "please come into the front room and sit down."

Anne turned slowly and with a beguiling smile answered, "Mother, I'm so tired I can scarcely stand. I never should have let Chris Schneider take me to the Forest Park Cottage for ice cream after dinner. And me having to get up at six tomorrow to go to work! I'm straight to bed now, as I am, without even washing my face! Kiss me good night, Mama." She embraced Mrs. O'Brien and was upstairs in one movement.

Her mother stared after her uncertainly, then slowly rejoined her husband and Will in the front room.

"I thought I heard Anne come in," Mr. O'Brien said, looking up from his paper.

"So you did, James. She has gone to bed, and I think we should all do the same." She took her husband's arm. "It may be a great alarm over nothing. He only bought her ice cream. Perhaps it can all be explained."

"How did she seem?" he asked.

"She was not herself."

The couple climbed the stairs together.

Margaret, Kathleen, a red-eyed Mamie, and Will huddled together until the clock struck midnight and then moved to retire themselves. Kathleen uttered a scream when she lighted the lamp in the bathroom to find Frank asleep on the hair-littered floor.

"What are you after here? In the middle of the night!" She shook the sleepy boy and cried, "You might have been a robber to murder us in our beds!"

"Oh, no, Kathleen," he protested, "I never did at all!" He was confused, awakening from his uneasy slumber to stand trial surrounded by shouting big sisters in the bathroom.

"Out of here now—you're a terrible disgrace!" Kathleen shoved him toward the bathroom door.

He paused, however, before the mirror, and glimpsing his semitonsured reflection, set up a howl of his own. "Margie said she would even me and now look at what she done to me!"

Margaret experienced an overwhelming revulsion at the sight of the squalling brat, the hairy floor, the hysterical Kathleen, and the limp Mamie, who had grasped her beads and taken refuge behind the linen closet door when the fracas began.

"I'll even you up all right," she said grimly, clutching Frank by his remaining locks and picking up her shears again. Frank wailed like a siren.

Anne's voice could be heard raised in protest from the far bed: "Please quiet down in there! How can I sleep? You're enough to wake the dead!"

As Kathleen yelped in indignation and threatened to pull Anne out of bed herself, a tight-lipped Mrs. O'Brien, clad in a bathrobe, appeared in the doorway and silence fell.

She stared coldly at each of them in turn, her gaze finally resting on Frank. "Come," she said, putting an arm around his shoulders. "Come to bed now—it's after twelve. Tomorrow before you go to Mack's I will finish your hair, and it will be a good job, too. The rest of you," she said, eyeing her daughters, "stay just as you are until I return. Don't move!"

She led her son into the rag-taggle room and gazed reflectively at the bed where Frank slept. It was occupied totally by the sprawling Owen and Tom. "Ah, well," she said, and gently but firmly rolled Owen into the middle and then, with her strong arms and hands, placed the somnolent Frank beneath the warm cover.

"Thank you, Mama," he whispered.

"You are welcome, I am sure. Good night." But at the door she paused and returned to his bedside and, to his joy, placed her lips against his cheek for a lingering kiss. "Good night, bonny boy," she said, touching his face, using the endearment she had pressed into service for all her sons when they were babies. Frank lay on the side of the bed, wondering at how unexpectedly the worst had become the best.

When Mrs. O'Brien returned to the bathroom she told Mamie to go to bed. "This regards you two," she said to Kathleen and Margaret, who were at that point weak from the day's tensions and distempers. "Now, Margaret O'Brien," she said, "I want you to know that you are never to touch a human being when you are angry. You picked up a shears and attacked that child's hair in temper. You, Kathleen, wrenched his arm and pushed him. No, I saw you! I tell you that I have raised ten children and I never once resorted to the rod nor the strap nor the back of my hand either. And nobody is going to lay violent hands on my child while God leaves breath in my body. The door of this house is open to those who disapprove of my ways. Good night to the both of you.

"And one more thing," she added, turning toward them again. "You two elegant young ladies—you should know that in this country, in this century, there are those who place all Irish people together with the worst trash from the Patch. Your father read to me from the paper where some Protestants have a club called the APA, against the Irish, and say they're not fit for society. And why? Because of the reputation for quick-tempered violence, and also for drink, which problem, Glory be to God, I have not yet encountered in this family. So if you want to label yourselves as brawling filth, raising your voices and venting your displeasure, oblige me by finding other premises to do it in. I say good night to you." She left the room.

In their bed a few minutes later, Margaret and Kathleen whispered frantically.

"To denounce us! To call us names! And not a word to that brazen creature with the black circles under her eyes!" Kathleen wept herself to sleep.

After a few tears of her own, Margaret began considering ways of controlling the rage that sometimes mounted in her. She thought that on the next Saturday she would consult Father Degnan. She had once done nine Fridays for the special intention of curbing her gluttony, and she had got the better of it.

The next morning at seven, after Mass, when Mrs. O'Brien was frying mounds of potatoes and sausages for the family breakfast, Mamie seated herself at the kitchen table and exclaimed in surprise, "Look! My eyeglasses! The bone scissors! Where ever did they come from?"

Owen pinched Tom and replied innocently, "The little gentleman brought them in, Mame, and laid them right on your plate. Didn't you see him?"

"Indeed I did not. What little gentleman has to do with my glasses and my scissors?"

Her mother placed a hot bowl on the table and said, "Stop your nonsense now and eat your breakfast. Your brothers will be coming down and wanting theirs." The kitchen table accommodated only six, so they did not all take their morning meal together.

"Oh, Mame, he was a darling little fellow! And certainly not a child, because he wore a beard and a straw hat. But how tall would you say he was, Tom?" Tom, choking on his effort not to laugh, decided to risk a wrenching cough instead, as a diversionary tactic. Mrs. O'Brien slammed down a bowl of hot cooked peaches and told them to hurry, if they were ever to get to work on time.

"About this tall, I would judge," said Tom, lowering his hand to a foot above the floor, "although it was hard to tell with that little dance he was doing." Mamie adjusted her glasses on her nose and peered at her brother's hand.

"Mary O'Brien," said her mother, "are you such a simpleton that two flippant schoolboys can flummox you like that?"

"I'm not a schoolboy!" Owen protested.

"Is it being a simpleton to believe your own flesh and blood when they speak to you?" Mamie asked.

Mr. O'Brien looked up from his plate of toast and remarked, "The smallest fully formed man who ever lived was not P. T. Barnum's Tom Thumb but another fellow entirely."

Will, Kathleen, Frank, and Margaret entered the kitchen together, and Will asked, "Where is Anne?"

Mrs. O'Brien, her back to the table replied, "Gone. Go,

boys, up the steps and get dressed now." When Owen and Tom had left the kitchen, she turned around, her face unexpectedly pinched. She described how she had encountered Anne leaving the house as she was returning from early Mass.

"I was that surprised to see her up and abroad at such an hour. She said the telephone company asked her and some of the other operators to come in early. So I said to have a bite of breakfast and she said no, she'd miss the trolley, and out she went. So I followed her to the sidewalk and watched her. At the corner of Compton Avenue, who should come along but Chris Schneider, in his automobile, and she hops right in. And *then*, what do you suppose?" Her voice dropped lower and she glanced nervously at the kitchen door. "He put his arms around her and kissed her right on the mouth!"

"Holy Mother of God," Kathleen gasped. "What happened then?"

"Off they went," said Mrs. O'Brien, "south on Compton, and wouldn't you know, Mrs. Mahoney was scrubbing her stoop and taking in the whole spectacle."

"For the Kinloch company you go straight down Washington—you don't need to turn any which way," said Will morosely.

Margaret, subdued from the exertions of the previous day, nevertheless put forth her opinion. "Isn't it time someone took a stand here? Shouldn't we talk to Anne and find out about this Schneider? We'll be the nine-day wonder of Francis Xavier if this continues unchecked."

Mrs. O'Brien looked thoughtfully at the iron stove and then at the members of the family still in the kitchen. "Frank," she said, "aren't you carrying for Mr. Mack today? It's almost eight."

"Mother, you said you would even my hair."

"Slick it down with water and I'll even it when you come home for lunch. Go now."

Frank left the kitchen with the seeds of revolt in his heart. Now it was his own mother, who never broke a promise, who was putting one over on him. He looked at himself in the foyer glass. A royal jackass stared back at him. He would be flogged before he presented himself at the butchershop in such a ridiculous condition to be the sport of Mr. Mack and the other butcher and half the neighborhood besides. He wondered if his mother was getting queer—she who scolded if a fellow's shirttail hung out behind even a little! It was all an upheaval over Anne, something so grown up and vile that they threw him out onto the streets to be a walking joke, just so he couldn't find out what was going on in his own family. He climbed the stairs slowly, sunk in gloom.

The boys' room was empty. Jim and John had left for Anheuser-Busch, Tom for the shoe factory, where he swept in the summers, and Owen for the knacker. Frank idly pulled open his drawer of the dresser and from under the shelf paper took out his book. What if he never went at all? It was a surprising idea. Frank felt that he was on the verge of something dangerous but intensely interesting. What would he tell his mother when she asked him for the quarter and the bones? That some big German boys swiped them. But what would he tell Father Degnan on Saturday? An answer instantly formed in the back of his mind: nothing. He was frightened and elated at the rapid progress of his thoughts. When he considered it, if they all lied and broke their word he was a poor sort of fish to tell the truth. The truth, of course, was what was on his mind.

The truth he wanted to learn was being discussed in the kitchen under his feet. On impulse he stretched himself out on the floor and pressed his ear against a crack in the painted planks. He heard nothing. A thought occurred to him. If he could climb between the bushes and the kitchen window, he would be able to hear what was being said inside and he would not be seen either. It was a difficult decision. He had never done anything deliberately terrible before—only spur of the moment nastiness of a minor kind, and then always accompanied by a brother or two. He breathed deeply and decided the thing was to be done. He would see if God really punished disobedient children after all, which Frank tended to doubt, thinking He was probably too busy blathering away with the Holy Family to even notice.

He picked up his pocket knife and a bag of peppermints he had been saving, put his book under his arm in case the vigil proved to be dull, and marched down the front staircase and out the door, slamming it behind him. Then he made his way down the boardwalk to the back of the house, and crept, heart pounding fearfully, under the big spirea bushes. Between the shrubs and the wall was a nice little green alcove where he and Tom sometimes buried things. He sat on his paper bag, sucking a mint, and put the rest in his pocket. The dark green leaves and the summer-dried gray St. Louis dust under him lent an acid tang to the already warming air.

He heard his mother's voice distinctly. "Will, give me a hand with this settling vat. Are you not on at 11:00 today?"

"I am," Will answered.

Then Frank heard crashing and gurgling noises as the tanks were filled with tap water and carried to the laundry room to stand so that the sediment would sink to the bottom. Frank idly flipped the pages of his book, *Pictures from Many Lands,* to a photograph of Mexico City featuring a palm tree. He wondered if such things still existed in this day and age. He had the same doubts about mountains and, for that matter, the sea, although his own parents had crossed it, but that was many a long year ago. He did not see how anyone could afford to keep such extravagant objects as palm trees from falling to progress. To judge from St. Louis, which was a normal place, bizarre natural objects had all disappeared. They called St. Louis the Mound City, but as far as Frank could see it was flat as a pancake. It was probably the same for mountains and palm trees. The Mississippi River, it was true, departed from the general rule. When he and John had thrashed this problem out, his brother had reasoned, "Look, Frank, in Mexico maybe they don't really believe in the Mississippi River, or snow, that we are so accustomed to. Instead they take palm trees for granted, and maybe parrots." Frank recognized the logic of it but remained unconvinced. Perhaps they still kept a palm tree in a park somewhere. When he was a world-renowned pugilist, he would visit Mexico City and ascertain the facts for himself.

His musings were interrupted by his sisters' voices saying goodbye to their parents and announcing their intentions to have it out with Anne that very evening. Some unintelligible comments from Will and the girls left the kitchen.

After a moment's silence Mr. O'Brien's chair was pushed back and his voice could be heard. "Put up a cheese sandwich for me, Kitty, and I'll be on my way, for I'm meeting my friend Pete Gentile and we have a long way to the end of the Laclede line and then a terrible expensive cab ride or a terrible long walk—one or the other—before we reach Hirschenroeder's office."

"Is he the World's Fair fellow?"

"The artistic painters' one, and he's handing out work to all and sundry."

"Is it as big a job as the Exposition Hall?" Mrs. O'Brien asked.

"As big as the Exposition Hall? Kitty, are you raving? This is the grandest enterprise in the history of the world! They could drop Exposition Hall in one corner and never notice it! Just in the decorative line they say there will be work for a hundred or more master artistic plasterers and two hundred assistants, and then a couple of hundred artistic painters and their assistants, and I don't know how many panoramic artists, glassworkers, ironwrights, mosaic tile artisans, and the rest! Why, Kitty, there is work going begging for artists of all kinds!"

Mrs. O'Brien responded soothingly: "It's certain then, James, that you will get some fine commissions."

"I'm inclined to doubt it," he replied gloomily.

"Whatever in the world are you doubting? Didn't you just tell me there was work to be had for the asking?"

"Oh, they'll have little use for virgins on the Fair Grounds," he said, and added hastily, "Of the painted adorational kind, I mean—nor Stations of the Cross either."

"Go on, James," she said. "Your friend will not wait for you at the car stop all day. There is bound to be some pieces of work for you. Don't forget you have more subjects in your repertory than only the religious. Your Osage is a grand figure and much appreciated, and so was your Père Marquette. So go now, and good cess to you."

Frank heard the sounds of chairs scraping and his father's departure. Then Will and his mother began to speak.

"It's an age getting them out of here." She was silent for a moment as the smell of coffee wafted out the window screen to Frank. "I believe, Will, that our Anne is headed into perilous waters. Margaret and I will speak to her tonight if I have to strap her to the chair. But today I was wondering if you couldn't find out something about this Schneider fellow. Your poor father keeps saying he saw his name in the papers not too long ago, it was nothing nearly like a bank robbery, and it will come back to him soon. But we shouldn't wait on events any longer. Can you track him down, Will, and get a notion of what the fellow is about? And if he's the ne'er-do-well he seems, couldn't you have one of your friends arrest him?"

Will's voice registered disapproval. "Find out is one matter, Mother—I'm way ahead of you there, and by the end of my shift tonight I'll have a whole history of Chris Schneider if he has a record to be traced—but arrest is a different question altogether. I'm surprised to hear you say such a thing. It would be a fine city, wouldn't it, if a fellow could be locked up just for kissing a police officer's sister?"

As his mother started to protest, Will interrupted her firmly. "Never you say another word, Mother. I'll go down to the station early, see, and have a look through the bags. And I'll tell you what I learn tonight when I come home."

Frank heard a chair being pushed away from the table and then his mother said, "Will, if you learn anything important, you've only to ring up Mack and Frank can run down the street and fetch me. Your father reached me that way not ten days ago when he left his sketches behind. So don't fail, Will—I'll be on the hooks, waiting."

"But is Mack's a Kinloch phone?" he asked.

"No, it's the Main, and what does it matter—I doubt that she's plugging any calls in today."

After that Will went off to work. Frank crawled through the spirea bushes to the corner of the house, stuck his nose out until he saw his brother pass on the sidewalk, and then quietly made his way down the street to Mack's. Perhaps his employer could be propitiated.

"Good morning, Mr. Macnamara. I'm sorry to be late," he offered gamely to the burly butcher's back.

Mack turned around slowly, cleaver in hand, his face as

red as the brisket he was cutting. At the sight of his delinquent runner boy, however, his expression of ferocity turned to one of glee. "Oh, come here, Heine," he called to the other butcher, "if you ever want to see what the Osage Indians done to a boy."

Frank smiled at them fixedly while they pointed at his hair and roared with hilarity. If they were amused enough, they might forget to tell Mrs. O'Brien.

"Ah, well, Frank," said Mack, wiping his eyes with his apron, "grab them packages there, and remember, today you get a dime and no bones."

3

JAMES O'BRIEN walked up the shady side of Washington Avenue toward the Channing Street stop, wearing his artist's getup. It was only an ordinary black suit, like those favored by clerks, but he had tied a wide strip of knotted lilac silk around his collar and on his head he wore a midnight-blue beret from France. These accessories, together with his thin drooping mustache, showed who he was as clearly as if he carried a sign saying, "James O'Brien, artistic painter, anxious for commissions." If he had been a truly successful artist, like Frederick Stoddard, whose paintings decorated the mayor's new offices, or like those whose Stations and Annunciations the most prosperous parishes competed for, he would be riding in a carriage of his own and wearing a suit cut to order in England.

On the other hand, he had never descended into that lowly category that all artistic painters dreaded. The soiled walls of private dwellings and hospitals, office buildings, and schools awaited the luckless artistic painter, the white overalls and peaked cap of the union men and the steady wages beckoning to those who could no longer afford to wait for another commission. From that slip down, James O'Brien had observed, there was seldom a leg back up.

On the whole, he had not done badly. For that matter, he had come a very long way from the destitution of his first years in St. Louis. The fact was, the times were getting better and better. New residential areas seemed to be going up everywhere and each new parish had to have a church. It was wonderful, he thought, all the marble and granite and limestone and bricks, the wrought iron and gold leaf and a hundred other materials Monsignor and the fathers were disposing all over the city to the greater glory of God. Wonderful, too, that anyone could swallow the nonsense that went with the buildings. Still, they kept many a workingman out of the Poor House on Arsenal Street, and besides, it was a great comfort to the women, who, God knew, needed solace. A fine-looking church was a joy to enter, he reflected—the only gloriously embellished space many poor people saw in their lives.

His steps took him past the recently completed church of St. Francis Xavier, a sight that never failed to lower his spirits, for its decorations had been entrusted to two of his competitors, Marray and Molloy, who themselves had to work around a prestigious triptych imported from Italy. James knew that the difficulty he had in obtaining commissions was due less to the delicacy of his compositions than to the diffidence of his manner. The truth was, he feared and disliked most other men, and presenting himself and his work before them was painful to him. More than once he had spent half a day getting to an architect's office only to turn around and leave when his name was called. He had acquired a reputation for oddness and might have failed in his quest for work were it not for his great friend, Pete Gentile.

Today Pete was waiting for him among a group of men milling about the stop, admiring the spanking new Laclede trolley car. "Hello, James! You ready? We gonna paint up the whole World's Fair?" He slapped James on the back and kissed him on the cheek. If another Irishman had tried to kiss Mr. O'Brien, it would have been a different thing altogether. But Pete was Italian and had Continental ways.

"I think they're artists," said one stout matron to another, lifting her skirts fastidiously as she stepped onto the trolley.

"I took Rosa down to St. Cronan's last week to see your Annunciation," Pete Gentile said to his friend as the two men boarded the street car. "We walk in and I say, 'My God! Look at that Virgin!' And what an Angel! The skin—that's your great secret. Like milk that glows. I never saw nothing so white. And you got her looking up at God, not down at the floor like some *poltroni* I could name. And her eyes, Jimmie—all rolled up in her head so just a little blue shows, and the blue is almost white, and her whites is almost blue! That's what a Virgin ought to look like!" He opened a bottle of wine he had stowed in his wicker work case and politely offered some to his companion. After James declined, he drank deeply, wiped his mouth with his handkerchief, and continued, "The trouble with you is you don't appreciate yourself. How much did you get for it?"

"Seventy-five dollars, including the spandrels."

"Let me tell you what will make you weep, what will make you gnash your teeth. Do you know that *porco*, Marray?"

"I do."

"Two hundred fifty for an Annunciation up at St. Alphonsus—a Virgin you'd spit at if she walked down the street, a *puttana*, black greasy hair hanging all over the place, eyebrows right across the bridge of her nose. And that Redemptorist priest, Eddie Kennedy, he has the nerve to say to me, 'Admiring our glorious new chapel, Mr. Gentile?' "

"Ah, well, Pete," said Mr. O'Brien soothingly, "Kennedy is a famous old flannel mouth from way back. You mustn't take it so to heart that there's them that admires the Marrays and says they are full of life."

"Life!" Pete Gentile exclaimed. "Who goes to church for life? To church for celestial visions, James—that's the thing. And that's where you got a touch like an angel!" He helped himself to another swallow of wine and pulled a nickel from his pocket for the approaching conductor. "Hey, what's he look so happy about?"

The conductor raised his hand to the men, refusing their coins. "No fares today, gents—rides on the house."

"That's a fact," said James. "I read it in the paper. Today is the maiden voyage of the Laclede Pavilion Line and it's free all day. A stroke of luck for us! Say, isn't it a fine-looking car? Cream and yellow. Did you ever see such seats in a public conveyance?" They inspected the cast nickel bars of the struts and framework and admired how the gleaming metal contrasted with the pale woven straw of the upholstery.

"Have a look at the observation platform," said the conductor. They followed him out the back of the car. Pete passed around cigars. All three men lighted up and leaned their elbows on the railing, watching the sycamore-lined street retreat in the heat haze of early St. Louis September. The breeze ruffled the garland of roses adorning the rear of the trolley.

"A good deal of building is going on—even without the Fair," said James. "I read the Masons are about to erect a structure that will be famous all around, and don't forget —when the Fair is over—the new cathedral!"

"There's no place else to be in the whole world but here right now. We're in the very center of the new century."

The streetcar ground to a halt, the conductor called, "End of the line," and the passengers stepped off into the dusty street at the eastern end of Forest Park.

"Where's the Fair?" James asked.

"A couple of miles further down Lindell Boulevard," said Pete. "There's going to be a car line right to the entrance when they get finished, but now they're still laying track. Come on. We'll get Benny to give us a lift." Pete took off his black jacket, folded it over his arm, and approached a knot of draymen watering horses at a trough on Kingshighway. He conversed with them familiarly, while James O'Brien hung back by the car shed, unsure of his surroundings, faintly queasy from the heat and the morning cigar, to which he was not accustomed. He was beginning to wish he had stayed in his cool third-floor studio, working on his drawings for the little Stigmatization of St. Francis for the rectory at St. Leo's. It crossed his mind that fairs were out of his line.

The carters were loading blocks of limestone from one wagon to another at a leisurely pace. Pete was joking with the men, helping lay straw between the rows. James O'Brien drew his watch from his pocket and regarded it sadly, wondering what time he would be back for his supper and his pile of newspapers. He admired the forms of the great restless horses at the trough, telling himself that they were a subject he would surely never attempt.

His friend finally came to fetch him and helped him up onto the straw-strewn stones in the wagon. They braced themselves as the wagon lumbered down the dusty length of Lindell Boulevard toward the great stone castle housing the works office of the Fair.

"I'll tell you the setup," Pete said. "It's all laid out regular. One! Two! Three! Hirschenroeder has a desk, see, so first you fill out your paper, talk to him, and he gives you a docket number."

"What if he won't?" James said nervously.

"What kind of talk? Who are you—a brat off the streets? Haven't you got your papers and all? When you got your docket number, you pick out three jobs. Then you got thirty days to submit the drawings. Wait until you see the crowds of workmen! And they say they can't get enough people to do the different jobs. But it's organized, Jimmy—really good, just like the army."

"Were you ever in the army, Pete?" James asked.

"My God, no, Jimmy. You think I'm crazy?"

James's misgivings over the whole venture deepened when he and his friend had finally made their way from the end of the boulevard, up the wide stone staircase to the Administration Building, and entered the artistic painters' work office. After a while, however, he managed to make room for himself before the specifications lists, and his apprehensions lessened as he read with great interest the projects being proposed. He realized that he could not read them all in one day and resolved to jot down only a few likely possibilities before consulting further with his friend. The description of the Palace of Machinery caught his eye.

> In the architecture of the great Palace of Machinery German features are dominant. The towers, entrances, and even the roofs will breathe a German influence. The two central towers on the north side are each to be 265 feet high. The building will be very rich in plastic detail and sculptural decoration. It will be one thousand feet long and cover ten acres. In the western end of the Palace of Machinery may be seen the power plant of the Exposition, capable of developing an aggregate energy of 45,000 rated horsepower.

James passed on hastily, thinking that such an extravagant building was not suitable for him. He glimpsed Pete across the room, taking notes before a board marked "ceilings." He examined the specifications for the Palace of Electricity and the Palace of Manufacture, but it wasn't until he came to the Traveler's Protective Association that James took out his fountain pen and note cards. He liked the description. The building would "cover an area 85 by 45 feet and be one story high." They were looking for an allegorical figure, representing the "Traveler's Friend," to grace the panel over the "very rich doorway." He could just imagine the nice little building, with its "separate ladies' and gentlemen's lounges and its complete telephonic and telegraphic communications with the rest of the country." He could also envisage the "Traveler's Friend." He thought of her as a large, smiling lady rather like an idealized nurse.

He was laboriously copying the details onto his card in his flawless script when Pete appeared at his side. "Let's go out on the steps and have our lunch, Jimmy. It's after twelve."

They found a brand-new medieval stone bench on the wide terrace fronting the Administration Building, and spreading their lunches out between them, they discussed their morning's findings. Pete Gentile looked at his friend in disbelief when James announced his intentions of competing for the $125 Traveler's Friend.

"James," he said, "tell me one thing. How many children you got?"

"Ten," he answered, modestly.

"How many alive?"

"Pete," Mr. O'Brien replied, "you know all my children are alive and, thanks to our good fortune, not one is dead."

"And Mrs. O'Brien—how many she lose to make ten that live?"

"Mrs. O'Brien brought forth ten perfect infants in as many confinements, and she never so much as had a bad time of it."

"Jimmy, look at me. I'm big as a house, my arm is as thick as your back, I got black curly hair all over my body, like a rug, and first little Pete was born dead, then the second little Pete dies after three days, then little Lena was born dead, and all we got to show now is big Lena. That's all. One girl. And my wife was that way I don't even know how many times anymore." He pointed his finger at his friend's face and said earnestly, "You got more strength in your runty little body than most of the men around here! You think just because you got no meat on your bones, and just because you got no heft to you, that you're not strong? False, Jimmy! Who else has fathered ten healthy children and not one rotten tomato? Give me that dumb Traveler's Friend card—I'm going to tear it up. You and me, we're going to paint the Palace of Electricity—two thousand dollars each." He reached for the card, but James stuck it in his inner pocket and stubbornly folded his arms.

"It's true, Pete, that the numerical odds are against such a run of successes, but it's Mrs. O'Brien who is the wonder of strength, and not myself at all. She compensates for me and keeps the race from degenerating." He took a bite of his cheese sandwich, watching Pete's face with an air of defiance.

"What are you talking about?" Pete uncorked his second bottle of wine and offered some to his companion. "Who's degenerating?"

"Look at me, Pete. I'm a step down from my father. He was larger and more colorful than me. So what if I had wed a little slip of a girl like Bridey Dea? Where would the strength have come from? She had a white face and hands like a child. I told her to find a great strapping fellow like Francis Farrell to compensate, and she said she'd have no use for a long drink of water like him. She wept and tore her handkerchief. Years later she married Francis Farrell anyway."

"And did he compensate like you said?" Pete asked eagerly.

"Somebody told me she died in childbirth, poor creature," said James sadly, "so I was never able to find out." He finished the cup of wine and said, "Would you mind if I had a bit more of this?"

"James! Help yourself."

"But Catherine—Mrs. O'Brien—the first time I saw her she was carrying a sewing machine in one hand like it was nothing. And Nora Barry was dragging *her* machine, barely able to move it, stopping every two feet to rest and complain. 'For the love of God, Nora,' I heard Catherine say to her, 'give me that thing, we're going to miss the car.' And she picked up Nora's machine in her other hand and ran. I was right behind them, walking up Franklin Avenue, and I made up my mind then and there that if she would wed me I'd have no other. And how right I was, Pete, to link my fortunes to such a bounteous nature as hers."

Pete sliced sausage and offered a piece to his friend on the tip of his knife. Mr. O'Brien shook his head. "I couldn't touch a fiery thing like that on such a blazing hot day as this."

The glaring sun seemed to immobilize the panorama before them—the immense stretches of gray stone steps leading down to further outsized terraces and walks, Lindell Boulevard itself an eternity of official space away in the distance. Fatigue welled up in Mr. O'Brien's body as he thought of the efforts still lying in store for him that separated the bench where he sat from his rocking chair by the electric fan in the kitchen.

"Why don't we put in our cards now, Pete, and come back another day for the rest? I don't think I can contemplate any more specifications today."

"What, are you crazy? We come all the way out here to

turn around and go home? What's a matter with you? I know—the Palace of Electricity got you scared. It's okay, we let it go. Marray and Molloy can have it, the *saltimbanchi*." He looked at his friend, who was leaning back against the wall, his eyes shut. There was no response.

Pete Gentile sighed and tried another tack. He pulled two cards from his pocket and tapped James on the arm. "I picked up a couple of little numbers just right for you and me, Jimmy. Neither one is artistic, but we'll knock 'em off in a few days each and make some easy money. Hey, Jimmy—you alive?"

James opened his pale blue eyes and answered softly, "You're a glorious fellow, Pete. Tell me about the little jobs and I'll face up to the Palace of Electricity in a day or two. I've a difficulty taking in a great deal all at once. My capacity is limited." He closed his eyes again.

"The first one is on the Pike, see," said Pete, drawing out a notebook from his pocket, "where it's going to be all gaiety and no uplift, cash and carry, shillings and pence! We'll take it in together some evening during the Fair, James. You'll bring Mrs. O'B and your ten children and I'll bring Rosa and big Lena. You listening?" James nodded affirmatively.

"So here's the place," he read. " 'The Temple of Mirth. Of all the Pike attractions the one best calculated to cure melancholia is that which will bear on its front the winking clown and the four grinning maidens. It will be variously designated as the Temple of Mirth, the Foolish House, and the Fun Factory. Screams of laughter will be heard issuing from within the mysterious portals. Those inside will find, as a source of all this hilarity, first a mirror maze in which the victim may wander for a long time, encountering his own image at every turn; then a succession of grotesque mirrors and a collection of cabinets, each one containing some surprise; and finally Dead

Man's Alley, ending with the circular slide. The mirrors, concave and convex . . .' "

"I beg your pardon for interrupting you," James said, "but I don't see where we come in."

"The winking clown and the four grinning maidens! The girls' heads will be molded in plaster, six feet high, and we'll color them in distemper. We have to use a ladder for the clown's head—he'll be on top. How about it, Jimmy? An easy day's work for an enormous sum?"

"I wouldn't have my name on it any place," replied Mr. O'Brien, "but I suppose it would be possible. Very well, Pete, we must live in the spirit of the times."

"This other job is right in your line. It's a mural for the Philippine Reservation. A great big splendid thing, thirty-five feet long and fourteen feet high, done on canvas in the studio and then mounted. Seven hundred fifty dollars. All we have to do is, here—let me read: 'portray the Samal Moros, the Negritos, the Visayans, the Lanao Moros, and the Igorrotes pursuing their typical daily occupations.' "

"I never heard of those people, Pete. Surely that isn't our sort of job at all. I could never stare at a bunch of savages long enough to paint them."

"James," his friend said, "you'll never have to lay eyes on them—you get photographs! We never go near the Filipinos. What's going to come along better than this?"

He pleaded with such intensity that James O'Brien capitulated. He took out his cards, his writing case, and his fountain pen, and asked his friend for more details.

They signed up for the Filipinos and the House of Mirth together. James insisted on the "Traveler's Friend." Hirschenroeder assured them that the commissions were only beginning to come in. He told Pete that "they might be lucky enough to get Puvis de Chavannes and his assistants to do the ceiling of the Palace of Electricity." Pete left the hall annoyed. The two artists descended the stone steps together, engrossed in conversation over whether foreign artists should be brought in over local talent.

"I've never had a big expanse of ceiling, ever," Pete complained. "All they give me was two little chapels and the Merchants' Exchange dining room with so many windows and woodwork that all I could squeeze in were the backsides of a few *putti*." He wiped the sweat from his face with a handkerchief. At the foot of the stairs they paused and looked around. Lindell Boulevard stretched before them, its dust gleaming in the heat.

"Let's take a cab to the trolley line," said Mr. O'Brien wearily. "I feel too tired and hot to walk."

"Gladly, my friend," said Pete, "but do you see one?" The streets indeed seemed deserted.

"I'll tell you what, Jimmy. Let's cut through the park to the trolley barn on Oakland Avenue. There's bound to be carters around the sites and maybe someone will give us a pickup."

Mr. O'Brien looked at his friend anxiously. "Do you think we can find some shade to walk in? I'm sure I was never so warm as today. Does it get this hot in Italy?"

"In Italy it gets this hot, but only in St. Louis does it get this lousy. Here, have a drink of wine—it will cool you off. Now tell me," he said as they crossed the road and entered Forest Park. "Mrs. O'Brien put in the strength and the size, but what did you have to balance her off?"

"I contributed aesthetic sensibility."

"Is that all?" asked Pete, astonished.

"I think that was the central thing."

"But did it come out the way you thought?" Pete asked excitedly. "Did the good features cancel out the deficiencies the way you planned?"

"Not altogether," said James, pausing in the roadway

and staring about a bit wildly. "Do you know where we are?"

"There's a spring up beyond that bend. Let's go soak our heads for a while, Jimmy. We'll cool off."

"Will turned out to look like a plaster cast of a god," Mr. O'Brien continued, "the last thing I had on my mind when I was laying my plans. And then Anne came along, with a head like a queen, and the next three girls are lovely too, although not the classical beauty you see in Anne. With the others, it's more in the flesh and will pass in time." He fell silent, staring ahead bleakly.

"Jimmy?" said Pete, alarmed at his friend's blank expression.

"Well, the children. They're fine enough to look at," Mr. O'Brien resumed, "but all garbled up as to temperaments and mentalities. Not one soul as stout as Mrs. O'Brien, and, on the other hand, not a trace of aesthetic sensibility in the lot of them. The only pretty things they appreciate are themselves. The girls, I mean. By the way, did you ever hear of a fellow name of Chris Schneider?"

Pete shook his head. They were trudging along the dirt road as it wound through the heat-baked fields of the park's western stretches. Not a cart or carriage was in sight. "I'm feeling queer," Mr. O'Brien said suddenly. He sat down on a stone at the edge of the weedy meadow and, to Pete's consternation, fell backwards onto the ground, his eyes fixed on the sky.

"James! Are you alive? *Dio mio*, what have I done?" Pete knelt by his friend's side, palped his face, pinched his cheeks, and rubbed his hands. Mr. O'Brien responded with a muffled groan. Pete undid the purple tie and collar, and fanned him with a sheaf of note cards. He started down the road toward the spring and then abruptly retraced his steps, to stare irresolutely at James's motionless white face. He was still wavering between his wish to bring some cold water back to splash on the exhausted countenance of his friend and his fear of leaving him unattended when he heard the sounds of horse and wagon approaching down the road they had come.

It was Benny Shields with an empty wagon, on his way to watering his horses. "For the love of God, Pete!" he exclaimed when he saw them. "Are yiz drunk?"

"Oh, Benny!" Pete cried. "Am I happy to see you here! Help me get him in the wagon. It is Providence that you come along like this. Here, we'll put him on the straw. Can you take him straight to his house on thirty-one hundred Washington? I'll pay you, so you don't lose the time. What do you say?"

"I'll take yiz—no need to pay me—but I have to pass by the depot and tell Kroger where I'm at," replied the carter.

"Wait a minute!" Pete jumped off the wagon and cut some sycamore branches with his pocket knife. He stuck them between the slats of the wagon's sides to form a leafy canopy over Mr. O'Brien. They stopped at the spring to water the horses, and Pete carefully poured a cold dipperful on his friend's face. James O'Brien tossed his head fretfully and muttered a complaint. He opened his eyes and asked for a drink. The water made him retch, then he fell asleep.

It was late afternoon when Benny Shields drew his cart up before the house on Washington Avenue. Mrs. O'Brien answered the door and had her prostrate husband placed on the bed upstairs. She sent Pete down to the butcher shop to call Dr. Kieffer and to tell Frank to bring ice.

She tended to Mr. O'Brien while Pete hung anxiously over her shoulder. "You should not have left him out in the sun, Mr. Gentile," she said severely. "He's not at all accustomed to it."

She put two pieces of ice in flannel and crushed them

between her hands, to Pete's astonishment, and placed the compress on her husband's brow. "He's frail—not like some," she said. "He was never suited to the rough life. He only cares for the indoors and fine things."

She sat by the bed and took his hand. "James," she said gently, "can you take a little ice in your mouth?" He formed a yes with his lips, but uttered no sound.

Frank knocked on the door to his parents' bedroom. His mother sent him back to the butcher shop with a warning to leave quietly.

As Frank pushed open the screen door, Mr. Macnamara and Mrs. Mahoney were discussing the O'Briens' activities that day. They didn't notice him come in.

"First Anne kisses a man on the mouth in broad daylight in an automobile, then the boy is late for work with his hair sticking up all over, then Will calls on our telephone and Mrs. O'Brien comes running down the street to talk to him, and whispers into the receiver, so I'd be surprised if Will heard her, and never says so much as thank you when she leaves, and now they carry the old man home drunk."

"They seemed like such a stuck-up bunch when they moved in, too," said Mrs. Mahoney. "How much for the knuckles, at the end of the day?"

"It's still early yet, but you can have them for a nickel."

4

Dr. Kieffer's carriage stopped before the door as the last light of day was fading. The family—except for Anne, who had not come home from work—gathered in the foyer to stare at him, humbled and awed by the presence of the physician and his driver. Pete Gentile came downstairs while Dr. Kieffer examined his patient. Margaret offered him and the driver tea in the kitchen.

"I'll have something stronger, if you got it," said the driver.

"Indeed we have not," Margaret snapped. "This house is total abstinence." Sipping his tea, Pete contemplated Frank, Owen, and Jim, who were facing him across the table. If he had not been told that the house was alcohol free, he would have sworn Jim was besotted with drink. Besides his reddened face and air of incomprehension, the boy reeked of beer.

"You work down at Anheuser-Busch, Jim?" Pete asked. The question was greeted with silence. Owen punched his brother to engage his attention.

"What do you say?" Jim responded after a pause.

"I asked you if you work at the brewery," Pete replied. Jim stared at him vacantly. "What do you do down there?" Pete did not relinquish a line of inquiry easily.

"I'm the mash kettle fellow, the third one," Jim said suddenly.

"The third one!" said Pete, trying to make sense of this piece of information. "How many mash kettles are there?"

Jim did not respond. He stared at his hands while Owen pantomimed idiocy behind his back. Abruptly he began to speak, addressing himself to Pete in great earnestness. "It's the hottest mash kettle—that's why I get paid the most of any of the mash men. They won't get back behind it for anything. It's not as bad in the winter. I work in my underwear. I watch the dial all day to make sure it doesn't go over a hundred sixty-five degrees." He lapsed into silence.

"Is there anybody with you, where you work?" Pete inquired, attempting to encourage Jim's conversation.

"I told you," Jim replied with some irritation, "the other men won't even enter the third room, it's that hot."

"You must get thirsty," Pete said. Jim looked at him suspiciously and Pete saw fear well in the back of his eyes.

"It isn't my fault," he said at last.

"Now who would blame you for getting thirsty, wedged behind a hot mash kettle?"

"It's the foreman," Jim answered. "He says we're not to pull off the hot ferment and drink it. But all the kettle men do. You can't help it."

"Maybe it's not good for your health, Jim," said Pete softly.

Jim arose from his chair abruptly and left the room. Owen chortled, holding up his brother's keys in triumph. "Every time I swipe his keys!" he cried. "Every time he forgets and thinks he lost them!"

Frank's face suddenly assumed an expression of rage. He turned on his brother, snatched the keys from him, and bolted from the kitchen, pausing at the doorway to shout, "You should all of you leave off badgering Jim! I'll tell Will and have you put in jail!"

Pete was disappointed by the display of fraternal ill will. He reflected that the loss of his little Petes and little

Lenas was perhaps less regrettable than it sometimes seemed.

Frank opened the door of the bedroom softly and saw Jim lying facedown on a cot in the corner. "You left these in the kitchen," he said, putting the keys on the pillow. Jim opened his eyes. He reached into the pocket of his trousers, pulled out a dime, and handed it to him. "Go to Hefflinger and get a real haircut," he said, turning his face back to the wall.

Frank left the bedroom clutching the dime in his fist, speculating that maybe Jim really was crazy. Everybody knew Hefflinger cut for five cents. Frank decided he would do what Jim said, let his mother and sisters like it or not, and he would keep the extra nickel besides. He hung around the door of his parents' bedroom, listening to the indistinct murmur of voices within, excited by his own rebelliousness and the aura of danger that seemed to permeate the house.

The presence of two strange men in the kitchen, the alarming but intriguing appearance of Dr. Kieffer, the collapse of his father and withdrawal of his mother, the unprecedented dime from Jim—all of these unusual events swirled together in his mind. He felt that there was a pattern to them, if only he had the knowledge to put them together in the right way. When the doctor and Mrs. O'Brien emerged from the room, he lunged into the doorway of the bathroom to hide, his heart beating wildly for no apparent reason.

"A combination of heat stroke and sunburn, Mrs. O'Brien," was the doctor's pronouncement. "Not fatal but not to be dismissed lightly either in a man of your husband's complexion. I'm leaving you the bottle of ointment."

The driver and Pete emerged from the kitchen at the

sound of the doctor's voice. Mamie, Margaret, and Kathleen crowded into the foyer behind them.

The doctor detailed a regimen of cold soaks and aspirin to bring down the patient's temperature. "One last thing, Mrs. O'Brien," he said. "You must restore the liquids he has lost, a little at a time. A sip or two of something cool every half hour or so should do the trick—not too much all at once. And you must get some oranges and squeeze him a bit of juice every four hours. I'll call around again tomorrow evening. Good night to you, Mrs. O'Brien, and to you, Mamie, Margaret, John, Owen, and Mr. Gentile." His driver pocketed the dollar that Mrs. O'Brien pressed discreetly into his hand, handed his employer his hat and cane, and escorted him out the door and into his carriage.

"Oranges!" said Mrs. O'Brien. "Where in the name of God are we going to get oranges at this hour of the night?" She looked at her children in consternation. "I can't think where such things are to be had."

Frank called down from the head of the stairs, "Mr. Prallee has peaches and strawberries for making ice cream and he stays open until eleven. I can go."

"Kieffer didn't say peaches and strawberries, he said oranges. You can go to bed!" his mother replied.

Pete took Mrs. O'Brien's hand impulsively and squeezed it. "I'll get him oranges—don't you worry. I got an uncle, he works at Soulard market, he lives over on Jefferson. I'll go over to his house—he'll know where we can find oranges."

"Mr. Gentile," said Mrs. O'Brien firmly, withdrawing her hand from his, "you have done quite enough for our family today. Your wife must be wondering what has become of you. I will say good evening to you now." She opened the front door and looked at him in a way that Pete could only interpret as unfriendly.

"But the oranges!" he said.

"Will can take care of his father's needs, Mr. Gentile. Have no fear. We appreciate your concern for all that it is worth."

The door shut behind him, and Pete found himself alone on Washington Avenue.

In the moonlit woods of Forest Park, on a narrow dirt lane, the Dion-Bouton was hidden amongst the shadowy foliage. The city was as remote from the dark depths of the old forest as another world. Anne lay faint in Chris Schneider's arms, lost in the sweetness of his kisses, his caressing hands, the smell and feel of his face and body.

"My beloved," he said softly, his mouth against her ear, "my queen, I want to take you home. Will you stay with me, Annie, and fulfill all my dreams, and satisfy our desires, this night?" She moaned and reached for his mouth. He pulled away from her, held her face in his hands, and looked into her eyes. "Say it, Anne."

"I'll do whatever you want, Chris," she answered.

"Then say it."

"Say what? Darling Chris, I'll say whatever it is." She moved to be kissed by him again, but still he held her face a few inches from his own.

"Say 'I'll sleep in your bed tonight, Chris, and we'll satisfy all our desires.'"

His somber eyes reflected a dim spark of light; she moved uneasily and tried to pull his hand from her cheek to kiss it.

"Say what I told you to say, sweetheart, and I'll take you home."

She shuddered, closed her eyes, and repeated the words in a whispered rush.

He embraced her again, caressing her breasts. "There's a little bird fluttering in your corsage, sweet girl. Are you afraid?"

She answered him in a voice that was nearly a sob. "Take me to your house now, Chris." He stepped from the car, started the motor, wiped his hands carefully on a rag from the glove-box, and settling himself once more behind the wheel, eased the vehicle into motion. Soon they left Forest Park behind them and headed west through deserted roads toward Maryland Avenue and Chris Schneider's house.

Will and Mrs. O'Brien settled down for a cup of tea in the kitchen as the hall clock struck one. The oranges had been procured and squeezed. Mr. O'Brien had ingested a half cup of their juice, sat bolt upright in bed, announced that by 1903 potable water would flow from every tap in St. Louis, and had fallen back into a deep slumber.

Mrs. O'Brien looked around the kitchen with an air of discontent. "Tom forgot to empty the ashes," she said.

"Never mind the ashes now, Mother," Will replied. "Let me tell you what I learned today, for my sins."

"Is Schneider a criminal then, Will?" she asked anxiously.

"The problem is," he answered, "what do you mean by a criminal? I only had a few minutes at the bags—I'll tell you why later. A dreadful investigation I'm assigned to—a grand opportunity—but at the wrong time, as you know, what with Anne carrying on and the old fellow all but expired upstairs. It's a wonder I had the chance to ring you at Mack's this afternoon."

"But, Will, is he a criminal or not?"

"To tell you the truth," her son replied, "he's been indicted twice and he has gone bankrupt once. Not the picture of a darling boy, Mother. On the other hand, to give the devil his due, the two indictments were dropped and it isn't a crime to go bankrupt."

"A bankrupt driving an automobile! Surely there's a crime someplace!" she cried.

"It said on his identification that he was a lawyer, certified for the Illinois Board. Those fellows can get by with murder. The only other piece I had a chance to look at was from the Town of Clayton Office of Realty Records. It said he had sold his house on Maryland Avenue for one dollar to a woman a few weeks before he went bankrupt."

"Who was the woman?"

"It said her name was Olive Taylor. That was all I had time to look at when Kieley called me into his office."

"Couldn't you ask Captain Kieley if he knows anything about him? Kieley has been on the force a long time. He might remember the name."

Will stirred his milky tea slowly, sending black leaves floating to the surface. "Do I spread my sister's behavior out on a police officer's desk like stolen goods to be pawed over?" he said at last.

"No," his mother replied, "but, Will, why do you have to mention Anne's name? Can't you just tell him you're after Schneider?"

"I've no business being after Schneider. I have to have a reason. I would be obliged to invent a fabrication." He sighed, rubbing his finger over the worn oilcloth of the table. "Listen," he said, "it's raining. Does that automobile of Schneider's have a top? I would need to fabricate," he repeated, "and I'm no good at the lie." He attempted a smile. "You never raised your boy to be a liar, Mother."

"I never raised my girl to be a slut, either—a wanton cause of scandal to the family and the nine-day wonder of the parish. I brought Anne up to be a lady, that the whole neighborhood admired when she passed. And now they've cause to talk about her." Her grim face wilted her son's feeble smile. "What are you going to do?" she asked accusingly.

"I'll tell you, I did confide in someone—not Captain Kieley, but my partner, Mike Egan. Listen, Mother," he said as Mrs. O'Brien attempted to interrupt him. "Hear me out. Mike Egan is my best friend and he swore not to say a word to anyone. And I'll tell you now, I helped him last year in a matter concerning his family, and it was more serious than this, and did you ever hear a whisper of it?"

"No, Will, not at all."

"There—you see how it is. Mike and I, we're the tomb respecting one another's secrets."

"What can Mike Egan do, though?" Mrs. O'Brien asked.

"He had a plan of action at the ready, just like that! Without a moment's delay, he says, 'Will, what are we waiting for? Tonight, we'll be by his front door, and when he comes, *whack!* we knock the bejesus out of him. And when he hits the pavement, we say in his ear to keep away from Miss O'Brien.' That's all. It couldn't be simpler, he says."

"So, Will! What did you answer?"

"Well, I said to him, 'Mike, police officers waylaying citizens at their front doors? How can you think of it? We'd both of us be kicked off the force, and maybe locked up ourselves.' So he says to me, 'How do you think the force takes care of its family woes? I'll tell you,' he says, 'if it was some fellow bothering Rose, I wouldn't hesitate.' So I thought to myself, Imagine bothering Rose! As like unto John L. Sullivan as two peas in a pod."

"It's almost two o'clock," said Mrs. O'Brien. "I think she's not coming home at all tonight, Will. Unless she has been in an accident with him and that satanic machine. Can I pour you a drop of tea? You're right about Rose Egan. She's not to be compared with our Anne and Mike is a roughneck sort of fellow—I wonder that he's such a great friend of yours. Still"—she paused and gazed reflectively at the black windowpane—"a good drubbing might end this whole matter once and for all." She lifted the teapot, watching her son intently. "But we must talk to Anne first and get some sense out of her. It is not only Chris Schneider causing the mischief here. It's herself that's in it—for half, at least."

"Oh, I wouldn't go that far as to blame Anne for wickedness," Will protested, "him being a lawyer with an automobile and a house and all."

"Doesn't he have any parents, that he could sell his house for a dollar to a woman?" she asked.

"That's the thought I had coming home on the streetcar tonight. What if tomorrow, after my shift, I was to go out to his house in Clayton and knock on the door?"

"What will you say if he answers?" Mrs. O'Brien asked.

"No. He's not supposed to answer—the woman is."

"What woman? Anne?"

"No, not Anne," said Will, irritated. "The one he sold his house to for a dollar."

"Ah," said Mrs. O'Brien, "that one—the reprobate."

"He's the reprobate, you mean."

"Isn't that what I just said?"

"Mother," said Will, "I think we're worn out, like two old rags. Let's be done with it tonight. We'll talk more in the morning."

"You go to bed. I'll just see if Mr. O'Brien can take a bit of juice and then I'll wait for Anne a few minutes more."

"I'll sit with you then. Go see to him." Will prowled through the pantry, finally picked up one of the remaining oranges, and peeled off the thick skin with his knife. This day has been nothing but misery, he thought. I might at least have an orange in lieu of comfort.

When Mrs. O'Brien reentered the kitchen, Will had dozed off in his chair. She put her lamp on the table and swept the orange peelings into the trash. "He's stirring and muttering," she said, "so I had to cool him off and get him to take some aspirin. Kieffer is a saint, and no mistake, always leaving the free medicine."

Will opened his eyes and then shielded them with his hand from the light. "He charges the Egans a dollar and a quarter," he said.

"That's because they don't go back twenty years the way we do. Kieffer never raises the old patients—he only charges more for new ones. Thank God, his sons are going to be doctors too."

"They may charge more, Mother. You better hold on to the old fellow."

Not the shadow of a smile crossed his mother's stern pink face. Will sighed, his shoulders sagging. "I would take off sick tomorrow and go to Clayton first thing in the morning, except that I've been put on special assignment. Me and Mike."

"Is it houses of ill repute or gambling dens, Will?" his mother inquired.

"Not the one nor the other," he replied, "but something far worse—and a terrible diabolical business it is. We're to work with police from Chicago and maybe Memphis and New Orleans too, and we have a special telephone wire hooked up. Even a police officer from New York may be assigned to us. Captain Kieley is mad with the excitement."

"Is it a gang of criminals, then, like the Porter gang?"

"No, this isn't a bunch of gangsters. It's more like a company of businessmen—smooth devils who run phoney employment agencies, fly-by-night operations."

"And what is so terrible wicked in that, Will, to arouse the captain and all?"

"It's a trick, you see," he replied. "They put advertisements in the little small-town newspapers for entertainers —girls who can sing or play an instrument. They want only blondes and redheads. And these poor hillbillies come to Chicago, or St. Louis, or Memphis, most of them on foot, all the way from their dirt farms. Some don't even have shoes. And quick as a wink, if they're halfway presentable, they sign some papers, and the next thing they know they're on a boat on the river. At New Orleans they load them onto an oceangoing vessel and they're taken to be sold. Kieley said blondes fetched $1,000 a head in Havana and Casablanca. For the brothels."

"Oh, my God, Will," his mother cried, "you don't mean it! What about their families? Don't they go after them?"

"It's all done so slick and so fast, and with the families being poor and backward, that it's a wonder if the police will be able to do something about it. The only stroke of luck was one brave girl from Iowa escaped from a house in Tangiers and made her way back to the New York police with her story. It took her two years to do it and she suffered something awful. I admire that girl's fortitude more than I can say. She told the police Jesus never left her side."

"The unfortunate creature! What her mother must have gone through," said Mrs. O'Brien.

A thump from the upper reaches of the house interrupted the conversation. "It must be James, getting out of bed, and here I am, gabbing in the kitchen instead of watching him the way I ought," Mrs. O'Brien said. She lifted the lamp and swiftly ascended the rear stairs, followed by Will.

Mrs. O'Brien dozed in a chair at her husband's bedside, a queer half-dream of an evil steamboat heavy in her mind. She woke spontaneously from time to time to inspect her patient, as she had done when Kathleen went through the crisis of her pneumonia and when Jim almost died from eating his father's jar of zinc white. She awoke to hear the clock chime six and, sighing, arose from the chair, smoothed her skirt, and leaned over the bed to peer at her husband in the morning light. His face was redder than she had ever seen it, and there were strange little puffs of swollen skin under his eyes. She washed his face with cool water and spread ointment tenderly with the tips of her fingers. He opened his eyes.

"Catherine," he said, "has Pete Gentile gone home? I hope you offered him some supper."

She stepped back from the bed and placed her hands on her hips. "Pete Gentile! Is that all that's afflicting you? He's long gone and good riddance to him. Go back to sleep. I'll bring you orange juice after I make breakfast. Or I'll send Vesta. Pete Gentile!" She moved toward the door.

"He's a wonderful Continental artist, Kitty," whispered Mr. O'Brien placatingly.

"I am not moved by Continental art," she replied, and left the room. Mr. O'Brien sank back into his pillows and his slumber again.

Anne awakened as the first light entered the crack in the draped windows of the house on Maryland Avenue. Fear tightened her stomach as she lay in bed, her eyes still closed. She wondered how late it was, and whether her mother would believe that the automobile had lost its capacity to function in the neighborhood of Chris's house. She reflected that much depended on how rapidly the interrogation could be gotten through. She remembered the sound of rain during the night and thought that perhaps her mother would accept the concept that rain had put the motor out. Provided Will weren't at home to contradict her with his authority on automobiles just because that lout, Mike Egan, had built some kind of contraption in his shed. Maybe the thing to do was to come home while Will was at work and have it out with her mother alone. And then what? She could say she was working the late shift. She cautiously opened her eyes and raised her body onto one elbow. Her thick, reddish-gold hair fell over her cheek and spread across the sheet. She pulled it behind her head and looked around the room.

A large lithograph on the wall portrayed an indolent nude lying on a sort of couch, her whole backside exposed in the most provocative manner. Anne looked away in embarrassment and then, slowly, let her eyes be drawn back to the picture. The creature did appear marvelously at ease, the tones of her flesh exuding a delightful complacency. Anne turned her glance to the figure asleep beside her. What a tableau for a gentleman's bedchamber! She thought of what her mother would say and smothered a giggle in the bedclothes. Suddenly the fear took hold of her stomach again and she rose from the bed to find the bathroom.

She returned to the semidarkened room a few moments later, stepping over her dress and underclothing, which were strewn about the floor. As she settled back into the bed, she noticed her reflection in an elaborately framed mirror on the wall. I look like a painting myself, she thought, and settling on to her stomach, she let one leg hang carelessly from the side of the bed. Piling her hair on top of her head with one hand, she regarded her image with great interest. She raised her hips tentatively and let them fall, admiring the effect on the picture in the mirror. Chris must see me. It will drive him to distraction, she thought. Turning to her lover, she slithered against his sleeping body and put herself to caressing him into wakefulness.

5

By MID MORNING a blanket of heat lay implacable across Missouri and Illinois. A feeble breeze rose irresolutely from the Mississippi River only to collapse a few feet up the levee onto the muddy cobblestones. Will and Mike Egan stood sweating outside Captain Kieley's office while their superior was closeted with the Commissioner. They spoke to Bailey and Derzie, who were coming off duty from the colored red-light district on Market Street.

"All's quiet on that front, lads," said Joe Derzie. "Not a sound last night but the pianos. The heat's done everybody in, I wouldn't be surprised. I thought you two was on special assignment."

"So we are," Mike Egan replied. "We're to rush in and arrest the Commissioner if he don't give Kieley what he wants."

The captain emerged from his office amidst the laughter and beckoned to his two aides. "Here's how it is, boys," he said. "We'll have to stay on until all hours this evening, to meet with the men coming in by train from Chicago. So why don't you take a long lunch and be back here by three. Get a haircut, why don't you." He disappeared into his office again and shut the door.

As the two men descended the steps of the station house a thought occurred to Will. "Mike," he said, "is Robert using your automobile today?"

"No," said Mike. "It's in the shed at home. In fact, I

have the use of it all this week. Say, what are you thinking of?"

"What I had in mind was a rapid excursion to Clayton, to have a look around," Will replied.

"I read your meaning, Will. In fact, I'm way ahead of you. I'm already pounding on his front door. But listen— shouldn't we wait until dark? Let's not beat him up in broad daylight."

"I'm not speaking of beating anybody up," Will said in annoyance. "You have a terrible violent imagination, Mike. I'm thinking of detective work, such as is our line fair and square."

"Clayton is not in our line, if you want to talk about lines. We've no business knocking on any doors in Clayton at all," Mike answered sulkily. "If you want to be particular."

They mounted the trolley that would take them to the corner of Mullanphy Street and Leffingwell Avenue, a few doors from the Egans' flat. They nodded to the motorman and the conductor, who tipped their hats, and seated themselves in the rear of the train.

"The book doesn't say that a policeman in uniform may not knock on a door outside his precinct," Will said carefully.

"It doesn't? I'll take your word for it. Still, what are you going to say to him if you don't want to hit him?"

"I don't intend to say anything to him," Will answered. "I thought we would check his yard, and if the Dion-Bouton is gone, we could ring the bell and talk to the woman."

"What woman? Is it Anne you think is there?"

"No, not Anne, for God's sake. The woman he sold the house to for a dollar. I figure that Anne won't listen to tales of indictments and bankruptcy, because a fast-talking fellow can explain away things like that to a girl. But if he's living with another woman, then surely she'll rid herself of him when she finds out what a scoundrel he is."

"What story will you tell this floozy of his?" Mike asked. "Providing she's even there."

"No story at all, Mike. You'll see. Are you up for it?"

"Not as much as I'd be up for punching his head directly. However, she's your sister, not mine."

They got off the trolley and walked up Mullanphy Street to where the boardwalk led to Mike's yard.

"You still have the Poles living in your yard?" Will asked.

"We do," Mike answered, "and Mrs. Petrofsky has been a blessing to Mother since the troubles we had. Did you ever meet the daughter, Frances? A grand girl, Will, I want you to know. A hard-working girl who's as good as gold to her mother."

They opened the door of the shed and Mike addressed himself to the tires of his vehicle. He tightened the nuts on the front wheels and then raised the hood. "It took Robert and me six months to build this thing and every other time we drive it we have to put it back together again. Hand me that stick, Will. I took her to the Beer Gardens by Sportsman Park for the polka a couple of times."

"Who, Frances Petrofsky?"

"Yes. Why do you act so surprised?" Mike asked, looking up from the motor of his homemade automobile to his partner's face.

"I wouldn't go to the Beer Garden to polka with any Pole that lived in my alley. That's all."

As they drove down Mullanphy Street Mike expostulated with his friend. "What difference does it make—Poles, Irish, Germans? We're all Catholics and Democrats, Will. We're all Americans, don't forget."

"I don't care about the nationality angle either," Will replied. "I'm not like that Father Johnny Quinn, when they said to him, 'What would you be if you wasn't Irish, Father?' and he says, 'What would I be if I wasn't Irish?' " Will imitated a brogue. " 'I'd be ashamed of meself.' " They laughed together, enjoying the sensation of freedom their outing was imparting and the breeze created by the moving vehicle.

"Well, then," said Mike. "Why wouldn't you polka with a Polish girl from your alley?"

"That's how a fellow ends up getting hooked, Mike," said Will solemnly. "No, I mean it! She's right there, cheek to jowl with your mother. What chance have you got if she decides she wants Grand Rapids furniture of her own?"

"Let's have a cigar." Mike steered the car to the curb and pulled two Hauptmann handmades from his pocket.

"Can you drive and smoke a cigar at the same time?" Will asked nervously.

"That's only a small sample of what I can do in this machine," said Mike Egan, spitting off the end of his panatela. He lighted up, blew a puff of smoke, and engaging his feet in a complex operation with the pedals and wheels on the floor of the automobile, caused it to lurch forward so rapidly that Will slid from the seat.

"Now you did it," said Will resentfully, rubbing ashes from his blue sleeve. "You deserve to end up in an apron, holding the baby for Frances Petrofsky."

"I wouldn't mind," said Mike Egan. "By next year I'll be making eighty dollars a month. What have you got against settling down anyway?"

"I got nothing against it, at the proper time. But you're young yet, like me. We have our lives ahead of us. Besides, I'm well off at home. With all of us working, even Frank and Tom bringing in something, there's money for a chandelier and a piano. I'm thinking when Jim gets a little older we'll go to Perry-Newstead like you and Robert did and buy the makings of an automobile together. Although I hate to think of Jim cranking a machine, much less driving one. Maybe John, then—except that he doesn't make near what Jim does at the brewery."

"So what age, then, would you consider getting put in tandem?" Mike asked.

Will took a long time with the question before responding. "When my mother dies," he said at last. "We'll all stay home while she's alive. And if God grants her the many years she deserves, as I pray he will, then maybe when I'm forty."

"Forty!" Mike exclaimed. "Oh, Will, I'll be wed long before you at that rate. Another year or so, when I have a bit of money put aside, and who knows—I may move Frances Petrofsky to somebody else's alley. The trouble is, Rose. She's a darling girl, but, Will, do you think any fellow is going to have her? She's close to thirty."

"Thirty is nothing for a decent girl who lives with her mother," said Will. "I don't know where you pick up such precipitation. Look at Billy Dolan—didn't he just get married? And Carmen Tierney is forty if she's a day. You were there at St. Leo's. Wasn't she a fine-looking bride? Her sister works at Kinloch with Anne. How far are we from Clayton, do you think?" Will asked, looking at the woods at the side of the road.

"That's the park," said Mike Egan. "Maryland Avenue is about a mile on the other side. Did you ever think about living in the country, where there's trees and all?"

"We don't take to the country," Will replied. "It's like Mr. Dooley says—we like the cities, where there's gas to burn and a police force to get on."

"I hope we have time for some lunch after we reduce this fellow," Mike said.

"We're not reducing anybody, Mike. I swear to God, you're worse than those toughs from Cass Avenue we ran in last week." They parked the automobile a few doors down from the Schneider house on Maryland Avenue, under the shade of a sycamore tree.

"Let's stroll by casually and just look it over," said Will.

They assumed their policeman's gait, swinging their clubs rhythmically together.

"If the boys from the Clayton station spot us here," said Mike, "we'll have a wonderful amount of fabrication to invent."

"Don't worry," said Will. "We'll tell them we're on the lookout for a high-class alley you and Frances Petrofsky can call home."

They glanced with studied indifference toward the house. It was set back from the sidewalk, surrounded by a low iron fence. Its shuttered windows and somber brick facade, rendered darker still by the porphyry pillars of the verandah, revealed nothing.

"Do you see any sign of the Dion-Bouton?" whispered Will.

"I'm hopping into the yard," said Mike, and before Will could protest he was over the fence and pushing through the hydrangea bushes. He reappeared a moment later, a smile on his face. "The shed is empty," he said. "The door is wide open. So the prey is at the mercy of the cunning detectives. Your sister isn't making a fool of herself for a poor man, I'll say that for her."

They opened the gate and advanced up the walk together. "Leave it all to me," Will said, ringing the bell by the door. After a considerable pause, they heard a shuffle of feet within the house, the lace curtain moved, and a wizened black face peered out at them through the glass.

"Who is calling, please?"

"Police," said Will. As the bolts and locks creaked, he

whispered to his partner, "That is the God's truth—we are the police."

A tiny, elderly Negro woman opened the door for them, her eyes coated with a bluish film. "Is Mr. Schneider in trouble?" she asked fearfully.

Will ignored her question. "We wanted to have a word with a lady name of Olive Taylor at this address," he said smoothly. "Is she perchance at home?"

"Why, she's at home, all right. I am Olive Taylor. Won't you please come in?" Will and Mike Egan exchanged startled glances and then followed the bent figure of the old woman into the dark foyer of the house. "Come with me to the kitchen," she said. "We can talk more comfortable there. I hope you can see in here. Mr. Schneider has me keep the shutters closed up tight all summer, so the heat can't get in, he says, but it gets in anyway. But I don't mind it nowadays the way I used to."

Will and Mike Egan groped their way down the gloomy hallway by touching the wall. "Don't you have any lights?" asked Will, barely able to distinguish his hostess a few feet ahead of him.

"Mr. Schneider had light bulbs put in all over the house," she said, "but I told him I'm not going to press them buttons unless somebody here to take the blame. I'll be glad to turn one on if you police officers will watch it."

They stood in the Stygian confines of what Will assumed to be a sort of pantry. He had the impression that his grasp of the situation was weaker than he had imagined it would be when he and his partner were driving out from the city. "Why should someone watch a light bulb?" he asked, in an effort to regain control of the interview.

"In case the electricity leaks out and causes an accident," she replied.

"That's impossible," Mike Egan interjected impatiently.

"You being police officers know the facts about electricity, I expect. Still and all, that's how Mrs. Schneider died, so I know it can happen."

"Push the button, Olive," said Will. "We'll take full responsibility."

A pool of light from an unshaded ceiling bulb illuminated a servants' kitchen, the green paint on the tongue-and-groove boards lining its walls cracked and peeling. The aged woman before them slowly pulled two chairs out from a table in the middle of the room, wiped the seats with her apron, and motioned her guests to be seated.

"It's been a long while since anybody come to see me. I think it was on my seventy-fifth birthday that Miss Grace —that's Mr. Schneider's sister—brought me a bouquet. Now, may I offer you officers a nice cup of coffee? It will only take me a few minutes to brew. Pevely brought me fresh cream this morning."

"Thank you, Olive, we'll be glad to have a cup of your coffee," said Will, directing a cold blue stare of warning at his partner, who was signaling petulance at the leisurely pace of their interrogation.

"You just call me Ollie, like everybody always does. Would you care for a piece of rhubarb pie I just took out of the oven last night and that's probably going to waste on account of Mr. Schneider dining in restaurants all the time this week?"

"We'll both taste your pie with pleasure, Ollie," said Will as the stooped figure laboriously made its way to the pantry, and then in an urgent whisper to his partner: "What have you got your monkey up about? Didn't I tell you to leave it all to me?"

Mike whispered back, furiously, "It's after one o'clock and we have to be back in Kieley's office at three. When am I going to have my lunch?"

"This is your lunch," whispered Will. "Rhubarb pie and coffee."

"It's made with fresh lard from Mr. Schneider's farm and not from the butcher shop at all. So you know it's *bound* to be good." She made her way back into the kitchen slowly, bearing an enormous mound of pastry.

"I was born in this house in the year eighteen twenty. Not in the house, but in the quarters back of the old place. Oh, my," she said, "these plates are all cracked. How can you enjoy pie on a nasty old dish like that? I'll just go into the dining room and get the Meissen ware. I *know* Mr. Schneider would be glad."

"Now there, Ollie," said Will, bringing as much authority to his demeanor as he could muster, "these plates are just fine. You sit right down here and tell us about yourself and how you came to buy this grand house for a dollar. You must have a clever head for business, to make a bargain like that."

She laughed to herself and shook her head as she cut large slices of pie. "I surely can't claim I was clever, officer, because I sold it back a year later for the same price. I sold it right back for a dollar." She chuckled to herself as she served the pie. Mike Egan sullenly regarded the plate before him.

"Now don't be backward," she said. "Let me pour your coffee for you."

"Why did you buy and sell this house for a dollar each time?" Will asked, knowing in advance what the answer would be.

"Because Mr. Schneider told me to. He showed me where to sign." She peered at Will, an expression of doubt crossing her features. "Did I break the law?"

"Did you know why Mr. Schneider wanted you to buy the house and then sell it back to him?" Will inquired.

"Gott im Himmel!" she exclaimed. "How would I know

a thing like that? When Mr. Schneider says to me, 'Sign,' I just sign. He is a lawyer, and gentlemen who are lawyers know all kinds of things." She looked dubious, as though her assertion failed to satisfy her completely.

A sudden smile lighted her face. "Say! I got a fine piece of ham in the icebox, left back from Sunday. How would you like a slice of it to go with your pie?" Will nodded his acceptance of the offer, and she turned her attention to Mike Egan. "Well," she said, "you tucked that rhubarb pie right in. How did you like it?"

"It was delicious," said Mike, holding up his plate. "Is there a little more?"

"Would you care for a slice of ham to keep it company?" Ollie asked.

Mike Egan inserted a napkin into his collar and spread it neatly over his chest. "I would indeed," he said. "Could I trouble you for a little mustard?"

"No trouble at all," she replied. "I got some in the box that Mrs. Schneider orders from Düsseldorf."

"Now which Mrs. Schneider would that be?" Will inquired. "The one that died from electricity?"

"No, not that one. Mr. Schneider's mother, that's in Paris now, buying the prettiest things you *ever* saw, like she does every year. Why, she gave Mr. Schneider this house—she'd give him just about anything, I guess. She done *this* to me." Turning from the icebox, she pointed to a scar across her face.

"How did that happen, Ollie?" asked Will.

"Oh, she hit me like that sometimes when her brown study came over her, but when they ended slavery in the whole United States of America, I told her, I said to her that I didn't expect to be hit anymore."

"What did she say?"

"That's when she gave me *this*." She pointed to her cheek again.

"What about Mr. Chris Schneider, Ollie. Did he ever hit you?" Will asked.

"How about some feet! I just remembered I got some homemade feet, the best you *ever* tasted, jugged up here in the back of my box. They go real good with a little potato salad I was saving for Mr. Schneider's supper, but I *know* he'll be dining out tonight, unless his young lady turns him down because of getting caught in the rain and having to sleep at our house. And I never even woke up when they came in."

"She slept here?" Will asked.

"I'll have some feet and potato salad," said Mike Egan. "Let me help myself, Ollie. You mustn't wear yourself out."

Will shot his partner a bemused glance. "Do you know the young lady?" he asked the old woman.

"I fixed her breakfast this morning, only I served it in the dining room, and I saw her as plain as I see you." She gazed on Will's face in a way that caused him a slight sensation of discomfort. "I lived here all my life," she continued. "I've never been anyplace but here. Where would I go? Everybody I ever knew is dead now, except for Mr. Schneider and my godchild, Maurice."

"Does he still hit you, Ollie?"

"It's just like I told the other police that time—the ones who thought my sauerbraten was so tasty. I don't have one word to say against Mr. Schneider. He's a fine man and his father set me free the day I turned twenty-one. This here Mr. Schneider takes after his mother's side. That's what Mrs. Schneider said."

"The one that died from electricity?"

"No, I mean the first one, Lucile, that got a divorce."

"Is that when the police came?" Will asked. "Was it to do with Lucile? Or the electricity one?"

"Both times they come and both times Mr. Schneider showed them how the facts got twisted all around, and they sat in the dining room and I served them a fine meal and they had some wine, too, from the wine cellar. They had a good laugh about women, all around. About Lucile, I mean. They never laughed about Emma. Poor lady—it was such a piteous thing to happen. And I found her! That's why I won't push those buttons—not for love or money—unless someone here to take the blame."

"Did Mr. Schneider hit Lucile?"

"Here. I'll show you the dent." She rose slowly from her stool. "Can you hand me my stick? The dent is in the parlor. You come along behind me."

Will nodded to Mike Egan, who pushed a last forkful of potato salad hastily into his mouth, wiped his lips with his napkin, and followed his partner and the hobbling woman into the cavernous hallway. At the door to the parlor, Ollie pushed another button, and in the light provided by a crystal chandelier, she pointed to a hole in the papered wall as big as a man's fist. "He says he's in no hurry to have it fixed up," she said. "He missed her head, *Gott sei dank*! With a great big old silver-headed cane." Turning toward Will, she said, "Would you please bend down a little?" He lowered his head and she stared fixedly at his face through her veiled eyes. "I never have a word of complaint against Mr. Schneider. I never tell any stories against him. But if the pretty lady that I gave breakfast was my daughter, or my sister, or any kin of mine, I would want her at least to have a look at that hole."

Will straightened his back and stood gazing at the torn wallpaper and the broken plaster of the wall. He sighed deeply and after a moment's pause spoke to the old woman. "You've been very kind, Ollie. Show us to the door now. I'll press the button for you."

"You aren't going to tell Mr. Schneider that I spoke out of turn, are you?" she asked. "Not after eating old Ollie's pie and feet?"

"I forgot to bring my book with me, more's the pity," Will replied, "so this visit is as good as wasted. You don't even have to mention it to Mr. Schneider."

"It will probably slip my mind before he comes back, with all the sweeping I still have to do."

"Goodbye, Ollie. Thank you for everything," said Will.

"Thanks for a grand spread," Mike Egan added.

"Goodbye now, officers. Just one thing you oughtened to forget."

"What's that, Ollie?" Will asked.

"Keep in mind how Mr. Schneider is a lawyer."

Will said nothing as Mike Egan drove back toward St. Louis and their appointment with the captain. He stared ahead of him, tapping his palm deliberately with his nightstick.

"I never really understood before today why a policeman is not supposed to be wined and dined or even accept an apple from a suspect," said Mike Egan, glancing tentatively at his companion.

Will merely grunted and continued staring out the window wordlessly. Pennsylvania Avenue was unpaved, and the automobile bounced awkwardly over ruts that had been worn by horse-drawn vehicles. Mike Egan suddenly turned his head and tipped his cap; the wheel of the automobile lurched precipitously to the right.

"What the hell are you doing?" Will roared.

"Wasn't that a Catholic church we just passed?" Mike asked.

"Keep both your hands on that steering thing," said Will. "I'll tip for the two of us."

"We should make good time on Delmar—they got

planks on it," said Mike, wishing for his partner's return from the intimidating solitude into which he had withdrawn. But the silence persisted past Union Avenue. Mike Egan whistled softly to keep himself company.

"Is that supposed to be funny?" Will scowled at him.

"What did I do now?" Mike protested.

"You're whistling 'After the Ball,' and let me tell you, it's a poor sort of joke," said Will angrily.

"I wasn't even thinking about Anne," said Mike. "The tune just popped into my head to cheer me up. It's true I had a bone to pick with her, but, Will, I'd never wish the poor girl a fate like this fellow Schneider."

"You were sore at her that time she wouldn't accompany you to the Ball. I didn't like that either, Mike. It was a slur on the uniform and I never will forget it. Remember, though, she said you could escort her the year you made captain, so it wasn't you she was against, it was only the rank." A chill smile crossed Will's face and abruptly faded. "A decent fellow wouldn't look at her now." He relapsed into gloomy silence.

A few blocks later Mike sallied forth again. "Schneider must be a terrible miscreant, wouldn't you say, Will? Two wives and one of them electrocuted and him beating the other one. Don't you imagine Anne will send him packing when she hears the tale? I know Rose would cuff a man down Biddle Street for a lot less."

Will took a handkerchief from his pocket, ceremoniously unfolded it, shook it out with a flourish, and blew his nose. Meticulously he refolded it and placed it in his pocket. He was silent again for several blocks before he spoke. "Anne and Rose are two different species, I'm afraid. It's a queer thing, Mike. I don't know what to do. If I tell Anne about our visit today, she may send me to the devil for sticking my nose in." Will slumped in his seat and pulled his visor over his eyes and then continued. "He sounds like he has a tongue for all occasions besides. What would you think, Mike, if we talk to the Clayton Police? Don't you have a cousin out there?"

"Lawrence Casey, do you mean? He's in Carondelet. Anyway, would it be decent to tell all that Ollie said, after how grand she was to us? What about your father, Will—can't he lay down the law to Anne?"

Will made a contemptuous noise. "The old fellow! He's not in the law-laying business. For God's sake, didn't you ever meet him? And besides, he's stretched out in bed, red as a beet from walking in the sun, and my poor mother up all night, squeezing oranges. Remind me to pick some up at Costello's, if he even has any, when we get off."

"Then it's up to you, Will. Tell her right out you forbid her to see the scoundrel again and there's an end to it." Mike didn't sound convinced by his own argument. "How old is Anne, anyway?"

"Twenty-three. Past the age of consent." Will resumed thumping his palm with his nightstick.

"What are you going to do?"

"I have to think on it some more, Mike. It surely cannot be that she goes on living in our house and being his concubine at the same time."

Both driver and passenger fell silent. A policeman on horseback crossed the street in their path and hailed them. Mike called, "Good day, Jack!" To his friend he remarked, "There's a lot to be said for the mounted duty. It's a benefit for the whole human machine to be out-of-doors on a grand animal like that instead of hanging out after cardsharps and hopheads." He carefully omitted any reference to prostitution, out of deference for Will's feelings.

Will pulled his cap off and rubbed his hair. "Tell me Mike," he said, "what do you do when you need more from a woman than the 'Beer Barrel Polka'?"

Mike whistled through his teeth and laughed. Will hardly ever condescended to entertain topics like that. "There used to be a little widow," he said, "ran a bakery on Jefferson Avenue. I won't mention her name. It was Gertie, to tell you the truth. She was left with four kiddies and a bakery to take care of. I used to drop over once or twice a week, in the mornings usually. When her kiddies went off to school. We'd have some stollen or strudel, and I used to bring her an Italian stuff she liked called anisette. It was cozy. She was good to me, Will, and I was cast down when she moved."

"Where did she go?"

"Back to Cairo, Illinois. She got married to some farmer from her hometown. It was the best thing for her and her kiddies, I guess. I certainly wasn't going to marry her. Didn't you ever wonder how come I used to always say I was going to the bakery in the morning?"

"No," said Will, surprised. "I never paid any attention."

"Since she went away," Mike continued, "I haven't done too much in that line. What about you?" He tossed the question at his partner with feigned casualness, reflecting that it was a cold day in hell when Will O'Brien unbuttoned and that he might as well take advantage.

"I take the streetcar over the Eads Bridge to Belleville. There's a very clean house over there, run by a German woman. She scrubs the whole place down with carbolic acid every day. Like you, I go in the morning. Not very often, though."

"What do you go all the way to Illinois for?" Mike asked.

"Well, Mike, Illinois is out of St. Louis altogether. It's entirely out of Missouri. It's like going to a foreign country. I'll never run into one of those girls on Market Street, to taunt me in my uniform, like happened to that luckless detective, Kramer, do you remember? What are you laughing about? You have your ways and I have mine. Anyhow, if one of the chippies moves back to her farm and gets married, it doesn't put *me* off my stroke. I'll tell you that. I don't know one from another. And I don't care to."

"But, Will," Mike asked, suddenly earnest, "don't you sometimes have a little feeling about one of those girls?"

"I had a little feeling once. The creature takes hold of my feet and says, bold as brass, 'Oh, look at them tootsies. You must be a cop! Ain't you the naughty one!' I had a little feeling then and there that I wanted to break her neck. Stop laughing, Mike! You might choke and I don't know how to run this machine."

"Oh, Will, for telling me that story I'll teach you after we get off tonight—how's that?"

"You're a pal," Will replied. "I'll take a raincheck. Tonight my mother needs me in more ways than one. What time is it?"

"It's ten to three and we're not far now."

Will tapped his blue-trousered knee with his stick and sighed. "I've little heart for the force today."

"Now, Will," Mike replied, "you know how vice always takes your mind off your troubles."

The automobile drew to the curb before police headquarters.

6

Mrs. O'Brien poured herself a cup of tea in the kitchen alone and settled her fatigued body into her chair. She thought over the day's events—the juice and aspirin for Mr. O'Brien; the hurried trip to Produce Row with Vesta, who could scarcely carry more than two or three big sacks of potatoes, so that she had all the rest to manage herself; the sediment tanks to be filled, lifted, and later siphoned; the fire to boil the clothes, the wringing and the hanging out; the toast and flaxseed tea for Mr. O'Brien; Margaret home from work unexpectedly and needing a hot water bottle; aspirin for her, too, and paregoric; the peas to be shelled, and now the rest of dinner to get. Vesta could scrub the stoop—it wasn't going to rain again for a while —and she could peel the potatoes. And tonight, she calculated, let them eat liverwurst. They'll disparage, but I'll be confounded if I'll be frying meat tonight when Anne walks in this door. I need to compose myself.

She washed her face and hands from the water in the basin and pushed her combs more firmly into her hair. She walked toward the front room.

"Mother?" called Margaret from upstairs.

"I'm busy," Mrs. O'Brien responded shortly.

She knelt heavily at the prie-dieu, clasped her hands together, and prayed for divine guidance. After the initial formalities, she addressed a brief request to the divinity. "Holy Father, help me to find the right words to say to my daughter Anne to bring her back from the abyss of sin to the paths of righteousness." She finished her prayer and knelt for a long while over her beads, fingering one by one the smooth olive-wood balls that had come all the way from Assisi to Galway, from Galway to Liverpool, and from Liverpool to St. Louis, whose faint, patient click had accompanied her through separation and loss, storm at sea, typhoid fever, marriage and confinements, stricken infants, and the many fearful months when James was unable to find work. The thought came to her mind: This is one cross I do not deserve to bear. She bridled and rose to her feet, pocketing her rosary. Deserve! she said to herself. If any of us got what we deserve, we'd all be in hell by now.

This idea restored her moral equilibrium and she stepped purposefully to the front door to make sure Vesta was scrubbing their stoop as diligently as the German neighbors up the block scrubbed theirs. She was watching her servant, who pretended to be unmindful of her gaze, when the red Dion-Bouton pulled into Washington Avenue.

Mrs. O'Brien folded her powerful arms over her bosom, her wide skirt filling the doorway from jamb to jamb, and fixed the couple emerging from the automobile with a baleful stare.

Chris Schneider lifted Anne from her seat and approached the house with one arm still about her waist. In the other he held red gladioluses wrapped in paper.

"Mother!" Anne cried. "We've been so worried about how worried *you* must be! You won't believe what happened to us!"

"I daresay," Mrs. O'Brien replied.

Mrs. Mahoney thrust her head through the first-floor window of the house next door. "What did happen to you?" she asked.

"Come inside," said Mrs. O'Brien. They stepped over Vesta and her bucket and stood in the foyer.

"Mother," Anne said, "Chris feels so bad that you've never been formally introduced. May I present my friend, Chris Schneider?" He stuck out his hand eagerly but Mrs. O'Brien's arms remained folded.

"You are no friend of Anne's in my estimation, Mr. Schneider," she said, "and I will thank you now to leave this house. I have grave matters to discuss with my daughter."

"Oh, Mrs. O'Brien," he said sorrowfully, "I can tell you're angry with me, and don't I deserve it! You must think I'm a terrible blackguard, but if you only knew the misadventures we encountered! We were enjoying a dish of ice cream at Dowd's restaurant with my aunts when the rain began. And we couldn't get the automobile to start! I almost broke my arm on the crank!" His plaintive appeal, the easy charm of his warm brown eyes and ready smile, his eagerness to ingratiate himself, his sleek appearance in his pale linen suit—all these attributes were registered in Mrs. O'Brien's mind as so many deficits against the account of his name.

"Mother!" Anne interjected. "Don't be angry at Chrissie. It wasn't his fault. Look at my shoes and stockings! We had to walk to his house in the mud. Thank God his housekeeper was there, or else what would we have done? She helped me get cleaned up and lent me a nightdress. She fixed up a spare room for me." As Anne embellished effortlessly, elaborations poured into her mind. "She made us tea and put rum in it so we wouldn't catch cold."

"Sweetheart," said Chris, "if you're going to be on time for the late shift at Kinloch, you better change your things now."

"Good heavens, Chris, I must run!" She was up the

stairs and into her room before her mother could gather her wits.

Chris Schneider turned toward Mrs. O'Brien and gestured fondly after Anne's retreating figure. "You've raised a magnificent lady, Mrs. O'Brien. You must be proud of her indeed." She eyed him dourly, but did not respond. She could feel the prayed-for strength of rhetoric building inside her mind, but she did not want to release it yet, lest its force be spent prematurely. He smiled at her and shyly held forth his tissue-wrapped flowers. "I would be much obliged if you would put these gladioluses in a vase," he said. "A little token peace offering, Mrs. O'Brien. It pains me to think of you being so frantic last night. I know how you must have felt. My own beloved mother has to live in the country for her health, and she worries about my welfare all the time."

Mrs. O'Brien, listening to his words, looking at his boyishly earnest face, knew a moment of fear—an emotion she had seldom experienced in recent years. She thought that the devil himself must appear much like the man standing before her—not red and ugly at all, but smooth and fair and pleasing.

"St. Bridget's is on your way downtown, Mr. Schneider," she replied. "Father Mulvihil always appreciates a floral offering."

"Anne tried to telephone the store on your block, Mrs. O'Brien. She even asked one of the operators to keep ringing, but evidently she didn't get through. Won't you say we're forgiven?" He held his arms out to her in a mock-dramatic gesture, as if to embrace her. He was laughing, at his ease, radiating the assurance of a man who knew that women found even his most transparent flattery endearing.

She had never encountered such audacity in such a

winning guise. She turned to the staircase and called, "Anne!" Her daughter appeared for an instant on the landing and then swiftly descended the stairs, swinging a navy-blue straw hat in her hand.

"Is that what you're wearing to work?" asked Mrs. O'Brien, gesturing toward the girl's carefully pleated dark blue dotted-swiss dress, with its white silk bow at the neck.

"Chris is taking me out for a bite after work, so I won't be home for supper," she replied. She moved toward her mother to kiss her goodbye, and at that moment Mrs. O'Brien felt that her time had come. She took Anne's slender arm firmly in her strong grip and stepped between her daughter and the smiling stranger.

"Anne and Mr. Schneider," she began, "listen carefully to what I have to say. Anne must go to work now—we don't want her to lose her position. You have my permission to drive her down to the Kinloch company, but, Anne, when you get out of work at ten I want you to take the first trolley home. Your brothers will be waiting for you at the stop. Then you and I and the rest of the family are going to sit down and settle this business once and for all. Do I make myself clear?"

Anne's face flushed with anger. She started to interrupt her mother but Chris touched her shoulder and shook his head.

"Fair enough!" he said. "Mrs. O'Brien, you are a woman with a wonderful capacity for putting things straight. We will do just as you say, won't we, dear girl?" Anne did not answer, but stared defiantly at her mother.

Mrs. O'Brien turned to Chris Schneider with magisterial scorn. "As for you," she said, "I request you to take your gladioluses and your lying mouth out of my foyer, and please make it your business not to come back. Anne!" She held the girl's arm. "Do you comprehend my meaning or not? Home right after work—your brothers will be waiting. What do you say?"

Anne mumbled her assent.

"Louder," said Mrs. O'Brien. "I can't hear what you are saying."

"I said *yes*, I'll be home on the ten-oh-two." She pulled away from her mother's grasp.

Mrs. O'Brien opened the front door and motioned Chris Schneider out onto the sidewalk. "Anne," she said, "bear in mind that you live with your family in a Catholic home. You must behave like a decent Catholic woman or it will all be up with you."

"Yes, Mother," she answered, face still reddened and eyes downcast. She and Chris Schneider drove off again in the Dion-Bouton.

Mrs. O'Brien watched them go, as did Mrs. Mahoney, who raised her window to say, "Catherine O'Brien, will you take a cup of tea with me? I'm in need of consolation for a dire trouble my old fellow has gotten himself into."

"I'm sorry for your trouble, Mrs. Mahoney, but I have no time for tea this afternoon. Good day." She reentered the house, closed the door behind her, and ascended the staircase, feeling that, with the help of God, she had placed matters in their proper perspective.

Chris Schneider drove around the corner to a quiet block on Garrison Avenue. There he stopped the car, leaned back upon the seat, and burst out laughing.

"Oh, Annie," he said. "Where did a grand old girl like her get a daughter like you? The way she looked at my poor gladioluses, I'm surprised they didn't turn brown! What do you say we split a bottle of champagne at Faust's place and then go home for a little nap? Say, Annie, are you crying?"

"It's your fault if I am!" She turned on him furiously.

"She talked to me like I was an animal, and you grinning and mocking the two of us all the time! You said you could get around her, and now my brothers are going to be waiting at the trolley stop. You're nothing but hot air, Chris Schneider!"

He hit her so hard and so suddenly that for a moment she did not realize that she had been struck. Then she began to moan, her face in her hands. He slowly unwrapped a cigar, clipped the end, lighted it, and blew smoke in Anne's direction. "Stop that noise, sweetheart," he said softly, "or I'll hit you again."

Anne stopped crying on a strangulated croak and stared at him in fear.

"Now say you're sorry, sweetheart, and come, put your hand where Chris likes it."

"I can't, Chris, not out here in public," she whispered.

He hit her again.

"Oh, God, Chris, what's the matter with you?" She doubled over in the seat. He leaned back his head, drew on his cigar, and smiled affably at a startled couple passing in the street.

"Come on, Annie, love, don't let's waste the afternoon." He stroked her reddish-gold hair and watched the blue welt under her eye dispassionately. "Come now, dear girl, you don't want Chris to get angry with you."

She raised her head slowly and wiped her mouth. She stared at the red stain on her white glove, then took it off and threw it into the street. She turned toward him, searched his eyes for several moments, and then said in a low voice, "I'm sorry, Chris. Please kiss me and tell me you love me anyway." As he moved to embrace her, she slid her trembling hand across his thigh.

Margaret emerged from the bedroom in her wrapper, her face puffy but alert. "Mother," she said, "what went on with you and Anne? I thought I heard a man's voice downstairs. It wasn't him, was it?"

"It was him, Margaret, but by the grace of God I was able to put him in his place, because I saw, as clear as day, that it was her will at stake, not his."

"What are you talking about?" said Margaret. "Isn't he the vile seducer that ought to be thrashed?"

"That's just it," her mother replied. "I was thinking and thinking along those lines. And then it came to me that when the first woman took the forbidden fruit from Satan she met him more than halfway, didn't she? He was not obliged to wrestle her to the ground and force the apple down her throat. She was so enflamed she'd have wrenched it away from him if he'd tried to hold it back. That's how it is with Anne now. Schneider is a scoundrel —surely he will meet the fate he deserves one day. But we must bring Anne back from the brink of the precipice, Margaret, ourselves, we must take her to see Father Degnan, and we must pray to God to turn her will away from sin."

"What if she went over the precipice last night?" said Margaret, "and it's too late?"

"Too late? How can it be too late? Isn't Mary Magdalene one of our most revered saints? We must make her repent, Margaret, and then Chris Schneider will cease to plague us."

"Sit down and rest a little, Mother," said Margaret. "You've had such a deal of uproar today, and this evening you will need your strength to put Anne straight."

"How do you know that?"

"I listened! What am I supposed to do when my sister's behavior is turning my family upside down, and everybody in the neighborhood is laughing at us, and this morning when I got on the streetcar, Alma Levy says to me, so everyone can hear, 'Oh, I saw your sister Anne out in an automobile with a swell-looking fellow. He sure was familiar with her. Are they engaged?' "

"What did you say to her, Margaret?"

"I said right back at her what a pity it was that she didn't have a brain as big as her mouth."

"You know how to answer them, anyway, and that's a blessing. I will sit down. It's been a long day and it's not over yet—oh, my Lord!" she interrupted herself. "I forgot poor James! He must be destroyed by thirst. We'll speak another time, Margaret."

She entered the bedroom apologetically. "James," she said, "are you parched waiting for me? I'll go fetch you a drink."

"Don't fetch anymore, Catherine, sit down a moment and talk with me. I'm feeling better and I haven't laid eyes on you today. Vesta brought me my lunch."

"Well, James, you must forgive me. Things were confounded today, but surely we're back on the right course now. The fellow Schneider was here with Anne, and I made no bones about it. She must come straight home from work tonight and account for herself." She did not mention Father Degnan, whom her husband especially despised ever since he had denounced artists from the pulpit as "Bohemians and anarchists." The sermon had mortified those O'Briens who had heard it, and Mrs. Mahoney had had the cheek to commiserate. When conversing with Mr. O'Brien, it was wise to speak as little of the clergy as possible—not because he was likely to react with anger, but because he backed off from her so readily. It took such a little mistake to snuff out his friendliness and send him back to his newspaper. He reminded her of a timorous piglet she had loved on a farm her father owned when she was a child. Precisely because it was smaller and less bold than its siblings, it was the one she invested with her affection. It was for little "Princy" that she saved the best morsels, and she was thrilled when he would stay for a moment to be caressed by her. The other stout piglets crowding around her feet she ignored. She cried when her father said that Princy was a diseased animal and killed him.

Mr. O'Brien was in unusually bright spirits. His wife reflected that perhaps an occasional boil in the midday sun might not be an altogether bad thing for him. It might peel off his dead layers and revive him, cleansing his outsides as the Black Draughts he sometimes consumed cleansed his insides. At certain times when Mr. O'Brien seemed to be in his most diminished phase, he would purge himself drastically and stop eating. He had read that if the human body was completely emptied of nourishment for a week, no disease could survive. He emerged from these ordeals, on the whole, rather more chipper than he went into them. His wife was deeply impressed by his behavior. She felt with humility the difficulty she had postponing breakfast until after Mass, and always hurried home when church was out for a piece of bread, at least, before she started preparing the family meal. Fast days were a great burden to her. She did not understand where her husband got the strength for his prolonged abstentions, without a drop of faith to sustain him.

"I thought I heard a knock on the door before," he said. "Was it Pete Gentile?"

"No," said Mrs. O'Brien, relieved to see him looking better and pleased with having reestablished her moral authority in the household. She permitted herself a small pleasantry. "It was the man in the moon." Mr. O'Brien looked delighted, his wispy gray hair a faint nimbus around his head, his pale blue eyes actually seeming to twinkle.

"No, Catherine, really—wasn't it Pete?" he put his hand on hers.

"I tell you, it was the man in the moon." Now she was smiling.

"Well, then, what did he want?" said James, enchanted to share a spot of whimsey with his serious spouse.

"He came to punish you for walking in the sunshine with Pete Gentile instead of walking in the moonlight with your wife." She tapped his chin with her finger.

Mr. O'Brien's thin face was illuminated with joy. Catherine hadn't made a joke since she said the hurricane of 1893 would blow over. He felt a swell of love and longing for her—for her honest pug face, her ample body, and her smell of Borax. He sat up in bed, put his arms around her, and attempted to pull her down on top of him.

"James!" she cried, "look out for my glasses!" As he released her from his grasp, the broken lenses slid from her bosom to the floor.

"Oh, I'm so sorry, Catherine, and those were your new ones, too." He was humiliated by the unfortunate clumsiness of his romantic venture. She reached to the floor laboriously, and picked up the pieces. "Be careful," he said anxiously. "Don't cut your fingers."

"It would take more than a little bit of glass to cut my fingers," she said. "My hands are good and tough. It's a punishment on me anyway, for my nonsense." She smiled at him gently. "I'll bring you up some cold root beer Vesta and I made last week. Then you go back to sleep."

They heard the sound of a man's voice at the door, speaking to Vesta.

"I'll go," she said. "Don't fret over the glasses, Jimmy." She stooped to kiss his forehead, left the bedroom, and descended the stairs. Mr. O'Brien wished she had not said it was a punishment on her.

Pete Gentile was standing in the foyer, holding an enormous watermelon. "Mrs. O'Brien!" he cried. "Look at what I got—a watermelon from St. Lawrence O'Toole!"

He thrust it into her arms. "Take it for your dessert!" She accepted the cumbersome fruit with good enough grace. "Come out to the kitchen, Mr. Gentile. Let's see if we can shove it into the box."

Mr. O'Brien's head emerged shyly from his bedroom. "Is that you, Pete?" he called down the stairs.

"In a minute, Jimmy," his friend replied. "The missus and I, we got a melon to push."

Mrs. O'Brien carried the fruit under her arm to the kitchen. "I thought James told me you lived over in Our Lady."

"I do, but I was painting some motifs at Lawrence O'Toole while the sodality was peddling watermelons. I figured with your big family you could use a full one." He had recovered some of his enthusiasm for large families as his memory of the preceding evening at the O'Briens' faded. They opened the door of the icebox and stared dubiously at the crowded interior.

"If I take those cabbages out there might be room," she said. "They belong in the cellar anyhow." She handed cabbages to Pete Gentile, who placed them on the table one by one.

"You got lots of cabbages, Mrs. O'Brien," he said admiringly after a while. "My wife, she buys one cabbage, she throws half of it away."

"She could always pickle it—it keeps a long time. I learned that from my old neighbor on Biddle Street, Mrs. Spiegle."

"I'll tell Rosa—maybe she'll try it. Although she's never cared much for cooking. She makes some spaghetti in ten minutes and *bang!* that's it. We go out to eat mostly." Noting Mrs. O'Brien's heavily tufted eyebrows rise in astonishment as she placed still another cabbage in his hands, he added hastily, "We got Nonna that makes the regular meals. Rosa works—she's the head accountant for Meyer Brothers."

"You don't say! Your wife is an accountant?" Mrs. O'Brien took the watermelon from him and slid it into the space vacated by the cabbage. It extended nearly a foot from the front of the box. "This is the biggest melon I ever saw. Maybe we could eat it warm," she said.

"It's no good warm. How about we cut a piece off?"

"I still don't think there would be room," she replied. "How did your wife happen to get such a wonderful, responsible position? I'm amazed, really."

"She's a prodigy with numbers," said Pete. "When she was a little girl, in Citta Cattolica, people used to pay money to watch her add. They took her to the bishop's residence one time. She was so famous he wanted to see her. He told her when the world began and asked her how many days since the Fall, and she had the answer in a couple of minutes. Imagine!"

"I cannot imagine," said Mrs. O'Brien softly, her eyes open wide. "She must be a great help to the drug company."

"A great help is right," said Pete. "Mr. Meyer had a special chair built for her. She can add up a column of numbers longer than that watermelon, and figure the breaks, all in her head, *snap*! And she never makes a mistake."

"Does she like doing such hard work instead of staying home?" Mrs. O'Brien inquired a bit apprehensively.

"Like it? That's her meat. She'd rather add those numbers than live. And listen to this—old man Meyer pays her fifteen dollars a week."

"Fifteen dollars for a woman! Why, it's unheard of. I hope you realize your good fortune, Mr. Gentile."

Vesta entered the kitchen. "Mrs. Mahoney for you, Mrs. O'Brien," she said.

"Tell her I'm busy. And, Vesta, these cabbages belong in the cellar, please."

"You know what we could do, Mama?" asked Frank, who had entered the kitchen behind Vesta. "We could put the melon in the sed tank. It's nice and cold."

"The mud would seep in and spoil it," Mrs. O'Brien said.

"No, it's all waxy on the outside. You're right, Frank. Let's do it," said Mr. Gentile.

Frank dropped his quarter into his mother's apron and said, "What should I do with the bones?"

"Put them in the box—there's plenty of room now," his mother replied. "I'll tell you what, Mr. Gentile—after we drop the melon, I'll ask you to have a cool drink with James upstairs."

Pete hastened to rid himself of the problematical gift and returned to the kitchen to receive a tray carrying two glasses of brown liquid. "What is this stuff?" he asked, on the odd chance it was a civilized beverage.

"Root beer," she said. "Go on up now, Mr. Gentile— you'll do James good."

"At least it's got a head on it," said Pete to his friend. "Here's to your improvement, Jimmy."

They clicked glasses together, and Mr. O'Brien's eyes peered happily over his root beer at his visitor, flecks of foam stiffening his limp gray mustache. "You must have made a favorable impression on her after all, Pete. Did you ask for this or did she offer it spontaneously?"

"She asked me if I wanted some! What do you think I am, a moocher?"

"No offense intended, Pete," Mr. O'Brien assured his friend hastily. "It's just that Catherine is heavy with starch toward outsiders most of the time. I take this drink as a good sign."

"I brought you a joke," said Pete. "To cheer you up. The motorman told me this morning. A policeman finds a dead horse on Pestalozzi Street, see, so he starts to write out a report. He goes, 'P-i-s, no, P-e-s-s, no, P-i-z, no,' and then he says, 'The hell with it. I'll drag him up to Grand.'" The two men chuckled together. "Don't tell your son who's a detective," Pete added.

"Oh, no, I wouldn't," said Mr. O'Brien. "Will doesn't tolerate any disrespect for the uniform."

"I also brought you a piece of good news. Hirschenroeder told Francis Bruenn and he told me that he's going to let us have the Filipinos. What's the matter—don't you feel good?"

"I think I'm still too sick to think about Filipinos, Pete. Let's wait until I'm well before we discuss that anymore. Tell me about Lawrence O'Toole. How is Marray's Assumption holding up?"

"It's all turning green and sliding off the wall. Serves them right. Every time I see it I laugh. Say, I brought you a picture." He unrolled a print and spread it on his friend's bed. "It's called *The Harp of the Winds.* Do you know what's so remarkable about it?" James held the lithograph up and studied it carefully.

"The first remarkable thing to me is the powerful impression it makes," he said thoughtfully. "The second thing is that the artist, Homer Dodge Martin, is blind. I read all about this picture in the *Art News* some years back."

"James! You're the eighth wonder of the world! You know everything already! But how did he do it—can you figure that out? I couldn't even draw a cross without my eyes."

"Maybe you could," said Mr. O'Brien. "Maybe it's a power that only comes out in us when the sight is gone. It's possible."

"If he laid on his strokes and let them dry in between, do you think he could feel where to place the next ones with his fingers? And paint the whole picture that way? But it seems unnatural to me, to be so methodical and to have to go so slowly, without seeing."

Mr. O'Brien continued to examine it with great interest. "It's the strongest possible composition," he said. "I'll never forget it, will you?" The two men discussed the picture's aesthetic qualities and its technical aspects. James concluded that it was artistically superior to Martin's earlier paintings, when the artist had still been sighted, precisely because it was unnatural. It was not only free from the visual domination of the subject, but even free from the influence of itself. The conversation agitated him, and at one point he tried to rise from his bed, to bring sketch pads and ink from his studio so that he and his visitor could experiment with drawing figures while their eyes were shut. Pete Gentile hastened to fetch the materials himself.

While the two friends tried their hands at being blind artists, the life of the house swirled beneath and around them as the family returned from work. Frank knocked on his father's door. "I wanted to know if you were still sick, Father. What are you doing?" Pete Gentile explained the experiment to the boy. "Oh, can I watch?" he said, "I won't make any noise."

"Leave us, Frank," Mr. O'Brien replied without opening his eyes. "Boys can't help making noise."

Frank shut the door behind him and sat on the hall steps, drowsily listening to the occasional murmur of the men's voices until he was roused by Owen, hitting the back of his neck with a pea. He told his brother to go away and stop acting like a savage. From his vantage point on the stairs he was the first to see Dr. Kieffer arrive.

Later he greeted his brothers and sisters as they came in from work, one by one, until it was time to set the table.

The family grumbled over the liverwurst without much conviction. The older ones were saving themselves for the impending battle with Anne. There was a general sentiment at the table that Will should be home, his absence leaving them feeling vaguely at risk.

"He is assigned to a grave case. He had no choice but to work late," said Mrs. O'Brien.

"A nest of cardsharps?" Mamie asked. As far as Mrs. O'Brien formally acknowledged to the family, the only vice in Will's jurisdiction was gambling.

"It's a confidential police matter, Mame. I ask no questions," she replied. The statement was close to being true; Will was so accustomed to telling his mother the day's events that she did not need to ask many questions. Where he left gaps in his schedule she never inquired.

"Where is Kathleen?" asked Jim suddenly, to everyone's surprise. He usually paid little attention to his sisters.

Mrs. O'Brien answered, "The photographer fellow, Andrews—he's taking her to the Olympia tonight to see a play."

"I don't like it," Jim said somberly.

"Why not?" asked his mother. "She is old enough to go to the theatre with an escort."

"This fellow on the afternoon shift at the brewery, he was mocking me. He said he saw my sister parked on Garrison Avenue in a red automobile with some sport. And I won't tell you what else he said. He's a tough guy. He thinks he can beat me. He's always aching for a fight. Tell her to stop it." He stared at his mother belligerently, folded a piece of liverwurst, and stuck it all into his mouth at once. He kept staring at her as he chewed. She lowered her eyes. There was no use making a scene with Jim at the moment.

She rose to clear the table. "We have watermelon for dessert," she said. "Mr. Gentile brought it."

Jim scowled more deeply still and stabbed a potato with his fork as she was lifting the serving platter. She continued to ignore him, but her hands were shaking as she carried the platter back out to the kitchen.

"You're nerts," whispered Owen loudly. "It wasn't Kathleen at all, but Annie."

Mamie carried dishes to Vesta at the sink. "I'll be off without the melon now, lest I be late," she said to her mother.

"Where are you going?" Mrs. O'Brien asked.

"To the French Mothers for the sewing. I told you yesterday."

"Be home by ten, Mame. We're going to have it out with Anne." Mamie hurried through the door and down the street in the warm fall dusk, pausing for a moment at St. Leo's to light a candle and say a brief prayer for her sister.

Mrs. O'Brien prepared a plate of potatoes and peas for her husband. There was no doubt but that it was too soon for liverwurst. She put the food on a tray with a cup of tea. She opened the kitchen door, stepped out upon the porch, and broke off a sprig of fragrant honeysuckle vine growing over the railing. She placed it upon the tray and carried it up the back stairs.

She and her husband were looking at the drawings he and his friend had made with their eyes shut when she heard the automobile stop in front of the house and Anne come in the front door. "What time is it, James?" she asked.

"It's only eight thirty," he said, pulling his pocket watch

from his bathrobe. "I thought you said she was taking the ten o'clock trolley."

Mrs. O'Brien stood up.

"I know you'll bring her to reason, Catherine," he said.

"To reason or to her knees, one or the other," replied Mrs. O'Brien, straightening her bun and untying her apron. "Here, James, let me stick this in a corner for the moment." She left the room and stood at the head of the stairs, looking at her daughter in the foyer below.

"Come to the sewing room, Anne," she said.

7

SHE WAS IN her big chair, Margaret at her side, when Anne entered the room, sporting a black eye and an unrepentant air.

"What happened to you?" her mother cried.

"I had an accident, that's what happened, after you spoke to me so harshly, and in front of Chris. I was beside myself all day!" She burst into tears and threw herself upon the settee.

"Margaret," said Mrs. O'Brien, "go to the kitchen and cut off a piece of the brisket and bring it up here, please." Margaret took the back stairs two at a time, praying that she wouldn't miss a word. Mrs. O'Brien wet a rag in the bathroom and wiped her daughter's face. "You've got powder on!"

"Yes," Anne replied. "I was so embarrassed to be seen like this that I stopped at the Grand Leader on the way home and asked Nellie Donnelly to lend me some. Not there! That's where it hurts!" And she began to weep again. The crying felt good. It somehow convinced her that the story she was about to tell was the truth, and if not the truth, then something even better. She rose and searched distractedly for a handkerchief, her exquisite features conveying a profound sense of injustice.

Her mother hastened to fetch her a clean one, almost running over Frank, who was listening in the hallway. She said only "Go to bed, Frank," in the most perfunctory way, so he decided to keep listening. When Margaret hurried by him she hissed *"sneak"* in his ear and gave him an unexpected shove that sent him sprawling. Despite the discouraging encounters with his female relatives, he continued to stay by his post, as he had no wish to go to his room, where Jim was passed out on the cot, snoring.

Margaret and Mrs. O'Brien attended to Anne's eye. Recovering her composure, Anne again turned to her mother accusingly: "I was unsettled in my mind by the awful names you called me," she began.

"I never called you names," Mrs. O'Brien protested. "I only said you had to come right home after work."

"I was so distressed," Anne went on, "that when my relief came I stepped straight out onto the floor without looking where I was going and one of the skaters, Charlie, came crashing right into me." She described the incident in detail, having witnessed, with great hilarity, just such a crash a few weeks before, when a roller skater had collided with an operator in the central switching room of the Kinloch company. "I landed in the pile of cords on the floor, with Charlie on top of me, and another boy, Louie, tripped over the cord Charlie was carrying. They're going like sixty in that room, and too bad for you if you end up in the middle." She looked at her mother to see how the old girl was taking it.

Mrs. O'Brien's face was an unrevelatory pink wall.

"Any number of cords got pulled out," Anne continued, "and a great lot of screaming went on—I can tell you that. Half the telephone conversations in St. Louis were cut off. It was a terrible imbroglio, believe me, and when Mr. Yesner fired me and Charlie and Louie, right in front of everybody, and me with my mouth bleeding and my eye hurt, I wished I was dead!" Anne finished with a flourish of her handkerchief. She experienced the warm glow that follows a successful creative effort. The story not only explained her shiner, her coming home early, and her getting fired, which Mrs. O'Brien would find out about on Friday in any event, it placed the responsibility for all of it squarely in her mother's lap.

Her triumph, however, was cut short when Margaret said, "Who hit you in the eye then—Mr. Yesner?"

"Nobody hit me on purpose," Anne protested. "It was an accident. I just *told* you, Charlie landed on me with his roller skates." She began to sob again.

"It looks to me like somebody smacked you right in the eye," Margaret continued implacably.

Anne emitted a howl of rage and Mrs. O'Brien hastily intervened to quiet her down. "All right, Anne, Margaret, that will do. We've had enough for one evening of crying. It's a terrible thing if you've lost your position, Anne, and I doubt that Mr. Yesner will give you much of a character, either, after what happened. Don't commence again! There's nothing to carry on so about! You can see how all these troubles descended upon us, can you not?"

"What do you mean?" Anne asked.

"You can see for yourself what a punishment it is on you for carrying on with Chris Schneider, and making a spectacle of yourself, and not behaving the right way. But now, Anne"—Mrs. O'Brien took her daughter's hand— "that you see the consequences, you can put a stop to it, and see Father Degnan, and do what he says, and then everything will be back the way it was and there will be no more said about it."

"No more said about what? About me and Chris?" She laughed, her eyes still wet with tears. "Are you imagining you won't hear more of Chris? If that's what you think, Mother, you're mistaken. I'll never stop seeing Chris—not as long as I have eyes in my head."

"How can you say such a thing?" Margaret erupted angrily. "Don't you realize you're disgracing yourself and your whole family? Do you know what people are saying about you? They're asking me if you are engaged, the way you throw yourself on him in public!"

"Then tell them yes! I'm engaged!" Anne reached into her bodice and pulled out a hundred-dollar bill, which she tossed across the table. "Chris said to buy whatever I want with it, so I'll buy myself a ring. Will that satisfy you?"

"Anne." Her mother stared at the bill and then at her daughter in bewilderment. "What is this money for?"

"It's for me, that's what it's for—for a lavaliere, or a ring, or whatever I wish. He gives me anything I want, he treats me like a queen, and if I want to marry him I've only to say the word!" Her cheeks were flushed and she was stammering with excitement.

"Marry him!" Mrs. O'Brien was thunderstruck. "Surely you don't ever mean to marry him, Anne!"

"Why not, if I choose to? I'm old enough, I want to be with Chris, and that's all I want! I *will* marry him if I want to! We love each other, we're bound to be together. Listen, Mother, you've no call to look at me that way— we're as good as married anyway, whatever you think about it!"

"Don't say any more." Her mother rose to her feet. "No more, Anne. You're going too far—stop now . . ."

"I'm already his wife in everything but name!" Anne screamed. The window of the house next door was heard to fly open, and Frank, out in the hall, wondered what she could possibly be that made her a wife in everything but name. He felt ill with the excitement and mystery.

Mrs. O'Brien regarded her red-faced, bruised, tremulous daughter for some moments in silence before speaking. "Come, Anne," she said at length, "let us sit down and talk calmly. Margaret, would you be good enough to fetch us some tea?" Margaret obeyed, astonished by her mother's quiet reaction to the revelation of Anne's delinquency.

Mrs. O'Brien took her daughter's hand and stroked it. "Soothe yourself, Anne. You're all overwrought and seeing things as worse than they really are. It's a terrible thing you've gotten into—there's no doubt of it. Sometimes a girl—a decent, God-fearing girl like you, I mean—makes a mistake, and she thinks then that she has to pay for it for the rest of her life. But that's not necessarily true. Anne? Do you follow my reasoning?" She touched her daughter's hair, watching her face anxiously.

"No," said Anne.

"What I mean is, in the King's English then, is that the sin can be forgiven, it can be washed away—you don't have to marry him. Anne? Do you understand? Even if different things took place that shouldn't have done, you don't have to get *married*. Father Degnan will tell you the same thing, I know. It can all be washed away. You don't have to ruin your life for one false step. Many's the respectable woman, Anne, who has atoned for a folly in her youth, and no one needs to be the wiser. We'll see Father tomorrow—I'll go with you. You'll make a general confession and then we'll see what's required. There will be special penance. Don't be frightened, he won't be too strict—that's what priests are for. If there were no sin, what would we need with the clergy?"

Anne took a sip of the milky tea her sister served her, and holding the steaming cup in her hands, she spoke softly, without looking at her mother. "You still don't grasp my meaning, Mother. I let Chris have me because I wanted to, and I'll marry him for the same reason, so we can always have each other and not be persecuted about it. That's all."

Margaret slammed her cup into the saucer, spilling tea on the sewing machine. "Oh, no," she began, "that is *not* all. That's only the start, you brazen tramp, you shameless tart, talking your filth to our mother, in our house. I'd like to pull that red hair out of your head and snatch you bald, so your ne'er-do-well sees what a forlorn, Godless creature you really are!" She paused, gasping for breath. She was about to pitch the contents of the teapot at her sister's head when Mrs. O'Brien restrained her.

"Margaret! Be still this minute!" Mrs. O'Brien hurried to the window and slammed it shut. She left the sewing room and reappeared, carrying an electric fan. She plugged it into the light socket and turned it on. Then she folded a piece of pattern paper and attached it to the rim, so that it clattered noisily in the breeze from the blades. "Do you want the whole parish listening to this conversation, Margaret? Anne?"

"No, Mother," said Margaret, pale and distraught, "it's just that I am pushed beyond my bounds by her. I cannot believe it's possible to say such things and not be struck down. I cannot believe I'm in my own sewing room, listening to my own sister spew such vileness. It's as if the whole world has stopped and I can't tell what's up and what's down."

Mrs. O'Brien settled onto the chair heavily, her gaze focused on a landscape of her memory. "You aren't twenty-four years old yet, Anne," she said. "You are in the best time of your life—you're healthy and free, without a care in the world. Don't you realize what it is to be married? At your age, you can have ten, twelve, fifteen children if you get married now. Why put yourself in the way to ruin your body, your life, for what? For romance? Surely, Anne, you have more judgment than to submit yourself to the calamities of married life, to destroy yourself and everything we have accomplished."

She gestured around the room, at the pier glasses, the dressmaker's dummies, and the sewing machine.

"How can you tell me I'm too young to be married?" Anne cried. "Didn't you marry Father when you were both nineteen years old? Do you feature keeping us here, slaves, until we're too old to care, like poor Carmen Tierney?"

"Your father and I were married when we were nineteen," Mrs. O'Brien replied, "indeed we were. We cleaved to each other and clung to one another for we had nobody else. Do you suppose that if I had lived with my father and mother in a spacious, clean, beautiful house like this, with a big bedroom I'd to share with only one sister, with a chifforobe all to myself filled with more dresses than a duchess, and hot meals, served to me by a servant—do you think it would have entered my head to get married at nineteen? Or your poor father either. If he had had a decent place to lay his head, do you imagine he would have wanted to *get married*? For what? If he had a place for all his things and almost trifling duties around the household? You keep half your salary, Anne. This man is a virtual stranger to you. Are you looking for chains to be bound with?" She did not permit her daughter to answer, but plunged ahead as if a dam holding back words had been burst.

"When I came to this country in eighteen sixty-nine," she continued, "I was fifteen years old. My Aunt Bessie in Liverpool sent me here to St. Louis to stop with her old neighbor, Maggie Callahan. I knew not one soul in the whole United States. I'd only the name of Maggie Callahan in St. Louis for comfort on this whole continent. When I arrived in New York, everything was stolen from me but the clothes on my back, my train ticket here, and a five-pound note I had sewn in my bodice. So that I had not even a mantle for the cold, and if I hadn't found Maggie, where would I have gone? Maggie and Brianey Callahan and their son Lawrence lived in the alley behind Biddle Street, in the yard where Kabelfleisch the carpenter lived. They had a kitchen with a stove and a room, that was all. Maggie and Brianey had a big bed in the room. Lawrence had a cot. He stayed there all the time because he had consumption. I slept out in the hallway on a pallet on the floor. I had a rag to hang from the ceiling for all my privacy. I hung my Sunday dress next to it." Mrs. O'Brien reached distractedly into her basket of darning and drew out a sock.

Anne had curled into a corner of the settee, her face hidden by her hand, her shoulders shuddering from time to time. Margaret sat bolt upright, her gaze fixed anxiously on her mother.

"There was a privy in the yard," Mrs. O'Brien continued. "Twelve families used it. I was frightened to go there because a man from Connaught with a face like a shovel used to wait there at night. I used to ask Maggie to go with me, or Mae Larkin, who lived down the hallway. Maggie Callahan was a saint, but she was simple. All she cared for in the world was Lawrence. She spent the whole day taking care of him—washing him, fixing what she could for him to eat, singing little songs for him. Brianey had an awful temper and when he drank he was like the devil. He said Maggie cared nothing for him, and him working all day to put bread on the table and sugar in the tea, and her saving all the best bits for Lawrence and nary a scrap for him. It was true. One day a neighbor we had, a woman from Italy, brought Maggie an egg custard with maraschino cherries inside. They came all the way from Sicily in a jar. She was the grandest neighbor to Maggie, only I forget her name. Wouldn't you know, Maggie let Lawrence eat it all, and the next day—oh, that's right! Her name was Mrs. Leone—she asks Brianey how he liked the custard. I thought he was going to kill Maggie that night. I lay on my pallet and said my beads while he shouted and threatened and cursed. Lawrence coughing something terrible. You've never seen anyone dying yet, glory be to God.

"Then, afterward," she continued, sipping the lukewarm tea, "he wouldn't give Maggie enough money. She said he was trying to starve the boy. But the dreadful thing that happened, I lay the blame on myself. Lawrence's pyjamas were all worn out, and it was winter. So I unpinned the pound notes and took them to the Boatman's Bank. A few days later they gave me American money for them. Then Maggie and I took five dollars and we went to Famous and bought Lawrence a beautiful pair of pyjamas. Cursed be the day, I remember them well. They were fine yellow wool and silk, woven together. We washed Lawrence's hair and dried it and put him in the yellow pyjamas. I remember how gay he was that evening, and when you think on God's mercy to him, it is wonderful.

"We were all smiling at some little joke when Brianey came in, and we all three of us froze at the sight of him, drunk and red in the face. He saw the pyjamas and it was as if he had lost his right mind. He said he drove dray in all weather twelve hours a day while Maggie and Lawrence stayed home by the fire and ate all the custard and never thought he might care for some. He swore and drank from a bottle of whiskey. Just when it seemed like he might quiet down and go to sleep, he became agitated again.

"I stayed in my corner and prayed Maggie wouldn't tell him I was the one who gave the five dollars. He started to shake Lawrence's cot, and Maggie crying and praying and begging him to stop. And then he did an awful thing. He picked Lawrence up, pulled off the pyjamas, and then flung him back on the cot stark naked. Then he put the pyjamas on himself, too small for him though they were, and made Maggie get in bed with him. I won't tell you the dreadful things he did then. He finally fell asleep, and in the night I tiptoed in to wrap Lawrence in my blanket. The poor child was dead. He must have passed away amidst all the horrible noises and nobody even noticed. I didn't know what to do." She paused and looked intently at Anne. Her daughter had pulled the pins from her hair and the ruddy tresses obscured her face. She did not look up when Mrs. O'Brien's voice stopped.

"What did you do then, Mama?" asked Margaret, moving her chair closer to her mother's.

"I was afraid to wake Maggie for fear of arousing Brianey, and I was afraid of going out to knock up the priest on account of the man from Connaught by the privy. Still I had to get a priest in a hurry, for poor Lawrence had only two hours post mortem for the supreme unction to do any good. And I wasn't sure when he had died. I was so ashamed to bring a priest into that room, without even the white cloth on the little table with the devotional candle, and poor Lawrence without a stitch. I was humiliated to be a party to such a bestial scene. I even thought, God help me, of climbing back into bed and letting Maggie find him in the morning."

She stared soberly at her darning, her fingers tirelessly weaving the needle back and forth across the hole, her face lost in the pain of the night she was describing. "I prayed to St. Christopher," she went on, "and my prayer was answered. It came to me to try the back gate, and if it was open I could slip down the alley, so as to avoid the privy altogether. Which I did. Father Degnan was down in St. Patrick's in those days. He came right to the door when I rang the little bell, almost as if he had been waiting. He was a young priest then, and every bit as harsh at thirty as he is today. But when it came to terrible troubles, he never failed a soul. Your brother Will says it's only the good times that enrage Father Degnan. So he came, and never a whisper of reproach, and we buried Lawrence from Mae Larkin's. Yes, Margaret, what else could we do? She let us lay him out in her front room. The whole time Maggie keened and Brianey stayed in bed. He didn't even come to his own son's funeral. In fact I was the one who paid for it. Maggie had not a dime put aside."

"Mother," said Margaret, "why did you never tell me about this before?"

"I wouldn't be telling you now except to answer Anne's question about why I was wed so young. It wasn't ten days later, Margaret, that the hand of fate grasped Brianey, for he woke up one morning spitting blood, and then you should have seen the way Maggie turned on him. He went fast—he was dead in six weeks. But what a six weeks! How dear he paid for his wickedness! He would plead with Maggie for a little care, but she only jeered him and taunted him and said ironies to him about his fine yellow pyjamas and all the good they were doing him. She had him thrown in Potter's Field, still in the pyjamas, with not a word said over him, like a dog.

"I've tried to put that winter as far out of my mind as it would go. After Brianey died, Maggie started drinking and using foul language herself. So Anne, you see, when I met your father on the streetcar and we used to converse on the way to work, and I saw what a refined person he was, that never cursed or passed remarks at all, and didn't drink or even spit, and that was as dainty as a girl and always spoke so nicely, I couldn't believe the good fortune that caused him to enjoy my company." She bit off the end of her thread and tied a nearly invisible knot before continuing.

"He was stopping at his Aunt Kate's, with eleven children in three rooms, and he was in despair for lack of quiet. He was so pale and thin from all the clamor debilitating him that when he finally asked me to walk out with him, we went to the cemetery. We used to sit on the bench in the sunshine and admire the peacefulness after we tended Lawrence's bit of a plot. One Sunday he said to me, 'Catherine, I've next to nothing now, and little enough in prospect, but if you'll have me, I'll be proud to share my lot with a fine woman like you.' So that's how it was. Father Degnan married us that summer and we moved down the alley from Maggie, so I could look in on her every day. We only had each other for keep and consolation until Will was born, Anne, and then you. And then all the others, in such a blessing of numbers. We haven't done so badly, though, have we? You'll never have to pass nights such as I spent under Brianey Callahan's roof and you need not hurtle yourself into a precipitous engagement, either, nor take on the awful burdens of matrimony. Especially since you've scarcely met, and you being so young. Anne? Anne!" Mrs. O'Brien looked at her daughter, stood up from the chair, walked across the room, and roughly pulled her hair from her forehead.

Anne was asleep.

8

LATE THAT EVENING Will and Mike were seated around the oak table in Captain Kieley's office with Foley and Cummings from Chicago. They were listening to Chief of Police Gillaspy explain the large-scale white slavery operation they were about to investigate. The hum of the electric fan blurred Gillaspy's voice and while Will attempted to follow the chief's words, his attention wandered. Thoughts of his sister in Schneider's bed and of the hole in Schneider's wall distracted him from the description of the cooperative crackdown being organized by St. Louis, Chicago, and Memphis.

"Thank God," the chief was saying, "a politician's daughter got herself caught in their net. He's a big shot, too, so we're getting all the cooperation we could ask for. The district leaders, prosecutor Folk, and Mayor Wells himself have promised to see it through. That's why you fellows are here. Desmond in Chicago picked his best men and we picked ours. This time we're going to get convictions that stick."

Will opened his blue eyes wide and felt himself flush. Best men! If he was the best, he thought bitterly, then crime was a safe way to make a living in St. Louis. His pencil traced wavy lines on the pad of paper before him. By "best" the chief meant "honest," he reflected, and surely he was that. Yet was honesty enough when it came to dealing with a serpent like Schneider?

Another doubt assailed him. Was it not deceit he and

Mike had just practiced on old Ollie? He was drawing bars over the wavy lines when the chief's words again caught his attention.

"This politician is a Swede from Iowa. His oldest girl, Tillie, takes violin lessons and features herself on stage like Paganini. The old man wants her to put down the fiddle and get married. That's where it all comes undone at the Jensens' house. She runs off to Chicago and answers an advertisement for musicians. The next thing she knows, she's coming to in a stinking cabin with half a dozen other girls, all sick as hell, all blondes, she said. Not one of them knows what hit her. A fellow comes in with some roust-abouts—he says they're going to break these girls in right. Tillie Jensen, she may not be smart, but she's strong and stubborn as a mule. She follows them out on deck, spies a great big long pole, and she hauls off and lays the fellow out cold with it. Then she jumps into the Illinois River, still with her pole. Instead of drowning, like she ought to, she's dragged to a little island of mud sticking out of the river. She lays there, more dead than alive, until that night a fellow comes by in a rowboat. Catfishing. He tries to take advantage, and I'll be cremated if she don't smack him with her pole, too. And takes his boat. She ends up on the levee of a little town name of Corona."

"By Harry," said Will, "that's what I call a woman."

"It is?" asked Mike, surprised.

"She goes right to the sheriff," the chief continued, "and stops with his wife until her old man comes for her. Now the whole clan of Swedes, and there must be I don't know how many thousands of Jensens alone, are swarming around their leaders in Chicago and Milwaukee and places like that. There's a newspaper, the *Sun*, arousing itself frantically and the Watch and Warders are coming from Boston to stage a rally on the levee this Sunday. Isn't that right, Sergeant Foley?"

"Indeed it is," replied the policeman from Chicago, "and it promises to be a grand spectacle, with ministers from I don't know what kinds of religions all coming to lead the prayers and do some singing."

"Protestants," said Will.

"Probably," Foley continued, knowingly, "and Tillie Jensen herself is going to make a speech, still carrying her pole with the flag stuck on it. Of course, the force will turn out strong in support of the cause."

"What's the cause again?" asked Mike.

"Why, to mop up the whole operation. Even some of the big houses in Chicago are going to help. They say this thing is giving vice a bad name and just encouraging the crackpots to make trouble for everybody."

"We don't have that much to go on yet," said the chief. "We have our work cut out for us, boys, and no mistake. Tillie said the boat was an old side-wheeler with no name on it she could see, but she did spot *Northern Belle* on a life preserver."

"She's not so dumb," said Will. "That's good observation."

"Ask her if she'd like a job in St. Louis," said Mike. "I'd feel safer with her and her pole in my neighborhood."

The chief waved his hand. "Let's break for supper, boys. I'll fill you in on the rest later. Oh, wait a minute. Here's a couple of names of employment agencies here in St. Louis that were advertising." He consulted a notebook. "Do you know anything about Barnett and Brown? No? How about T. J. Fagin, Cooper, and Schneider?"

"Schneider?" said Will sharply. "What's the first name?"

"That's all I got," said the chief, "and they may be fabrications anyway. Coogan in the first precinct will know tomorrow, if anybody does. Let's go."

The men retired to the back room of Joe Ward's saloon down the street, where the police had eaten since Headquarters closed its kitchen the year before. The men from Chicago and the men from St. Louis sized one another up over the hash, potatoes, and beer Joe Ward put before them.

"How long you been working?" asked Foley.

"Four years, the both of us," said Will. "We only got put on vice this year, though."

"How come you're still in uniform?" asked Foley.

"Because I want them in uniform," said Captain Kieley. "Tomorrow, though, plain clothes for you two."

"You got any vice to speak of in a place like this?" Foley inquired condescendingly.

"Some," Will answered. "It's hard on a man to have to go all the way to Chicago just to get his ashes hauled."

"We got gambling, too," said Mike eagerly. "We even have roulette and some other French business. The Chinamen smoke dope, but they don't bother anybody."

"Sometimes, Mike," said Will.

"Oh, that's right. We had one Chinaman last week went screaming up Gratiot Street . . ."

"In Chicago," said Cummings, leaning back in his chair. "Let me tell you about Chicago. This Englishman wrote a book where he said that in Chicago we got the most vice of any place in the world. Any place." He paused for a moment to assess the effect of his words on his listeners. Noting their blank expressions, he decided to emphasize. "More than Paris, more than London, more than New York! The payoff from our madams alone is a million and a half dollars a year! That's right. Think on it. The God's truth." Cummings signaled to Joe Ward for a refill and continued expansively. "We got a pike that's nothing but sporting houses. One of them, run by the Everley sisters— it's like a king's castle. They charge fifty dollars a trick— twenty for the girl, twenty for the house, and ten for the protection."

"Fifty dollars?" Will registered skepticism. "What do they throw in, a new set of clothes?"

"Nothing extra is included," replied Cummings. "If you want a drink, you have to pay for it besides. But it's a glorious place, with fountains and mirrors and unheard-of things. One fellow I know—he's a big Democrat—he says they let loose a spray of perfume and a whole herd of orange butterflies to crown his achievements, you might say." Cummings leaned back in his chair, swallowed his beer, and thought fondly of Chicago's magnificence. Mike glanced at Will to see how his partner was taking the news from the big city.

"You mean they let bugs crawl on a fellow while he's getting his wick dipped?" Will snorted contemptuously. "That's a dirty way to run a house. Here in St. Louis, you're in and out for under a buck, and there's nothing crawling up your hide, either. That's one thing Mike and me are very particular about—the girls have to get checked out for lice and different vermin every couple of days—don't they, Mike? Your Chicago cocksmen are different from the ones in St. Louis—fifty bucks with bugs would never go here." Will pushed his plate away and gestured to Joe Ward. "Let's have another round of St. Louis brew for the men from Chicago."

"Maybe what the big Democrat thought was perfume was really bug spray—don't you think that might be it, Will?" Mike Egan offered helpfully.

Before Will could express an opinion, Foley came to his partner's aid. "We've got a House of All Nations up there that offers everything in the world. What do you want— you want a Gypsy?"

"I don't want a Gypsy," said Will, offended.

"No, but what I mean is, say you want a Gypsy, or a Russian, or a señorita from Spain—they're all there, under one roof. It's educational. Can you guess what woman has got the biggest following, so that you have to make an appointment a week in advance? Can you guess? You'll never figure this one. It's Ti-Ti, the Pygmy girl. No, it's true! She's only about four feet tall, and she's all tattooed. You should see them lining up for Ti-Ti! They say she's mean as the devil and depraved. They say she's put away ten thousand dollars. She's got her teeth filed to little bitty points. A couple of weeks ago the governor of a populous state came back three days in a row for Ti-Ti."

"Don't say which one, now," interjected Cummings.

"I didn't say which one. Anyway, the point I'm making is that you have somewhat of a worldly type of bordello in Chicago—not just the neighborhood cathouse. Places like the Everley sisters' and the House of All Nations—they attract the distinguished clientele."

Will blew his nose at some length before replying. "Well, Mike," he said at length, "I'm truly mortified for the home town. We think we're the nuts when we can get the girls at Mother Johnson's to use soap and hot water. And hardly a one with a bone in her nose. I'm not surprised the 'distinguished clientele' heads for Chicago when it has a mind to lower itself in style."

The chief and the captain continued their private conversation earnestly, ignoring the give-and-take occupying the rest of the table. When they rose to leave the saloon, the men followed, speaking of relatives and acquaintances on the two city police forces.

"Is Clarence Walsh still in the eleventh precinct up there?" asked Mike. "I used to see him sometimes—he was an old towny of my father's."

"Walsh is an inside man now," said Foley. "His eyes got too bad on him for the beat. They figured his white cane hurt confidence around the ward."

"Give him my regards, if you see him. Tell him Mike Egan says he's better off inside, from what I hear about Chicago."

It was nearly one in the morning when the chief dismissed them with instructions to report back the next day at eleven. Will and Mike bid the "last-outers" good night and descended the steps together. The deserted street still gave off the odors of heat and horses and the peculiarly dank exhalations of the river a few blocks away.

"I could stand a trip to the bathhouse," said Mike. "I'd like Bones to go over me with his rolling pin for a while."

"Tomorrow," said Will, "before we meet with the chief again."

"Say, Will, you got bathtubs with pipes in your house. How do you like that?"

"It's a great improvement in one way, but in another I miss the company down at Bones'. If my mother can spare me, I'll meet you there about ten."

Mike cranked up his car and they started west on Locust Street. "I could see your surprise, Will, when the chief asked about a hoodlum name of Schneider," he said after a pause.

Will sighed and wiped the sweat from his face. "It's a common name, Mike. There must be a hundred of them in St. Louis. How much trouble could one fellow cause, anyway? Tomorrow is soon enough for more bad news. I hope my mother isn't sitting up for me when I get home. I'd like to lie down and go right to sleep."

The house was quiet when Will let himself in the front door, and he was asleep before Mike had backed the automobile into its shed.

9

WHEN ANNE opened her eyes the following morning, she was confused to find herself fully dressed on the sewing room settee. "She could have woken me up," she grumbled to herself. She rose to inspect her eye in the looking glass. The purple bulge depressed her. She splashed water on her face in the bathroom and pulled a brush through her hair. I don't know whether to get undressed or dressed again or what, she thought discontentedly. What time is it anyway? She fumbled for her watch, but it had stopped. She heard sounds from the kitchen and realized that the family was having its breakfast.

I don't want to eat with that bunch giving me the once-over, she thought. How about I climb into bed until this eye goes down enough to paint. I wouldn't go out with Chris today anyhow, looking like this. She worked her way out of her clothing and then stopped, holding the French silk stockings Chris had bought her to cheer her up after her eye started to swell. She held them up to the window and laughed. They had tiny red hearts woven into the black silk. They cost ten dollars and Chris couldn't get enough of her when she put them on. She leaned against the window frame and looked at the wall of the house next door, thinking of how she and Chris had carried on up in his bedroom on Maryland Avenue, her wearing only her red hair, her black eye, and her French stockings. He sat her on his lap before the big glass and made her watch their reflections while he put money, one bill at a time, in the tops of her stockings. She tried to think what made it all seem so funny and happy. Perhaps it had been the champagne. It wasn't so sporty last night, though, she thought, suddenly angry, having to listen to my catechism and that whole tiresome blather about Maggie Callahan; what that had to do with anything I'd like to know. And with my face hurting so, and that was her fault too because she made Chris and me have a fight. I wish I really was going to marry Chris and be shut of this lot of donkey Irish. She tiptoed into the room she shared with Mamie, but her sister was gone. She put on her nightdress and shoved her stockings into the bottom of the chifforobe.

She crawled into bed, reached for one of the newspapers on the floor, and aimlessly turned the pages. Mamie had gotten into the habit of taking the papers after her father was finished reading and clipping them. She spent many evenings poring over them in bed, her nose almost touching the paper, cutting articles of her own. Anne found her unbearably tedious. Mr. O'Brien and Mamie clucked over their Teddy Roosevelt or their "Safe and Saners" like two old dears at St. Honoria's Home.

And Mame didn't throw the papers out when she was finished either, so that the room was beginning to jam up. The stacks of newspapers almost touched the large plaster crucifix on the wall.

I have to get out of here, Anne thought nervously, flipping through the advertisements in the *Globe-Democrat*. I wonder what Chris would say to leading me to the altar. He tells me I'm his queen and he'll give me whatever I want, so why not? She put down the paper and stared at Mamie's new needlepoint picture of St. Theresa without seeing it. She was thinking of the right way to break the news to Chris. Her revery was interrupted by Mamie's entrance into the room.

"Anne!" her sister said. "When did you get into bed? Mama says you were in an accident. Are you hurt?"

"Mame, dear," Anne replied, "I'm destroyed and too weak to go downstairs. Would you bring me my breakfast on a tray? I'll love you forever for it, Mamie."

"Oh, Anne, and here I am late for work already," Mamie cried. She was very slow and had lost her previous job by arriving long after the others, although she made up for it by being the last to go home at night.

But Anne coaxed her sister and a while later Mamie appeared carrying a loaded tray. Anne blew her a kiss and said, "Mamie, you're a darling. Run now, so you'll get to work on time." She stirred her porridge carefully, lost in her thoughts of Chris Schneider and matrimony.

Dr. Kieffer's carriage stopped before the house. He looked in on Anne after giving Mr. O'Brien a clean bill of health, and if he had reservations concerning her collision with a skater, he took care not to express them. He had decided early in his medical career to accept his patients' lies with gentlemanly courtesy, since often as not, in his experience, they served some purpose or another in the patient's life, and it was not his to say whether the purpose was worthy or not. He recommended that she stay in bed a few more days, as that seemed to be what she had in mind anyway.

Will and his mother had a few moments alone after the family dispersed. He told her the details of his trip to the Schneider house, and what Ollie Taylor had said. She told him about Anne's black eye. They looked at one another bleakly, neither wishing to put into words the thought that occurred to them both.

"I don't know what's got into me, I'm that tired today," said Mrs. O'Brien, seating herself laboriously at the kitchen table. "Will, she says she wants to marry him.

Could you talk to her? If you told her about his other wives and all those horrors . . . ? I tried to reach her on sensible grounds last night, but she fell sound asleep while I was speaking to her."

"You're more than a little peaked today, Mother," said Will. "Why don't you get some rest? What if I give Frank a couple of dollars and let him bring in corned beef and cabbage from Dave Dwyer, so you don't have to worry about dinner."

"Liverwurst last night and Dave Dwyer's corned beef tonight? Your father will be saying I don't earn my keep around here."

"Father will say that?" asked Will incredulously. "When did Father ever say the least reproach against you?"

"It's true," she said, wavering. Yet not cooking meat for her family left her feeling vaguely at risk. She stared glumly at the roses on the oilcloth.

"So shall I give Frank the money?" Will asked, feeling with some anxiety her attention wandering from him.

"Yes, please do—here's the money." She pulled two bills from her apron pocket. "You're a grand comfort to me, Will."

"How can I tell Anne about Schneider without getting her back up? And what will she do but run to Schneider and denounce me for a meddler? Maybe we should wait a bit. A fellow like that, he could get tired of her tomorrow. Kieffer says she has to stay down for a few days. You look like you're the one who needs the rest. Why don't you go back to bed?"

"In the daytime?" she asked in honest surprise. "Who ever heard of such a thing? I'll be fine, Will. I have my ironing to do. As you say. Perhaps we can wait a bit now, since she's housebound. I'm to see Father Degnan this afternoon."

"Shall I call Kinloch and say she isn't coming in?" asked Will.

"Didn't I tell you? She's fired."

They looked at each other uneasily and then Will arose from his chair. "I must go now," he said. "How do you like me in plain clothes?"

"Have you your service revolver?" she asked.

"Right here." He patted his chest holster. It was a wonder how his mother hovered over his revolver. As long as it was under wraps, she thought the world of it. Once, however, he had pulled it from its holster to show it to her, and she had screamed, blessed herself, and implored him to put it away. He kissed her briefly but tenderly and went into the hall to place his straw hat on his head in front of the mirror before leaving for the bathhouse to meet Mike. His mother put herself to boiling starch.

Mr. O'Brien breakfasted on the tea, toast, and orange juice his wife had brought to his bedside before she went to Mass. He looked at the snowball flower in the jelly glass she had put on his tray. The more he gazed upon the multiheaded mound of whitish petals, the more he saw. There's enough detail in just this flower to keep me drawing for a year, he reflected sadly. And if the light here was better, it would be so much the worse.

10

FOR THE REST of the day and the two days that followed, Anne stayed in bed most of the time, rousing herself only to bathe and wash her hair. The latter operation required Mamie's assistance, and Anne calculated that when she and Chris were married, she would want a girl who could do hair as well as clean.

She had several mutually unsatisfactory conversations with her mother. Mrs. O'Brien proposed to bring Father Degnan around for a sick visit, but the suggestion provoked such a display of ill-temper on Anne's part that she backed off.

A messenger arrived on Friday with a bouquet of red roses and a letter for Anne. Mrs. O'Brien unhesitatingly threw the flowers into the ash pit and pocketed the letter. She moved restlessly about the house, trying to decide whether to give Anne the letter or burn it or read it and then burn it. She entered Mr. O'Brien's room to ask his advice, but saw that he was in his studio and therefore was not to be disturbed. Taking off her apron and pinning her rats more firmly in her hair, she went out the front door, telling Vesta she would be back in an hour with the fish.

Father Degnan told her that under no circumstances should she open the letter or destroy it. She was to hand it over to Anne with the injunction to haul herself out of bed immediately and report to Father for confession upon pain of the direst consequences to her immortal soul, to say nothing of the family's reputation, if she failed. Mrs. O'Brien delivered the letter and the ultimatum simultaneously.

Anne read the letter quickly and, with a hint of a smile, tucked it under her pillow. "Mama!" she said gaily. "Why are you pulling such a puss at your little Annie? I'll go see your old stick of a priest. I'll see him tomorrow afternoon. How's that? Now would you do your girl a good turn and bring up a cup of tea and some of that bread that came this morning? With jam?" she added to the departing figure of her mother.

She stretched her legs out before her under the sheet, enjoying the voluptuous sensation of extending her body as far as she could. It was almost time to get up, all things considered. If she was to meet Chris the next afternoon, she had details to take care of. She bounced her hips experimentally for a while, seeing how much upward thrust she could command, discontinuing her exercise abruptly when her mother entered the room.

"Thank you, darling Mama," she said. "Why don't you have a bit of a rest—you're looking tired."

Mrs. O'Brien answered tartly, "I'll take care of my own health, much obliged to you anyway," and left the room.

In the late afternoon Frank walked home from Mr. Macnamara's store, pausing to pull a hollyhock from the bush by the gate. Instead of going to the kitchen in search of his mother, as he usually did, he mounted the stairs and knocked on the door of his sister's room.

"Come in," she said.

Frank poked his head around the door and held the bright red flower out to her. "I heard you were sick, Annie," he said, "so I brought you something. May I come in?"

She was seated tailor style on her bed, holding a hand mirror, a box of combs and ribbons before her. "Frank!"

she cried. "What a loving boy you are! Of course you may come in. Isn't it glorious! Look on top of my dresser— there's a little pink china slipper that would just hold a hollyhock." Frank filled the slipper from the basin, stuck the flower in it, and placed it on the table next to her. He looked at her expectantly, waiting to be told to leave.

"Come, give me a kiss," she said instead, and held out her arms to him. "Sit down by me here and talk to me, Frank. I'm no end of bored with everybody going off and leaving poor old Annie by herself." She pouted beguilingly.

He sat on the edge of the bed, being careful not to crush the silks strewn about the coverlet. He gazed in wonder at her smiling face. How could he have ever, even for a moment, preferred Kathleen or Margaret or Mame to this one? There was no comparison, the shiner notwithstanding. Her hair hung loose around her shoulders, her lacy white nightdress was unbuttoned at the neck, and her face was open to his gaze.

"Frank!" she said. "What would you most like to do if you could do anything in the world?"

He hung his head, feeling dumb. Nobody had ever asked him a question like that before, and he didn't know the right answer. He searched for a way to tell her that whatever he would like to do, it would be better with her.

Finally he said, in a low voice, "Annie, I would like to go on a trip someplace with you." She leaned back against her pillows and laughed. She seemed all rosy and quivering, except for the dark splotch under her eye, which Frank avoided looking at. He laughed when she did, for the sociability of it.

"What a funny fellow you are," she said at last. "I'll tell you what? How about if in two years, when you're thirteen, you and I go to the World's Fair together—just the two of us, Frank. We'll take in all the sights and have lunch in a restaurant."

"Oh, Anne," was all he could reply, unable to believe such an outing could take place in the world as he knew it.

"It's settled, then," she said. "Our secret, mind you." Suddenly serious, she added, "Could I trust you to do an important favor for me?"

"Anything," he answered earnestly.

"Would you take this envelope"—she pulled a letter from under her pillow and held it out to him—"and this penny to buy a stamp at the corner so you can drop it in the box for me? Do you think you could do that without telling a soul?"

"I'll hide it under my shirt," he said solemnly. "No one will notice it."

"You're my honeybunch," she said, blowing him a kiss. "Run now, and be sure you don't lose it."

He bounded from the room, down the stairs, and out the front door, past Tom, sitting on the stoop. "Where are you going?" his brother asked.

"Nerts to you," Frank replied.

The following day, after lunch, Anne rose from her bed to prepare her toilette. Mamie was pressing her light green dotted-swiss dress for her. "It's awful good to wear just for Father Degnan, Anne," her sister said, sighing, carefully inserting the point of the iron into the pleats that embellished the cuffs of the dress.

"I want to show my respect," said Anne, buffing her nails. "I'm not going to put on some old drab thing to go to church." She drew her pale bronze-colored shoes from the cotton bags where she kept them and lovingly inspected the silk laces and the curved heels.

"Your French dancers besides?" Mamie looked at her incredulously.

"They're the only thing I can wear with this dress," Anne answered impatiently. "Come on, Mame. I could have finished pressing it half an hour ago." She tied up her shoes and whisked the dress from the ironing board over her head. "Button me behind, Mamie, dear—I cannot reach," she said.

"Anne," said her sister timidly, "I've no wish to put my nose where it doesn't belong . . ."

"Then don't," said Anne, kissing her cheek. "I'll see you later, lovey dear. Thanks for the help." At the door she turned back. "If Mama wants to know where I am, tell her I have a date with a priest."

She swung down Washington Avenue to Grand and entered Mueller's Pharmacy on the corner. She seated herself on a high stool and waited for Mueller to funnel gasoline into a can for a customer.

"Be careful what you are doing with this stuff," Mueller scolded the motorist, following him to the door. "If you're going to light that cigar, don't do it in front of my place.

"Damn fool," he muttered angrily, as he wiped the lid of his gasoline container with a cotton rag.

Anne tapped her nails on the counter. "Can you help me, please?" she asked.

"I help the one when I've done cleaning up after the other," he said, "and not before. This is a pharmacy, a professional place of business—not some kind of saloon." He looked up at her sharply. "If you want a poultice for that eye, I won't sell it to you." He rinsed the rag out carefully at the sink, hanging it up to dry.

"Why not?" she said.

"Because it's too late to do any good. You should have come right after he socked you."

"Nobody socked me, Mr. Mueller," Anne said, standing

up, "but if a customer pops you one someday, I won't be a bit sorry." She marched to the door.

"Miss O'Brien," he called, "I beg your pardon—such delicate customers I'm not used to. Sit down by the window and I'll make up a paste for your eye." He opened a drawer and withdrew a jar of white cream. He ladled a portion of it onto a sheet of glass. Then he put drops of orangish liquid into it with an eyedropper. He mixed the pigment into the paste with a small spatula. The door opened and Mrs. Mahoney appeared.

"Glory be to St. Patrick and his Blessed Mother!" she cried. "If it ain't Annie O'Brien, just like I thought it was, going by my door just now."

"It must have been somebody else," Anne replied coldly.

"Mr. Mueller," said Mrs. Mahoney, "could you take a minute from what you're fixing up there to hide Anne's black eye and give an old lady something for her piles?"

"I could," said Mr. Mueller, "but I'll be God damn if I will. First come, first serve, Mrs. Mahoney—it don't matter to me, eyes or piles. I lose money either way."

Anne applied the cream to her face with the tips of her fingers, examining herself in the druggist's mirror. "Too pink," she said. "Try it again, Mr. Mueller." He returned to his jars and tubes.

"I'll just say my beads while I'm waiting," Mrs. Mahoney whined.

"Go ahead," replied Mr. Mueller. "If you want to say your beads in a Lutheran pharmacy, that's your lookout. This is America." He brought a new blob of paste to Anne. "Try this one," he said. "I added just a drop of green. No, what's the matter? That's what cuts the orange. You'll see." They peered together at Anne's reflection in the glass. "A little more there," he said, pointing at her temple. "Now! How's that? Gibson never painted a prettier face."

He pinched her cheek. "I'll put it up in a little jar for you in case you need it again. Although I give you some free advice, Miss. Find yourself a different suitor. This one doesn't suit you." He laughed, handing her the package.

"Was the fellow that punched you the same one as has the automobile, Anne?" Mrs. Mahoney inquired as Anne was leaving the store.

"No," she replied, "the same one who kicked you in the rear." She slammed the door behind her.

The sky was darkening as she stepped back onto the sidewalk; a faint flash of heat lightning was echoed by a rumble of thunder. Mr. Bopp was rolling up the awning before his shoe store. She saw the Grand Avenue trolley approaching and ran for it. She waved at the dray driver in her path who had to check his horse to avoid her. She settled back onto the canvas seat with a gasp, her heart pounding fiercely.

I shouldn't have been made to run like that, she thought. Not when I've been in bed sick.

Drops of rain splashed on the window as the streetcar lumbered south on Grand Avenue. Peering through the streaked glass at the Tower Grove Park stop, she saw Chris struggling to install the tonneau cover on his automobile. The red Dion with its brass trim glistened in the rain, radiating excitement and promises from its shining surfaces to her as a Christmas ornament does to a child. Holding her hat with one hand and her skirt with the other, she descended from the car and ran to Chris. They embraced in the rain and climbed, laughing, into the car. Curled against him in the moist confines of the front seat, Anne buried her face against his shirt.

"Say, sweetheart, let's celebrate!" Chris said. "We'll go to the Oriental Gardens for dinner and I got ringside seats for the fight tonight."

"Chris," she answered, "first you have to kiss me." He obliged.

"Then, dearest, you must wait outside the College Church while I have a date with Nappy Degnan."

"Church!" he exclaimed. "What's that all about?"

"It's my mother, darling." Anne produced her set piece with considerable aplomb. "She says she will put my suitcases on the sidewalk if I don't square things with Father D. today."

"Let her then, Annie! What do you care about the hurrumphing old party?" He kissed her neck, hanging about her ear in a way she found especially lovely. "You can come and live in my dresser drawer."

"She won't let me, Chris," Anne said, laughing, carefully monitoring her irascible lover to make sure he stayed in a jovial frame of mind. "She says she'll never allow me to marry you—that I must wait until I'm forty and then she and Will are going to decide on a policeman for me."

He looked at her in astonishment. "She said that?" He threw back his head and laughed. He seemed vastly amused by her mother's alleged threats. He put his head in his hands and chuckled to himself. When he straightened up suddenly, Anne's stomach clenched in fear. She had no way of predicting what Chris would do next. She was not at all prepared when he drew a small box from his pocket and dropped it in her lap.

"Let me put it on, Annie," he said softly, as she held the ring up to the window. "Let me put it on your finger, and then we'll go together and tell this priest of yours to sweep out his church for the wedding. I'm planning on next week because the week after that I have to be in Chicago."

Anne was stunned. For a moment she could not comprehend the meaning of his words. She allowed him to place the heavy emerald in its gold setting on her finger in silence.

"What's the matter, Annie?" he demanded. "I like to see a girl smile when I tell her I'm marrying her."

She turned to look at him searchingly. "Are you saying we're to be married, Chris? In church?"

"In church?" he replied. "Why not? We have to get married someplace, don't we? So give me a smile and a kiss, pretty girl, and I'll start this machine so we can run down your old priest. I don't want to miss the first round of this fight and I hate to rush my dinner."

As he moved to climb from the car she caught his arm. "Dearest," she said, "when did you decide you were going to marry me?"

He turned and smiled at her, all the honey-sweet charm concentrated in one expression. "Last Saturday at Tony Faust's," he said, "while I was dancing with Summertime."

The realization that her scheme to lead Chris to marriage had been unnecessary struck her as very comical. She was ebullient by the time they drove back up Grand Avenue toward St. Francis Xavier. Turned sideways in her seat, she twirled the loose ring around her finger, chattering to amuse him, checking her eye in her hand mirror from time to time.

"Who is 'J.A.S.', Chris," she asked, peering at the inside of her engagement ring.

"My mother," he replied. "See the date on there? That was the day they got married. Don't lose it, *Liebkuchen.* It's worth as much as this automobile."

Father Degnan was just leaving the rectory to relieve Father Mara at the confessional when the red Dion, its lamps ablaze, stopped before his door. He viewed the flaming-haired young woman in the green dress and hat and her well-turned-out escort approach as if they were an apparition from hell come to talk him into selling his congregation.

"Father!" Anne exclaimed. "Lucky for Chris and me to catch you this way! May we have a word with you? It's awful important."

"A word, is it!" The priest scowled at her. "A word indeed! The only words I'll have with you, Anne O'Brien, will be in the confessional, and they begin 'Mea culpa,' and until I hear an act of contrition from you, and a full one, too, and until you have repented of your scandalous behavior and repudiated your partner in infamy . . ." The exercised priest's voice was moving into its more resonant registers when Chris interrupted him.

"I beg your pardon, Father—excuse me, please—you are quite right to be so incensed at my fiancée and me."

"Your what-is-it-you-called-her?" Father Degnan asked, eyebrows elevated.

"My intended," Chris replied, seriously. "Miss O'Brien has done me the honor of agreeing to be my bride and we have come to ask you to join us in holy wedlock."

Anne stifled the wild giggle mounting in her throat at the sight of the old priest's open mouth, like a crack in a rock. He quickly recovered himself and pointed out that marriages would be discussed when and if more urgent spiritual businesses had been attended to as they ought and that he would hear Anne on her knees before he would speak to her in his rectory, and other admonitions to the same effect.

Chris addressed the hostile priest in his most engaging way. "What about it, Father, if we signed up to get married now, and then Anne can say her confession when you're not so busy. We want to be wed soon, Father, to put an end to all the unfortunate talk in the neighborhood and to make up for our sins."

A grim smile crossed the priest's face. "If you're thinking marriage is where you pay for your sins, I wouldn't be the one to say you were wrong. Come in, then. I'll write down your names to start the inquiries. These things all take time." He led them into the darkish room, fumbled to light a lamp, and motioned to them to be seated.

"Anne O'Brien," he said, "I baptized you, gave you your first communion, and confirmed you. You are aware that you are now in a state of mortal sin."

"Yes, Father," she answered, her head lowered, afraid that if she noticed his mouth again she would be unable to control herself. The whole scene seemed to her to be teetering on the edge of unbearably hilarious farce. She focused her gaze on her new ring to calm herself and noticed that her hands were shaking.

"And you, sir—what might your name be?" the priest inquired.

"Chris Schneider, Father."

"Christopher Schneider." The priest wrote the name on a sheet of paper. "What is your middle name?"

"Not Christopher, Father. Christian Rupert is my name," he said.

"*Christian!* Did you say *Christian?*"

"Yes, Father," Chris replied meekly.

"What the hell kind of a name is that?" The priest stood up from his chair, threw his pencil on the desk, and glowered at his two visitors. "I never heard of such a thing! Were you baptized with that name?"

"Yes, Father—at Christ Church, right here in St. Louis, on Manchester Avenue."

"Christ Church! You're a Protestant! I knew it! I knew it! No Christian was ever a Catholic!" he cried.

"Oh, Father Degnan," Anne began, and suddenly stopped. "Did you say that no Christian was ever a Catholic?" She glanced at Chris, and the laughter took hold of them both. She tried to choke it back down her throat, to cover her mouth so that it would not come out, to keep the words from tickling her entire body, to avoid seeing Chris, who was doubled up pretending to tie his shoe; she tried to think of skeletons and gallows, to avoid looking at Father, to deaden her face. At length she took a deep breath and had the courage to raise her eyes to the priest. She exploded with laughter and was able to control herself no longer. Tears ran down her cheeks and her stomach ached.

Father Degnan walked to the door and opened it. "Out!" he said. "The two of you. You have profaned this house. I will pray for you, Anne O'Brien, that God in His infinite mercy will pluck you from the abyss that yawns at your feet, but I can do nothing for you while such sinful, willful depravity rules your soul."

11

THEY STOOD under a street lamp, exhausted by their levity. "Oh, Annie," Chris said at last, "I cannot tell who I like better, your priest or your mother. You must have had a sporty time growing up." This remark set Anne off again; she felt delightfully dizzy at seeing her whole world ridiculed through her lover's eyes. She felt as if shackles had been abruptly struck from her limbs, ones so ancient and familiar that she had not known they existed until she saw them lying on the ground, smashed.

"Are we on Spring here?" said Chris. "I know a place around the corner on Olive where we can have dinner. Come, sweetheart. It's starting to rain again."

"Don't you have an umbrella?" Anne asked, as hand in hand they ran down the block.

"I had one," he replied, "but I gave it up for Lent." He had to stop again, while Anne clung to him, laughing.

The stone house with its shuttered windows gave no appearance of being a restaurant. Only the carriages lining the street before it hinted of the life within.

"Good evening, Mr. Schneider," said the dark man in evening clothes who admitted them into the somberly lighted hall, from which they emerged into a brilliantly illuminated purple and silver reception foyer. Its ornate mirrors reflected Anne's flushed face and disheveled coiffure. "I think I'd best straighten my hair, Chris," said Anne.

"It's to the right, dear girl," he replied, turning to speak to a portly middle-aged man retrieving his topcoat. When Anne, revived, joined him, they climbed a flight of stairs and were admitted to a lavish dining room filled with people whom Anne found extraordinary. The room was crowded and noisy, an orchestra was playing, and as they followed the waiters through it, weaving among the tables and chairs, some of the diners greeted Chris by name. A dark-haired woman in a black dress, with rouged cheeks and nearly naked breasts caught his arm as he passed by. He kissed her quickly on the shoulder, whispered something in her ear, and continued across the room.

"Here you are, Mr. Schneider," said the headwaiter, opening a mahogany door into a tiny room lined in mauve silk containing a table and a velvet banquette seat. "Shall I let you have some privacy, Mr. Schneider?" the headwaiter asked.

"No, Henry, that's all right," Chris replied. "Leave it open for now. And send Maurice on the double. I'm going to the fights tonight."

Anne looked out the door in wonder. "Chris," she said, "what kind of a restaurant is this? Who are these people? That lady in the shiny, silvery dress—why she looks like an *actress*. She's got rouge and powder on. I can see that from here."

"She *is* an actress, you poor thing. That's Mabel Hite and she's appearing in the *Sultan of Sulu*. She's tarted up like that all the time." He put his arm around her and pulled her against his shoulder, as the waiter appeared in the doorway. "Maurice!" Chris cried. "Tonight Mr. Schneider is celebrating his engagement." Maurice's melancholic black face betrayed no reaction to the news. Unperturbed, Chris continued, "Let's have a bottle of Krugg '98 and three dozen oysters on the half shell. And hurry it up, sport. I don't want to miss that first round."

"No more Krugg '98, Mr. Schneider," said the waiter. "I

got Dom Pérignon '93 if you want. Oysters come in this afternoon, all the way from the Atlantic Ocean. I'll bring them right up."

"Maurice! If one of them is bad, do you know what I'm going to do to you?"

"Yes, sir, Mr. Schneider."

"And don't pull my leg about the Krugg either. On the double, Maurice."

"Yes, sir, Mr. Schneider."

"Chris!" Anne put her arm through her fiancé's and leaned against him. "This is the funniest place I've ever been to!"

"How many places have you ever been to, sweet Annie?" He kissed her cheek. "Wait until we get to Chicago. You'll see joints that make Caesar's look like a sausage vendor's."

"Is this called Caesar's restaurant?" she asked.

"It's not a restaurant at all. It's a club. You can do anything you want here—not just have dinner. But you have to belong. See that little lady over there?" He nodded toward a dark-haired woman in a low-cut blue gown pouring wine into the glass of her dinner partner. "That's Maud Berri—you've heard of her. Now she gets ten thousand a year from that fat old rep she's sitting with, and she does all her acting in private." The expression of annoyance that had settled over Chris's features disappeared when Maurice came bearing a bottle of Krugg and a platter containing a bed of chopped ice filled with oysters.

"Just like you ordered, Mr. Schneider," he said, popping the champagne cork and filling their glasses. Anne squeaked when it hit the wall over their heads. She sipped the champagne tentatively.

"Not that way, Annie," said Chris. "Pour it right down."

"Oh, Chris," she protested. "I can't do that!"

"Pour it down, beloved, or I'll pour it down for you."

She glanced at his face, and noting his expression, she put the glass to her mouth, closed her eyes, and swallowed the liquid. It seemed to sit somewhere in the upper part of her throat.

"Now, Annie," he said. "Watch me. I'm going to show you how to eat an oyster."

She looked in dismay at the objects before her on the platter. Surely Chris wasn't going to put vile-looking blobs like those in his mouth. They reminded her of a slug she had once found crawling in the coal bin, causing her to scream in fright. Her lover squeezed a wedge of lemon upon one, doused it with an orange-colored sauce, deftly loosened it from its shell with his fork, and popped it into his mouth. She watched, fascinated and repelled, her own appetite quite extinguished.

He refilled their glasses, raised his in a toast, and said, "Here's to my darling bride." She downed her betrothal toast quickly, eyes shut, hoping it would settle lower in her gorge than the first glass had.

"But, Chrissie," she said as the thought occurred to her, "Father Degnan isn't going to want to marry us now."

She tried to smile engagingly at him, but a large gas bubble in her esophagus lent a sour cast to her features. Chris, swallowing oysters, did not seem to notice.

"Father Degnan had his chance, beloved. We'll be married up in Chicago then—or when we get back. Now eat your oysters. I got a bet with a fellow on the first round."

"In Chicago? Oh, Chris, I don't know what my mother will say."

"You don't know what your mother will say? Annie, I don't want you to be afraid of your mother anymore. That won't do now. Now you have me and I'm the one to please, dear girl." He unbuttoned the back of her dress and ran his hand over her shoulder and breast. "Here," he said. "I'll serve up your oysters for you." And presently he held a fork laden with the delicacy to her mouth. "I'll feed you, pretty baby," he said in a husky voice.

She thought of explaining that she wasn't hungry, but Chris's manner was not conducive toward rebellion. A smiling, moon-faced man stopped by their table, temporarily postponing Anne's ingestion of the oysters.

"Steve!" Chris said. "Aren't you the deuce of a fellow! Annie, this is Steve Velle, who just won a thousand dollars on a bet! Tell Annie what you did—it'll make her laugh."

"Well, Miss Anne," said the man, "I drove my horse and runabout right through the front door and up the main staircase of the Fly Club in Kansas City. A fellow bet me a grand I couldn't do it, but I won!" He smiled happily, remembering his triumph. Anne obliged both men by an appropriate display of amazement, admiration, and pleasure. She encouraged him to elaborate on his account of the feat, hoping that the oysters might get lost in the telling. They were joined by yet another man, older than the first.

"Eddie!" said Chris. "I thought all you boodlers were supposed to be in jail!"

"I'm out on bail, Chris. You'll see, it'll all blow over by next week when Roosevelt comes to town."

The men's talk turned to politics and Anne was beginning to feel relieved as the prospect of her forced feeding seemed to recede, when suddenly Chris interrupted Steve Velle's remarks. "That's enough, boys," he said abruptly. "Stay out of jail, Eddie, and Steve, rake some hell for me." He turned away from his friends, picked up the fork again, and extended it toward Anne's mouth. "Down the hatch, my girl," he said. "Swallow your medicine."

A desperate plan passed fleetingly through Anne's mind. She could excuse herself, walk calmly to the ladies' room, and then make a dash for home. By running as fast as she could, dodging through alleys, she could be barricaded in her room before Chris even got to looking for her. She could mail him the ring, dye her hair black, and take a different name. The fork pressed lightly but firmly against her lips.

"Let's go, Annie," he said, an edge to his voice. She closed her eyes and opened her mouth, submitting to the oyster as she had so often allowed the wafer to be placed on her tongue, obedience and defiance so intimately wed that swallowing and gagging became one act.

"Good girl!" said Chris. "Now have a glass of Krugg to wash it down." He snapped his fingers. "Maurice! Another bottle. And don't keep me waiting this time." After the waiter brought them the fresh champagne, Chris Schneider closed the door to their little room. As Anne, eyes glazed, forced the remaining oysters down her throat, he caressed her, laughing at her discomfort, kissing her cheek and neck.

"Something new to learn every day, sweetheart," he said, drawing her hand across his thigh. "Finish those things and Chrissie will teach you to do a trick I bet you never even heard of."

When they left Caesar's place they found that the weather had turned unexpectedly cool. Anne was shivering in her thin cotton dress. She held Chris's arm for warmth and for steadiness as they walked back toward his automobile. A wave of nausea took her when they reached the Dion, and she vomited into the gutter. He lent her his handkerchief, patted her shoulder, and said to her fondly, "You're a grand sport, sweetheart. Don't worry—you'll get used to it."

Mrs. O'Brien was ladling soup from the pot on the stove into bowls, which she placed on the kitchen table.

"Why aren't we eating in the dining room?" Kathleen demanded querulously. "Where's Vesta?"

"She had to go to Union Station to get her mother," said Mrs. O'Brien, "and with the lot of you coming and going at all odd hours I'm not going to set up the dining room. Owen! I said slice the bread, not mutilate it! Give your father a piece."

Mr. O'Brien was seated in his rocking chair, his stack of newspapers once again at his side. His face was marked with red blotches, but otherwise he was much the same.

"I thought Anne was going to see Father Degnan," Kathleen said. "She should have been home an hour ago."

"She must have an enormous amount of sins to tell!" Owen cried, falling to his knees and clasping his hands together. "Father! I have sinned, and sinned, and sinned . . ."

"Owen!" His mother's voice brought him to his feet, but he continued to grimace fear and repentance when she turned away from him. "Aren't you going to the theater, Kathleen?" she asked.

"Yes, we're going to see *The Gambler's Daughter.*"

"I thought you saw that on Wednesday," her mother said.

"I saw it on Wednesday with Walter Curran. Tonight I'm seeing it with Johnnie Gilmore."

"You told me you didn't like Johnnie Gilmore anymore," Mamie said

"I don't. But what am I supposed to do on Saturday evening?" Kathleen asked, her voice rising.

"You could come to the euchre at St. Cronan's with me, Kitty," said Mamie. "We always have a lot of fun and it's for a good cause."

"Where is Anne?" Frank asked.

"None of your business where Anne is!" his mother

cried. "Your sister's life is not yours to question, Frank, so just hold your tongue."

"I'm sorry, Mother." Frank looked at his soup and vowed to be quiet for the rest of his life.

"Zola died," said Mr. O'Brien suddenly, looking up from his newspaper. His family fell silent for a moment, each member contemplating the information according to his own lights.

"Well, good riddance to the atheist," said Kathleen indignantly. "It's too bad they didn't put him on Devil's Island with the other one."

Mr. O'Brien looked at his daughter in dismay. "Of all the ignorant statements I have heard pronounced in this kitchen," he said at last, "that takes the prize for stupidity. And vulgarity," he added as Kathleen opened her mouth to protest.

"I don't see what you're picking on me for," said Kathleen, tears welling in her eyes. "Everybody knows that Zola sided with a Jew against the Catholics."

"When did you become the defender of the faith?" asked Mr. O'Brien. "You're not religious enough to be entitled to be anti-Semitic."

"I'm religious and I'm not anti-anyone," said Mamie quietly.

Kathleen's mouth quivered as she spoke to her father, her voice rising shrilly. "I may not buy all the hocus-pocus but I won't stand by while all the Catholics are persecuted by Jews!"

"What hocus-pocus would you be referring to?" asked Mrs. O'Brien, swinging her ladle a bit wildly from the pot.

"Ow! Look out!" Owen cried, wiping soup from his hair.

"I'm a good Catholic and I like all the religions," Mamie said more loudly.

"Catholics persecuted by Jews!" Mr. O'Brien exclaimed. "Kathleen, are you raving? Do you even know who Zola was?"

"Charlie Noonan told me all about it, and he was at West Point, so he should know. Zola was an atheist and an anarchist, hired by the Jews," Kathleen explained triumphantly.

"I left one benighted country behind me only to land in another," said Mr. O'Brien sadly. "Didn't you even read about it in the newspapers?"

"How can I read the newspapers after you and Mame get through snipping them to shreds?" Kathleen cried.

"Sadie Bierman, who works next to me, is my friend," said Mamie. "She prays for me in Jewish and I pray for her our way. Next week we're going to take the dinky together out to Richmond Heights where a lady has a talking dog and we're going to visit him."

"A talking dog? You're going to Richmond Heights with a Jewish woman to see a talking dog?" Kathleen was screaming. "Now do you understand?" she demanded of her father. "What do you say now?"

"More soup," said Jim, holding up his bowl and glowering at his mother.

"What are you hurtling black looks at me for, I should like to know," Mrs. O'Brien exclaimed, red-faced and flustered as she spooned soup into his bowl.

"He's cracked, is why," said Owen, diving under the table as Jim turned on him.

"I'll buy you your own private subscription to any newspaper published in St. Louis if you'll read it, Kathleen, and I'll pay for it gladly," Mr. O'Brien said.

"The story about the little dog who talks was in the *Globe*," said Mamie. "Well, wouldn't you pay a dollar to hear what a little dog has to say?"

"Do you have to believe every imbecility you read in

the newspapers?" Mr. O'Brien cried, rising to his feet. "I'm going back to bed." He gathered together his newspapers and started up the rear stairs, followed by Mrs. O'Brien.

"James," she said, "what about your soup?"

"How can I enjoy my soup in the midst of this superstitious mob? I don't want it."

His wife stared mournfully after him. "Now see what you've done," she said, addressing no one in particular. "The first night he's been down since Monday and you have to create a fracas."

Frank approached his mother timidly. "I enjoyed my soup, anyway," he said. She patted him absently.

Mamie was sniffing, head bowed, while Kathleen harangued her, when Margaret entered the kitchen. "Where is Anne?" she asked. "What aren't we eating in the dining room?"

Mrs. O'Brien slammed her ladle onto the table. "I'm going upstairs to be with poor James. Serve yourselves. And I don't want to see any dirty dishes when I come back down." She placed a slice of custard pie on a plate and climbed the stairs, leaving her disgruntled family to its own devices.

"What am I to do, James? She should have been back more than an hour ago. I'm sure she's with him again." Mrs. O'Brien looked at her husband in shame, humiliated by her daughter's dereliction, her children's outbursts, and her failure to hold them together in one decent, cohesive mass.

Mr. O'Brien, mouth full of custard, raised his eyebrows and shoulders to convey bewilderment. He would never tell his harassed spouse his real conviction—that if Anne had spent her formative years learning about what went on in the world, about the vice and crime and disease lurking on every side of their brick house on Washington Avenue, instead of wasting her youth on dresses and Masses, she would have been far less likely to fall victim to the likes of Schneider. He felt utterly defeated. Mamie was the only one who even looked at a newspaper, and all she seemed capable of gleaning from it were talking dogs.

"Catherine," he said at length, "where is Will?"

"He's all tied up now, James, with a white-slavery investigation, more's the pity, and God knows when he will be home. John and Jim are going to the Delmar races. They know I don't like it, but they're full of defiance tonight. They blame me about Anne." She looked at her husband apprehensively to see if he was of a mind to give her what she needed. He was.

"They've no call to blame you for anything, Catherine. You're too good to them—and to all of us." He put his hand on hers. "It's you I care for, Catherine. You came before the others, and you still come before them. Don't devour yourself over Anne. Surely she will recognize her folly before long."

"I'm afraid, James. I think Anne is lost."

The couple sat together in silence in the darkened room, unable to bring each other peace of mind, unwilling to part.

12

ANNE DID NOT APPEAR the next day or the day after. Will and Mike Egan made another excursion to Clayton, to learn from Ollie that the couple was at the Schneider farm in O'Fallon, Illinois.

"At least that's what Mr. Schneider said, officer," Ollie volunteered, "although I found a map of Memphis on his dresser when I went to tidy up. He has business *all* over—*every* kind of business goes through Mr. Schneider's hands. He's got a desk with different papers for any number of companies."

"Let me see those papers, Ollie," said Will.

"I *know* you won't get old Ollie in trouble, because I know you're not those regular Clayton police," she said, moving slowly toward the room with the dented wall.

"Miss Anne is surely a fine-looking lady, and sunny, too—like a little chick in the house. As old as I am, I would *surely* hate to see any misfortune befall her." She opened the drawer of an elaborately carved ebony desk, revealing row upon row of letterheads and envelopes. "You won't touch anything, officers," she said. "I'm sure you'll be careful. I read those letterheads years ago, before my eyes went bad on me. Old Mr. Schneider taught me how to read, and I showed Maurice. Even though it was against the law long time ago."

"Look at these, Mike," said Will. "There must be twenty business names here. 'Schneider and Church, attorneys at law; Fagin and Schneider, Collection Agency; Fagin and

Sons, Collection Agency; Schneider, Church, and Fagin, Employment.' My God, Mike, lend me a pencil so I can write them down."

"Where is the farm in O'Fallon? Do you know how to get there?" Mike asked.

"I haven't been out there for twenty years. Maurice would know—he brings me back hams and sausages every fall. But I think you're wasting your time in O'Fallon, because Mr. Schneider had me pack his gray suits and his black shoes. He wouldn't have use for those in the country, would he?"

"Ollie," said Will slowly, shutting the drawer. "How is she? Do they . . . get along together?"

She stared at the carpet. "So far as I can tell, things are all right between them. Just remember, though—loving as he is, Mr. Schneider got a real short fuse."

Will throttled a sudden impulse to ask Ollie for advice. He seemed pitiable to himself, a great stuffed dummy policeman, unable to defend his own sister. He regarded the drawer sadly and then turned out the electric light.

At the door he paused and drew a piece of paper from his pocket. "I'm going to give you a telephone number," he said. "I want you to call me if they come back here. Just leave the message, 'Tell Will hello,' and I'll know. Agreed, Ollie?"

"No, sir," she replied. "I've done too much for my health as it is. He knows I never leave the house."

"What about Maurice?"

"No, sir—not Maurice either. What do you think would happen to us?"

"We would protect you, Ollie," said Mike Egan earnestly.

"I would never want to hurt you gentlemen's feelings," she said, "but you can't protect Maurice and me any more than you can protect Miss Anne. If there was a crime Mr. Schneider committed against the law though, and if he was put in jail, that would be a shame, wouldn't it?" She searched Will's face with her curtained eyes.

Will heard the plea in her voice and silently shook his head. They thanked her soberly and headed back downtown in Mike's automobile.

"Did you hear about O'Hearn?" Mike asked after a long interlude of silence.

"What about him?"

"He shot Larry Manion from the second ward," Mike Egan answered. "Dead through the heart."

"Was he on duty?"

"He was not," said Mike, "more's the pity. Still, how hard can it go with him? He's been on the force for ten years and has a good record."

"Too fast on the draw. I remember him from when I was a rookie. What did he shoot Manion for?"

"Do I know?" said Mike. "The cut of his jib. A lot of problems are solved that way. Every trade has its little rights, Will. Doesn't Mack on your corner have more roast beef in a year than the rest of us combined? Anyway, if you decide to do anything, count me in."

Will looked at his partner. "You're talking like a mug. This isn't Oklahoma. It's bad enough for me, her brother, to risk getting thrown off the force for her, but you, that she wouldn't look at twice, ready to go up the long ladder and down the short rope! For what? A tramp who doesn't care about her own family, about her mother! Let her rot." Will's face was drawn, the robust inner righteousness that had always radiated from his countenance now replaced by bitterness and doubt.

"Even if you mean it, and I don't think you do, what about Mrs. O'Brien?"

"Tell me what you would do, Mike," Will asked wearily.

"Shoot him in the back on a dark night. The easiest thing in the world."

"Ah," said Will after a silence. "What's the next easiest thing?"

Mike Egan fiddled with the instruments on his dashboard a long moment before replying. "The trouble is," he said at last, "there is no second easiest thing."

Will was in good spirits the following Thursday morning as he came off his shift. It looked as if they were building a pretty case, with all its ends tucking in neatly, against half a dozen shady businessmen and entrepreneurs who were operating a large-scale white-slavery operation, although there did seem to be some ambiguity about whether all the girls left involuntarily or whether, in point of fact, some had not sought out businessmen with propositions of their own. No matter, said Kieley, the testimony of that stout Swedish girl with her pole would carry the whole case. They might even bag the former city councilman, currently under indictment for boodling, who seemed to be the leader. Will thought fondly of Tillie Jensen, imagining her clean, muscular blondness walloping her captors and their bosses. He was whistling as he stepped from the streetcar, pleased at the prospect of a promotion and a raise, and of white-slavers at bay. It crossed his mind that capital punishment was applied much too charily in certain cases. It would be grand to see the lot of them swing.

"Will! Wait up!" He heard his name called and turned to see Frank running toward him. "Do you want a French cruller? It's still warm." Frank handed his brother a pastry from a paper bag.

"Thanks, I don't mind if I do." The brothers walked

companionably together down Washington Avenue, eating their doughtnuts and enjoying the chill sunshine.

"Why aren't you in school?" Will asked. "It started yesterday, didn't it?"

"I quit, Will," said Frank. "I got myself a job instead."

"Why did you quit?" Will asked in surprise. "You're only in seventh grade."

"I can give Mama three dollars a week on the back of the baker's truck and free bakery goods besides. She said she was short last week on account of Anne."

"You should go to school, Frank. High school, even. I'll give Mama more money if she needs it."

"But, Will, I hate those nuns. Yesterday, when I went to my new class, Sister Theresa said bad things about me in front of everyone. I'm not going back to her, no matter what."

"What did she say?" Will asked.

"A stupid thing, and at lunch some German boys tried to shove my head in the toilet. I'm not going back."

"Never mind the German boys. What did she say?"

"She read my name off and said she hoped I had better morals than my sister, or she'd have me sit in a special seat away from the rest of the class. This way I'm home from the baker's by twelve and nobody talks bad to me."

Will felt cold. "A nun said that to you in front of the whole class? Frank, are you telling me the truth?" As they crossed the threshold of their home together, still deep in conversation, Will picked up the mail from the box by the door. He was flipping through it when his mother and father came down the stairs, side by side.

"Look," said Will, startled. "A letter from Anne!" They walked into the kitchen. Mrs. O'Brien put on her reading glasses, opened the letter, and read it aloud.

Dearest Parents and Family,

Please don't be angry at me for running off! Chris and I *are* going to get married as soon as he straightens out his business affairs in Chicago, and we are *very* happy. Won't you write me a note and say you forgive me and will be happy too?

Much Love from your *awfully sorry* daughter,

(signed) Anne O'Brien (soon to be Schneider!)

P.S. Maurice, the boy who works for Chris, will come on Saturday for my things. Will you *please* be my dear and pack my good chambray waist, my three silk camisoles, my green velour, the gray silk with the black frogs, the Navy blue Eton jacket & skirt (would you please see if the hem needs tucking & if so, the thread is in my second drawer), the black moiré *and* the hat that goes with it, the pale gray shantung three-piece ensemble, the waist you just made for me (the white, not the ecru, it's too tight in the bust), the other white with the foulard, also my good stockings. The rest you might as well pitch or give to Mame.

Mrs. O'Brien put the letter down and stared intently out the window.

"Catherine!" said her husband. "You look as if your eyes were popping out of your head! Blink!" She blinked, but continued to wear the same astonished expression.

Mr. O'Brien invented gallantly in an effort to soften the stricken visage of his wife. "I knew a girl once who ran away with a Protestant," he said. "She was a ninny, just like our Anne. After the baby was born they came back to Fethard and were married at the rail. He turned out to be a better Catholic than she was. You'll see, Catherine. Anne will come home."

"If it be His precious will," she said, still strange about the eyes.

September-
October 1902

13

ANNE CAME BACK a week later. The bell rang insistently at three o'clock in the morning, and when Mrs. O'Brien opened the door, an automobile drove off down Washington Avenue. She was about to close the door again when she saw Anne lying on the sidewalk. She roused Will, who rang for an ambulance and the police surgeon from the call box on the next street. They rode with Anne to the Female Hospital on Arsenal Street.

"I know Dr. Powell," said Will. "He owes me a favor. It will be all right."

"I want Dr. Kieffer, too," said Mrs. O'Brien.

"We'll have Kieffer, too," he replied.

They put Anne in a ward accommodating ten women. A stove stood in the middle of the bare but clean room. Mrs. O'Brien helped the nurse to get Anne out of her clothing and to wash the blood from her face and throat. She was so badly beaten as to be almost unrecognizable. She opened her eyes only once, when they tried to slip her underclothing over her head.

The nurse reappeared with a scissors. "It will be easier on her if we cut the chemise," she said. They enveloped Anne in an outsized hospital gown. The nurse apologized because it was patched.

"It's no matter at all," said Mrs. O'Brien.

The police surgeon appeared in the doorway and the nurse rose to attention. "Good morning, Dr. Powell," she said. "The patient is ready to be examined." She motioned to Mrs. O'Brien, who retreated behind the stove. Will accompanied the surgeon to his sister's bedside. Dr. Powell looked at Anne's head and neck. Turning to the nurse, he said, "You'll have to cut the hair. It's matted with blood and I cannot see what has happened. Clip this part here and sponge the scalp with alcohol."

He and Will exchanged remarks in low voices while Mrs. O'Brien lifted her daughter, with infinite care, so that the nurse could cut the tangled knots of blood-soaked red hair. Mrs. O'Brien picked up a clean lock from the floor and put it in her pocket. She heard the surgeon say to Will, "If she dies, you have a good chance for manslaughter, but if she pulls through, it all depends."

Mrs. O'Brien gently lowered her daughter back onto the pillow. "Anne," she said softly, "do you hear me?" The eyelashes fluttered but the girl was silent.

Dr. Powell returned to the bedside and the examination of the patient. At length he turned to Will and said, "I must ask her a question, but her throat is so injured that she may not be able to speak. Miss O'Brien, can you answer a question?"

Anne's eyes opened briefly and shut again.

"I am Dr. Powell, the police surgeon. I must ask you if you know the name of your assailant. If you can tell me that, I will be able to give you something for your pain and you can go to sleep."

Her hand moved on the sheet.

"Can you write it?" he asked. The hand moved again.

Will put a pad of paper on her bed and a pen between her fingers. He was panting. "Write the scoundrel's name, Anne," he said. "Don't be afraid. He'll be in jail by tomorrow."

She hesitated, made marks on the paper, and then dropped the pen. Will snatched up the pad and took it under the lamp's light. "Oh, God," he said, and turned the pad over to the surgeon. She had written only a single word upon it: *accident.*

Dr. Powell gave her an injection of morphine. "She has a broken collarbone. I cannot set it so it will just have to heal," he said. "Her nose may be broken, too—I cannot tell yet. I don't think she had a fractured skull, but I want nurse to watch her closely tonight and call me if she lapses into coma."

"I will watch her," said Mrs. O'Brien.

"I am deeply sorry for your trouble, Mrs. O'Brien. Will here will tell you that unless she lodges a complaint against the man, there is little the law can do. Even if she does, the law is much too cute in domestic cases, if you ask my opinion. Is it possible she is telling the truth and it really was an accident?"

"What do you think?" Will asked indignantly.

"I think she was beaten on purpose," said the surgeon, shaking his head. "I'll be back here at six. Good morning." He left.

Mrs. O'Brien and Will sat by Anne's bed, a screen separating them and her from the rest of the ward. The nurse brought them a small oil lamp, saying she was obliged to extinguish the overhead electric light she had turned on for Dr. Powell. "We have an empty bed, Mrs. O'Brien, if you would care to lie down."

"Oh, no! Not at all. Will and I will just sit here quietly, in case she needs us. Thank you for your kindness, nurse."

"It isn't often that we have a respectable girl with family in this ward, Mrs. O'Brien," the nurse whispered. "It's a terrible pity that such ruffians are allowed on the streets, begging your pardon, officer—I'm sure with you on the force you'll have him locked up right away, and he'll learn what it is to touch a girl with police in the family."

Will grunted and hunched forward, head down, his hands between his knees.

"You must be unnerved," said the nurse. "Shall I fetch you a cup of tea?"

"Please," said Will.

"Don't bother yourself," said Mrs. O'Brien.

"No bother in the least. I keep the kettle on at my station all night. It gets lonely here." She returned a bit later, carrying tea things and biscuits on a tray.

"Nurse!" one of the other patients cried. "If you're making tea, would you bring me a cup. I'm wide awake."

"It's two hours before breakfast," said the nurse. "Go back to sleep."

"I can't."

"Then be quiet anyway."

The nurse poured the tea and carefully passed the cups to Will and his mother. "Thank you, nurse," said Will.

"My name is Frances Gilles. You can call me Fanny," she replied. "I hope your wife isn't worried that you're here all night." She brought another chair to Anne's bedside and sat down between Will and his mother.

"I'm not married," said Will.

Mrs. O'Brien looked up sharply, her fingers frozen on a bead. "Don't let us take you from your duties, Miss Gilles. I'm sure you have your hands full with these women."

"Oh, them," said Frances Gilles. "They'd wear me out if I let them. You have to know where to draw the line. It's different with a well-brought-up lady like your daughter, Mrs. O'Brien. I'm happy to look after her, the poor darling, all destroyed as she is."

"Will," said Mrs. O'Brien, "when can we take her home?"

"We'll ask Dr. Powell when he comes back."

A low moan escaped from Anne's lips and she turned her head on the pillow restlessly. Her mother took her hand and spoke to her softly.

"Nurse!" one of the patients called. "I need a bedpan."

"Wait," said the nurse.

"I can't wait!" the patient cried.

"Oh, very well," said the nurse, rolling her eyes at Will. "I'll be right back."

When she was out of earshot, Mrs. O'Brien said to her son, "Must we countenance that creature all night long? Will, can't we bring Annie home? This is a horrible place."

"Have patience—the night is nearly over. Fanny must go off duty in the morning," he answered.

The police surgeon returned shortly after dawn and took a long time with his patient. At last he summoned Will and Mrs. O'Brien. He told them that Anne was out of danger and that they should go home. He said that she could not be moved for another ten days. They said good-bye to her sleeping form and walked out into the early morning sunshine on Arsenal Street.

"I'll come back here as soon as I get breakfast for everybody," Mrs. O'Brien said.

"For the love of God!" Will exclaimed. "Can't you let them get their own breakfast? What are you planning to do, go home and start cooking Malta-Vita for that bunch? Why can't Kathleen and Margaret spend some time in the kitchen instead of slavering over themselves in front of the looking glass so much?"

"Will, you're raising your voice to me right out on Arsenal Street." She stared straight before her, face and neck reddening, hoping nobody from Francis Xavier was lurking behind the curtained windows of the houses they passed, listening to Will's harsh voice.

"Forgive me, Mother." He put one hand on her shoulder. "You're not the one I should be venting my spleen on. But I won't let you fix breakfast. Let them eat the crullers Frank brought home yesterday. I'm going to take you to a place over on Maclind Avenue, in the next block, where Mike and I go sometimes when we're in this neighborhood. We'll sit at a table and be served." Mrs. O'Brien let herself be led by her son, although it seemed to her indecent to be going to some kind of a restaurant at six thirty in the morning with a hungry throng waiting for her at home.

"They're entitled," she said by way of protest.

"Not today," Will said resolutely. He opened the door and escorted her into the All-Night Green Tea. Once seated, she began to tremble. Will pretended not to notice the slight movement and buried himself in studying the menu.

"Have some lamb hash," he suggested, "or the fried haddock Mike says is good here."

She let Will order for her, but picked at the dish when it arrived. She stopped quivering after she had her second cup of tea.

"Will," she said firmly, "Anne has been punished for her sins, and if it helps to save her immortal soul, we may yet learn to thank God for His infinite grace. But Schneider—when is he to feel the sting of the whip? How long can he be allowed to lay violent hands on Anne? Now, Will, today"—her voice was low but intense—"go with Mike, arrest him, throw him into a cell, put him in irons. *What are you waiting for?* When he has beaten the last breath from her body, then will you act? Will! You must strike him down for this or none of us can breathe!"

Will felt himself struggling for air. He undid his collar and wiped his face nervously. "Mother," he began, and then paused, drinking deeply of his ice water. "Mother, let me speak with Kieley, but I'm afraid Dr. Powell is right. If Anne will press charges, we have a case against Schneider. If she says it was an accident, though . . ." His shoulders slumped. "Unless we had a witness . . . we would need somebody who saw it happen, who would swear to it in court."

"A witness!" his mother cried. "*I'll* be the witness then. I'll swear I saw him strike her, and you will, too, and so will the rest of the family. Witnesses! Is that what's causing you to hesitate? Aren't there twelve of us? We'll all swear in court, Will—we'll swear on ten Bibles, if it will put that demon from hell behind bars."

Will's gaze was fixed on the cutlery but his mind was engrossed with the spectacle of his entire family perjuring itself, one by one, in a court of law, each in his own way. He could imagine Kathleen's excited stammer, Margaret's red face, and Jim's alcoholic miasma as they lied picturesquely under oath. He saw the serpentine Schneider, reducing them to confusion and contradiction with laughable ease.

"You're the only one who could even pick him out of a lineup, Mother," he said. "That day I saw him with the goggles and cap—I wouldn't recognize him again."

"What's a lineup?" she asked fearfully.

"Oh, well, Mother," Will replied, exasperated, "if you don't even know what a lineup is, and I remember describing one to you, how do you plan to flummox the whole St. Louis court system? And him a lawyer?"

She looked at him accusingly. "What are you saying, then? That we are powerless to protect our own? That he has the license to do that to Anne's head?" When Will did not answer her question, she rose from the table. "Thank you for breakfast. Tell the family I am with Anne."

Will watched her leave the restaurant, longing to run after her, to tell her that he would assault Schneider, that he would satisfy her need for revenge, to fuse once more with her into the double fortress of righteousness they had always formed together, the two who kept the ten.

He wondered if he should speak to Kieley. Perhaps he was being too timid, too mired in detail; perhaps Kieley, who was older and more experienced, might see a different way out of the narrowing tunnel that lay before him. Still, he had never much cared for the captain, and airing his family's miseries to the likes of his superior seemed a hard thing—one more humiliation in the demeaning series. He thought of Mike Egan's recommendation that they simply shoot Schneider and be done with it. He was lost in thoughts of hiring an assassin as he left the restaurant and started north on Maclind Avenue. It was more difficult to hire an assassin than people credited, he thought self-pityingly. Or, rather, finding one without grave risk of compromise was impossible. The image of the word *accident* on his pad of paper made him clench his teeth in anger.

"Will!" a voice called to him, and a young woman leaned out from the window of a narrow clapboard house he was passing. "What are you wearing a puss like that for?" she asked. "Hookers getting you down?"

"Good morning, Jenny. I'm surprised to see you up so early," Will replied.

"I ain't been to bed yet, sweetie—not to sleep, at least. You want to come in and rest your feet a little?"

Prostitutes sometimes invited Mike and Will to hole up for an hour or two during a shift, particularly if the weather was bad. Will usually refused, but Mike took advantage of the chance for a nap on the warm couch of a cathouse back room on occasion.

"I didn't know you were over here on Maclind, Jenny," said Will.

"I just moved in last week. That old neighborhood was going down. It's good trade here, with the Insane Asylum and the Female Hospital right up the street. Come on in and see my stuff."

Will opened the door and Jenny led him to her room, decorated with plaster of Paris statues of moderately erotic inspiration. She lowered the drapes, turned on the light, and laughingly opened her robe to him. "Here's my stuff," she said, "what do you think?" Will responded instantly to her provocation, flung himself and her upon the bed, and possessed her in what seemed to be one motion.

"Gee, Will," she said as he lay spread-eagle on top of her, "I never figured you was such a hot pistol." She patted his head kindly. He didn't stir. "How about rolling over, though, hon—you ain't no bantamweight, you know."

Will eased himself from her body and onto the bed, where he promptly fell into a deep sleep. Jenny regarded her visitor philosophically, calculating that while he was not exactly what would be termed a sport, it did no harm for a girl to have a cop's head on her pillow from time to time. She made herself an enormous breakfast and consumed it, studying the racing returns as she ate.

Will awoke as suddenly as he had performed the other actions in her presence that day and dressed hastily. She reflected what a shame it was that so many of the really grand-looking fellows were either priests or cops—their mamas' favorites. Not that the two callings ruled a girl out altogether, but it certainly diminished the friendliness.

Will wished her good day and started out the door. He caught himself and returned to place a dollar bill on her dressing table. "Gee, hon," she said, "keep the buck. Treat's on me."

"Not at all," said Will, leaving the money despite her protest. He hastened out onto Maclind Avenue and away from her door.

During the weeks that followed, the domestic life of the O'Brien family slipped out of its established routines. Mrs. O'Brien spent a large part of the day at the hospital, arranging her visits to coincide with Anne's meals and with the arrival of Dr. Powell. She guarded the protective white screen around her daughter's bed and saw to it that the other patients kept their distance. Anne had difficulty swallowing and could not speak. What was worse, she seemed totally limp, both physically and morally. Mrs. O'Brien did not press her for response. She merely stayed at Anne's side, her hands occupied with her sewing or her rosary. She permitted Margaret and Will to come and go as they wished, but restricted the other members of the family to brief visits, firmly escorting Kathleen to the door when her agitated shrieks struck Mrs. O'Brien as intolerable.

Without her mistress to supervise her, Vesta spent more and more of her time in bed, partly because at last she had the chance to sleep as much as she had always wanted to, partly because she was bone weary, and partly because the complexities of her responsibilities frightened and overwhelmed her. She found it difficult to handle the washing and ironing alone, and soon a mass of soiled clothing was overflowing the laundry room, reproaching her so keenly that she jammed it into a large box and covered it with a bit of carpeting. She spent much of the day seated upon the box, attempting to compile a shopping list.

Mamie insisted on preparing supper and Kathleen on helping her, but by the time they returned from work, donned their aprons, and resolved their differences as to the menu and the division of labor, the hour was far advanced. Jim grew increasingly surly and stopped coming home for supper at all.

Mr. O'Brien arranged to consume a bowl of crackers and milk after returning from his visit to the hospital at a time when no one else was in the kitchen. He spent the rest of the day, in his studio, immune, by long-established custom, to the vicissitudes of his household. An occasional thump or howl from below stairs wrenched his attention from the minute drawings of St. Francis's hands to which he was devoting himself. He flinched as the disorder invading the family impinged itself upon his mind, but comforted himself with the thought that soon Anne would be home and Mrs. O'Brien would set things to right again. One day he heard knocking at his front door and, peering out the window, saw Pete Gentile on the sidewalk. He retreated quickly from the window, and at length, when no one answered, Pete retraced his steps up Washington Avenue.

Anne was released from the Female Hospital two weeks after being admitted. They installed her in her old bed, Mamie being exiled to a cot in her other sisters' room.

The weeks that followed were the happiest Frank had ever known. He arrived home from Diarmada's Bakery every day at noon, laden with as many breads and pastries as he could carry unaided, a perquisite of employment that the good-natured baker seemed to enjoy watching him exercise. He was frequently rewarded by an uninterrupted interlude with his mother, as she worked around her kitchen at their lunch and preparations for the evening meal, in which his bakery contributions played a worthy part. He told her about the prizefights the Missouri Athletic Club was sponsoring and about the diamond one of the combatants had won. "Johnnie Rohan, Mother—he's on my route. He showed it to me. It was a real diamond set in a black silk thing with his name on it. He said it might be worth fifty dollars." His mother smiled absently, and although she did not comment, Frank's heart was warmed by her apparent acceptance, if not approval, of his story.

The cherished hour with his mother was not the end of his day's bliss, however, for when she had prepared his lunch, she put it on a tray with that of his sister Anne and sent him upstairs with it. Frank and Anne took the meal together, he chattering to her, serving her, rising from his chair to pace the room and gesticulate, she smiling at him from her pillows, occasionally uttering a word in her hoarse whisper. "Don't talk, Annie," her brother cried, anxious lest her throat crack completely. The joy of having an immobilized, voiceless adult all to himself for hours every day made him euphoric. He plied her with a kind of pastry she enjoyed, called the Santa Fe, dipping it in tea so that it could slide smoothly past her injured throat. He played long games of chess with her and read aloud from the newspapers and from a novel called *Richard Carvel*, which he did not understand. He had never talked so much before. Words seemed to flow from him as water from an unknown spring that had long lain unsuspected, waiting to be tapped.

He did errands for her, buying her *eau de toilette* from Mr. Mueller, mailing her letters and picking up envelopes for her at the post office. They bore the initials C.R.S. in a corner, which bothered him obscurely. He stole a red glass ring from Doran's Dry Goods and told her he had won it in a fight. She wore it on her right hand and kissed him. Any other grown-up would have called him a liar, but not Anne. Dr. Kieffer came by from time to time, examining Anne briefly and conferring with Mrs. O'Brien at greater length over a cup of tea in the front room. The front room was being used much more than usual. Father Degnan appeared several times, and he, too, devoted more attention to the mother than the daughter, which was understandable, since when he entered Anne's room she rolled her eyes up into her head and seemed to be relapsing into coma.

"There has been nary a word from that one," Mrs. O'Brien told the priest. "If he is vanished, Father, as well he ought, do you think she can be brought back to reason?

Could Reverend Vander Sanden be entreated to grant a dispensation, do you suppose? If only she could take communion again, I know it would have the effect."

Father Degnan drank from the glass of whiskey that Mrs. O'Brien provided, to her chagrin, after his first visit, when he had contemptuously rejected her offer of tea saying "those Father Mathews Clubbers are a lot of mugs." She hid the bottle behind the coal scuttle when he left.

"It isn't a matter of dispensations, Catherine, nor of Vander Sanden, nor of Archbishop Kain, nor of the Pope himself. For all of that, it isn't a legality issue but a spiritual one. It is Anne who must turn away from sin and repudiate the tempter. Until she is so inclined, no formalities will avail."

"What can I do, Father?"

"Try to persuade her, and in the meantime pray, and I must tell you, Catherine, prepare yourself to be disappointed. Above all, pray." He downed the whiskey, rose, offered her his blessing, and departed.

To her mother's efforts at communication, Anne responded by rolling her eyes and pointing at her throat, and although she had strength for chess with Frank, she was abruptly weakened by the appearance of Mamie and her magazine, *World of the Catholic Girl,* or Margaret with a rosary all the way from Lourdes.

Kathleen presented herself in the doorway one evening, a bit wild about the eyes. "Anne," she whispered, locking the door and kneeling beside her sister's bed, "I'd give anything if you'd tell me what it's like. I promise, I won't say a word to Mother. But please tell me. Is it disgusting? How does he do it? *Please, Anne!* What are you laughing at?" Her face expressed such a mixture of lust and revulsion that Anne chuckled noiselessly to herself when she looked at her. "Anne, don't make fun of me!" Kathleen protested.

"I'm sorry, Kitty," Anne whispered, "it's only your face that tickles me. You better go now—you're making my neck hurt." As Kathleen retreated, in her dudgeon, Anne pressed her throat between her hands to ease the ache.

14

Mrs. O'Brien spread the contents of her apron pocket out on the kitchen table and examined the piles of bills and coins thoughtfully. There was not enough. "I'll have to put Macnamara and Dr. Kieffer on the long finger," she said to herself. Mamie had been fired again for lateness and was consuming carfare with nothing to show for it. Mrs. O'Brien counted the money once more and frowned. It seemed to her that she was shy five dollars, yet in such troubled times could she trust her memory?

It would be a great relief if the Little Stigmatization of St. Francis were finished and the commission tucked into her apron. Yet James appeared less to be approaching the completion of the work than retreating from it. Each time she entered his studio, he was engaged in more minute preparatory drawings. That morning, when she brought him his tea, she found him bent over a paper covered with thumbs, each one viewed from a slightly different angle. This struck Mrs. O'Brien as excessive for a $75 job that would end up in the dim recesses of St. Leo's rectory, where nobody would probably ever give it a glance. Nevertheless, her husband was an artist, and she did not question his methods or intentions any more than he involved himself in how she boiled the linen or scoured the stove. She sighed and placed the money in the stack of envelopes marked "Boatman's Bank," "Laclede Gas Company," "Grand Leader," and "St. Francis Xavier." She remembered James referring to Fiona Lynch as "worse than a washerwoman" because she belabored her husband about money. I'll give Arthur the tuckpointer two dollars on account, she decided. The rest I leave to God—at least for today. She closed her ledger and put the remaining coins back into her apron.

She walked to her knife rack and pulled from it a long cleaver, almost as hefty as an ax. Alexander was said to have resolved a dreadful knot with just such a blade, she reflected, and when it came to the strength of her torso and shoulders, she was sure she was the equal of any Greek, if the Corriopulous family down the block was an example. Alexander was not a Christian, of course, and it was not to the pagans she should be looking for guidance, although James was familiar with a great many stories about heathens who had solved their problems in original ways, and sometimes those tales reminded her more of her own struggles than did the lives of the saints.

The old people used to say a few words now and then amongst themselves about old-time things, but the priest called them superstitions.

"There must be justice afoot in the world," she said aloud, and startled at her own voice, she returned the cleaver to the rack.

It was a rainy afternoon in mid-October. Life had settled into a sort of uneasy routine, and Mrs. O'Brien was not expecting anyone when she heard the bell beside the front door ring. She screamed in fright when she opened it and saw him standing there. He was in the foyer before she could slam the door and, to her horror, sank to his knees and attempted to embrace her skirts. "Mother," he said, "do you know what I have suffered?"

"Let me go, you insane scoundrel, you fiend from hell— unhand me!" With a thrust of her leg she pushed him to the floor.

He rose to his feet, brushed himself off, and addressed her with eyes full of tears. "Mother," he said, "I have not slept one night . . ."

She did not permit him to finish his speech. "Don't call me Mother! Are you mad, to say such words to me? James! Help!" she shouted up the stairs. "Oh, James, please come at once!"

Mr. O'Brien had seen the Dion-Bouton pull up before his house. He stood at the sink, heart pounding, scrubbing ink from his nails. He knew he had to descend the two staircases and finally face his daughter's seducer, but first his fingers had to be clean. A few fine black lines around his cuticle absorbed all his attention, to the point where his wife's calls scarcely reached him.

"James! *Please* come—it's him!" Mrs. O'Brien called again, but still her husband could not seem to relinquish the soapy little brush and the effort to eradicate the faint shadow on his fingertips. He scrubbed more and more vigorously, mumbling, "Just hold on, Catherine, I'll be right there," until abruptly, her entreaties ceased.

"What am I doing?" he cried, flinging the brush aside. He picked up a rag, hastily wiped his hands upon it, and headed down the stairs. He arrived on the second landing as Christian Schneider and Anne were moving toward the front door.

"You're not leaving your home to go with this devil!" Mrs. O'Brien cried, her arms against the door.

"Mother, I have to be with Chris. I belong to him," said Anne, avoiding her gaze.

"Then go, Anne O'Brien," said Mrs. O'Brien, opening the door, "go with your tempter and your nemesis, for he can be no husband to you or any of his so-called wives, but know this: If you leave the house with Schneider, you will never enter this door again."

"Mother, please," said Chris, now openly weeping.

"Goodbye, then," said Anne coldly, and taking her lover's arm, crossed the threshold of her house for the last time.

Frank entered the house a half hour later, carrying a bouquet of asters he had picked in Mrs. Wind's yard by reaching through the fence from the alley. He was astonished when he found Anne's room empty. He called her name upstairs until the door to his parents' bedroom opened and his father appeared.

"There's no use calling Anne, Frank," he said, in a voice like ashes. "She's gone."

"Gone?" Frank asked. "What do you mean?"

"She has gone away for good this time. Now, please—your mother is afflicted with a pain in her head—be quiet and don't disturb us."

He closed the door again and the boy was left alone. In his grief he wandered through the empty house until at last he made his way back to Anne's room, where he threw himself upon her bed. After the initial spasm of anguish, he arose in anger and began searching amongst her belongings. He found only one of the letters he had brought her from the post office, stuck in her chifforobe with a strange-looking pair of stockings. He read it, conscious of and glad for the sin incurred.

While he did not comprehend most of its sentences exactly, the tone told him why Anne had left. "My silken glove," the letter began, and after Frank had read it, he tore it to bits and flushed it down the toilet. He took a scissors and cut the black stockings into tatters and then ripped open her pillow with the point, burying his face in the feathers.

"I posted her letters to him and picked up the answers," he repeated to himself. "I was the one. When she couldn't even walk, I did her mailing for her." He took the bottle of cologne and poured it into the toilet, tossing the scraps of black silk on top. He broke her hand mirror and sprinkled the shards in the bowl, cutting his finger. The chess pieces and the asters were next, followed by handfuls of the feathers from the pillow. He was hacking up her nightdress, which still gave off the aroma of her body, when Kathleen entered the room.

It was well after midnight before the house quieted itself, less calmed than stuporous. Convulsive sobs were still to be heard coming from the room Kathleen shared with Margaret, and in the rag-taggle room only Frank was still awake. He lay with his eyes open, staring at the dim orange glow coming from the overcast sky outside the window. The faint stink of the slaughterhouse that clung to Owen nauseated him, the whistles and grunts emitted by Jim grated upon his nerves, Tom's horrible mop of hair was pressing against his neck, and the fact that John's bed was empty because he had not yet returned from the races seemed to him especially unjust.

He thought that if he fell asleep, he had no wish to wake up, no desire to make his own breakfast quietly, alone in the predawn kitchen, no impulse toward the baker's wagon and his morning rounds of the residential streets of St. Louis. He saw his life stretch before him without her like an endless track whose trolley would never come. He crawled out of bed, crept into his clothes, and silently tiptoed into Anne's room. He fumbled in the dark chifforobe and pulled out an old Mother Hubbard she used to wear around the kitchen. He held it against his face and, stretching out upon her bed, fell asleep at last.

Three days later, at headquarters in the Four Courts building, Captain Kieley was instructing his men. "The prosecutor hasn't given me the final word yet," he said, "but I don't mind telling you boys that it's a pretty sure thing we'll get indictments. There's a couple of big names involved. No, Will, even you don't know about this part yet. I'll tell you the truth," he said, leaning across his desk toward the two policemen. "Even I don't know everything yet. The chief and Desmond in Chicago, they're laying back together, see, until the prosecutors give them the green light. It won't be long now, though, and there will be something in it for all of us. I promise you that. My wife is ready to go back to her mother—that's how little she's seen me! And for you fellows, I know it's been the long pull." He looked at Will and Mike Egan expectantly.

Mike managed half a smile. "That's what we've been waiting to hear, Captain," he said. "Grand news, right, Will?"

"Oh, the best," said Will.

"What's the matter with you two lately?" Captain Kieley asked. "You look like a pair of dead mackerel. Every time I speak to you, O'Brien, I get that fish eye of yours right back at me. My God, I know it's hard staying up all hours and not being home much, but you're young—who can stand it if you two can't?"

"It's not the hours, Captain," said Will hastily. "Mike is doing me a favor by worrying about my troubles with me. We'll snap to directly—you can count on that."

"I'm sorry for your troubles, Will. Powell told me about your sister. How is she?"

"Gone," said Will, surprised to hear himself telling his superior about it anyway. "With him. The man, I mean—the one who did it."

"Ah," said Kieley sadly, "she left of her own free will with him, did she?"

"She walked right past my mother and out the door," Will replied, a lump suddenly forming in his throat.

"I wish I had known about it sooner, Will," said Kieley. "We might have been able to reason with the fellow."

"I don't think he's reasonable," said Will.

"Sometimes there's different kinds of reasoning that can be applied. What's his name?" Kieley asked.

"Christian Schneider."

"Chris Schneider? Son of Augustus Schneider that owned the quarries?" asked Kieley in surprise.

"Yes, that's the one. My brother-in-law." Will laughed shortly. "Do you know him?"

"How do you like that? I knew his father. My uncle Bob used to haul for him, oh, way back. He took me along one time on the wagon, when I was just a little fellow, out to a quarry in a place called Rock Hill. Limestone. He said to me, 'That nob in the knickers over there—that's Gus Schneider, the boss, and I couldn't ask for a better one.' The old man had a grand reputation, but I don't know what happened to the son. He's a different story. I don't have to tell you." Kieley appeared to hesitate, then he unlocked a file drawer under his desk and fumbled for a bit with its contents. He finally pulled out a folder and flipped its pages nervously.

"Look here, O'Brien," he said, "this is an odd sort of thing, but I'll tell it to you straight away. Schneider was a partner in one of the agencies that advertised for girls. I put it on hold because I had nothing more to go on—no witnesses and no complaints—whereas with some of the other agencies we have a whole case just waiting for us. But I'll leave it to you. If you can dig up something that will nail Schneider to these riverboat white-slavers, go ahead—if you think it will help your sister in the long run." He pushed the dossier toward Will, who opened it and looked at the advertisement and the statement from the manager of the office building on Sixth Street and Olive.

"Let's go down there, Will," said Mike Egan eagerly.

"All we need is a little something on him—just enough to get our hands on him, even if it couldn't hold up in court. Will, forty-eight hours in custody and you know we can make a new man of him."

"That's altogether the wrong ticket with Schneider," said Kieley sharply. "You can't teach him any lessons, you thick mick—he wrote the book. If you got real evidence against him, that would be one thing, but I don't want my people harassing a man like that. Do you understand me, O'Brien?"

"I do, Captain," said Will, soberly, "and you're right. Could I look at this and think it over?"

"Let me know in a couple of days. You're not a hothead." Kieley glanced at Mike Egan. "I hope yours cools off before you get into trouble. Here," he said, handing a green card to Will. "This is a cooper on Broadway, name of Bowers—he sold barrels to the *Northern Belle*."

Will and Mike hopped on the streetcar going west on Clark Street. They flashed badges at the conductor and took seats facing backwards. "Don't feel bad about Kieley calling you a hothead, Mike," said Will. "It's me that's acting queer, not you. If I had done what you said in the first place, the whole thing would have been settled by now."

"Your hash would have been settled, you mean. I don't know, Will, it seems like things are more complicated than they used to be."

"You sound like an old lady," Will replied. "Haven't we always been devious? Look at Adam and Eve."

"Well," said Mike Egan, "look at them. They both sinned and they both got bounced for it. I call that straightforward. Nowadays they'd get a lawyer and you'd never hear the end of it."

"We have to be cuter, is all," said Will. "We'll send

him up for white-slaving, and we'll all know it's really for Anne."

"If we need a witness I could ask Frances Petrofsky. She'd swear to anything if I asked her to," Mike offered helpfully.

The cable connections of the car emitted fizzling crackles and the smell of ozone as they descended from it and started down the dusty sidewalk to Ralph Bowers' place of business. As they walked, Will pictured Frances on the witness stand.

"She'll have to get on line after my mother and the rest of the family, but thanks for the offer. Let's think on it, Mike. We don't want to hurt Schneider just a little bit."

"Either way, you lose your sister," said Mike quietly.

"What do you mean?" Will stopped and stared at his partner.

"Well, Will, for God's sake, she loves him!" Mike replied.

Will felt an abrupt impulse to push his partner off the boardwalk and into the path of an oncoming wagon. Mike suddenly seemed to him intolerable, an intrusive voice destroying his privacy, as implacably opinionated and inescapable as a spouse. He wished he had Arthur O'Connell for a partner, that went through the day asleep on his feet.

"What's the matter? Why are you pulling a face like that?" Mike asked.

"It's the filthy smell down here," said Will, walking on. "I wish there was a law against stinking."

They traversed the shed with the barrel marked "Bowers" on the roof and found themselves in a yard where a burly man and a black boy were stacking staves. Mr. Bowers was delighted to have the opportunity to describe his dealings with the *Northern Belle* to the police. When Will asked him if he had observed anything out of the ordinary, he turned to his helper and said, "Melville, you can listen to what I'm about to tell because hearing the way I explain things helps your education. But we keep these secrets under our hat, agreed?"

"Yes, sir, Mr. Bowers," the boy replied.

"Didn't you deliver some barrels to the *Northern Belle*?" Will asked.

"That's just what I wanted to talk to you about. The strangest thing happened. Melville and I hauled three gross on board, at the foot of Gratiot Street, and I says to the roustabout, 'Who gets the bill of lading?' So he says, 'Cooper,' and points to a doorway. So I knock on the door and go in and I says to the fellow, 'Cooper! Let me tell you a fact about yourself! One of your ancestors was a barrel maker!' Well, this fellow gives me a terrible look and then he leans down and picks up a grappling hook. 'Get off this here boat and don't say my name again,' he tells me. So I got out of there right away, you can bet, and I told Malachy Dunne just what I'm telling you that afternoon when he came by the shop on his beat."

Will looked thoughtful. "Anything else you noticed about the packet?"

"Foul-looking crew—the most unfriendly bunch I ever saw," said Bowers. "Can you imagine going after a workingman like that, when he's offering you an educational story? What's become of the world?"

"If you want to know something funny about that packet boat," said the barrel maker's helper, "ask me."

Will turned toward the boy, who rewarded him with a gap-toothed smile. "Tell us what *you* saw, young fellow," he said.

"Women's drawers hanging on a wash line on the bottom deck."

"What's so funny about that?" Mike asked. "There's a

woman on a packet sometimes. I even heard of a woman roustabout once, name of Alberta."

"Twelve or so pairs of drawers?" asked Melville, skeptically. "And how come that big fat one push me away so mad when he seen me looking at them, flapping in the breeze, pretty as a picture?"

"You're a sharp lad," said Will. "We thank you for your cooperation. Mr. Bowers, Melville, I bid you good day." The policemen made their way back to the streetcar stop. Mike Egan was excited. "Every little bit fits together, Will. Do you think Kieley will be glad to hear about this?"

"About what?" Will asked.

"Melville!"

"Come on, Mike," Will said impatiently, "what do you think a smart lawyer would do with a colored boy on the stand, talking about ladies' drawers? Melville would be lucky if he didn't end up in jail himself. Wasn't there another lynching only yesterday in Woodriver?"

They waited by the trolley tracks at the corner of Broadway, and when the car did not appear, they decided to walk.

"I need the exercise, Will," said Mike. "My machine isn't as full of steam as it used to be."

"You look the same to me," said Will, glancing at his partner.

"I'm not twenty anymore," Mike continued, "and don't I know it? Summertime, Will—it doesn't last forever."

Will scowled. He knew what was coming next. "In that case, Mike, you had ought to put your hands up without a struggle and get married."

His partner's face lighted up. "Funny you should mention it. Frances and I were talking on Sunday about going to see Father Garvin. Only he's away, so it would have to be Father Harty."

"If I were you, I'd wait for Garvin. Father Harty is Roman," said Will, relieved at finding a bright side to his partner's predicament.

They stepped off the boardwalk onto the cobblestoned street to avoid a construction site. They waved to a man with a wheelbarrow hauling dirt.

"What's going up there?" asked Will.

"Donk Brothers," his partner replied. "A new coal yard. How about if we stop for a beer? The A.O.H. in the next block has got my neighbor Hibby McFarland for bartender."

A pile of dirty rags lay against the brick building housing the Ancient Order of Hibernians' clubhouse. As the two policemen passed, an eye opened amongst the heaps of tattered clothing and a voice said, "If it ain't Egan and O'Brien, I'm a monkey's uncle." They stopped and Will addressed the derelict on the sidewalk.

"Where have you been, Carmine?" he said. "I haven't seen you sleeping at the station house lately. You haven't got a girl friend now, have you?"

An expression of delight transfigured the soiled features of the old bum, and from his toothless mouth he emitted sounds of pleasure. "I'm as dry as these here boards," he said. "How about slipping an old fellow a nickel?"

Will dropped a coin in the filthy hand protruding from the mound of debris. "Seen anything lately, Carmine?" he asked.

"Come closer and I'll tell you something queer," the bum said.

"How long has it been since you got deloused?" Will asked, eyeing his informant distrustfully.

"Oh, it's been a while, back a little, I forget," he answered vaguely.

"I'll listen to you from here then," said Will.

"I need more than a bucket of suds to tell you this story, I need a bottle of Southern Comfort."

"Tell me a queer enough story and it's yours," Will agreed.

"It's you mentioning girls reminded me. Couple of weeks ago, I was keeping well, sitting in front of a building on Olive Street. I saw a good-looking fellow lead one girl after another from that building down to the levee. And he came back each time alone, and a little while later he was walking down with another one. He must have taken four different girls down there and left them."

"What kind of girls were they, would you say?" Mike asked.

"Oh, the right kind," said Carmine, describing immense curves in the air with his hands, an obscene leer illuminating his wrinkled features.

"Lookers, were they?" asked Will approvingly. "Did they have valises?"

"I don't recall. But one girl, she was carrying an accordion, and she didn't have no stockings!"

"How do you know?" asked Mike.

"I looked! How do you think? I don't miss much from where I sit," he cackled to himself.

"Would you know the man if you saw him again?" Will asked.

"If I wasn't too sick. Now, O'Brien, how about the Southern Comfort?"

"It will be waiting at headquarters for you tonight when you come after you get deloused. That way you only have to make the one trip. Just ask whoever is at the desk when you come in," said Will.

"Sure?" asked the bum anxiously.

"Don't I always keep my word?" Will replied, annoyed at being doubted.

"Write it down, so you're sure," the old man begged.

"Goodbye, Carmine. Keep your eyes open down there," said Mike as they turned toward the entrance of the A.O.H.

"I like Carmine," said Will. "It's a real blessing to have a drunkard on the streets who isn't Irish."

"I guess he wouldn't look any better on the stand than Melville," said Mike Egan glumly. "Judge Hannon wouldn't let him in the door."

"Now you're getting smart, Mike." They entered the clubhouse, breathing its familiar odor of stale beer and cigars, and the lace-curtained door swung shut behind them.

The next Saturday, when Frank had finished his rounds on the baker's wagon, Mr. Diarmada was filling his arms with rolls. "What about this stollen?" he inquired. "I'll never sell it now—it's too late! Here, let me put it under your arm—you can carry it, have it tonight with your coffee." He beamed fondly at the wan boy.

"Frank," he said, "you don't look so good. You sick?"

Frank shook his head.

"What about your sister. She still sick?"

"She's better now, I guess," Frank replied miserably.

"Well, then," said Mr. Diarmada, "I got a treat here for you. Have you ever gone to the theater to see a play?"

"No, sir," Frank answered.

"Look at here, sonny. Two tickets to see *The Wizard of Oz*, playing at the Olympic. My customer, Pat Short, he gave me six. I'm handing you two of them so you and your sister can go cheer up at a stage play. Now promise me you'll go!"

Frank stared at his benevolent employer, unable to reply. When Mr. Diarmada repeated his request for a promise, Frank thanked him and said he would go. Embracing his bags of rolls and his stollen, the two tickets tucked into his cap band by Mr. Diarmada, he hurried home, dodging down the alley when he saw a group of German boys on the steps of Prallee's candy store.

After delivering his money and bakery goods to his mother, he went looking for Mamie. He found her in the dining room, writing a letter of application to the St. Louis Tent and Awning Company. "How does this sound, Frank?" she asked. "Dear Sir, I am writing in response to your announcement in the *St. Louis Star* for an opening for a typist. I was just fired from Bokern Realty for being late all the time."

"It sounds fine, Mamie—but do you have to tell them you got fired for being late?" he asked.

"You see, Frank," she replied, "if I don't tell them and they find out, I figure they would hold it against me. But if I tell them in advance, and they hire me anyway, that way they won't be angry with me."

"But what if they won't hire you because of your being late?" Frank asked.

"Don't put gloomy views in my mind, Frank," she said earnestly. "I do my best and trust the Lord."

"Mamie," he said, showing her the tickets, "how would you like to go see a stage show with me tonight? Mr. Diarmada gave me two tickets for *The Wizard of Oz* and said to take my sister. After all, you're my sister too."

"I promised the nuns I'd help serve the supper at Mount St. Rose tonight, Frank, or else I would be glad to go. Why don't you try Kathleen—she's so unsettled since Anne left, it might do her good."

Frank knocked on Kathleen's door, was admitted to her room, and repeated his offer to her. "Are you mad?" she cried, sitting up in bed. "Do you think I would be seen on a Saturday evening going to a children's play with a twelve-year-old boy? Wouldn't I be the laughing stock of certain parties? Take Owen, if Mother will even let you go, which

I doubt. Shut the door behind you." She slumped back onto her pillows, mumbling to herself.

Frank sat on the steps in the hall and looked at his tickets. Mr. Diarmada had said to take his sister, so Owen or Tom would not do. It really was Margaret or nobody. He was trying to think of a way to make the play sound appealing when his father came down the stairs.

"Father," he said. "Did you ever hear of a play called *The Wizard of Oz*?"

"I did," said Mr. O'Brien. "They say it's a grand show for the young and the old alike." He continued down the stairs to the kitchen, followed by Frank. Mrs. O'Brien and Margaret were fixing lunch.

"Why do you ask about *The Wizard of Oz*?" Mr. O'Brien inquired.

"Because I've got two free tickets. Would you like to come with me, Margaret?" Frank asked.

Before she could answer, his mother turned toward him angrily. "There will be no play going around here, young man. This household has become terrible lax, and haven't we been punished enough? Tonight Father is coming by to lead the rosary. We talked about it this afternoon. It will do us all a world of good. Those of us who care to join, I mean." She ladled ham hock and bean soup into the bowls. "Go tell Kathleen and the boys that lunch is ready."

Frank walked slowly up the back stairs again, feeling trapped. Mr. Diarmada would never forgive him if he wasted the tickets to the stage show. Frank's fear of his boss was all the more intense because Mr. Diarmada had consistently treated him kindly. His generosity cast a deep shadow over Frank, who felt that such unhoped-for goodness must inevitably reverse itself, that he would surely misbehave and alienate the generous baker. He experienced mounting anguish as he thought of how Mr. Diarmada would look when he saw the two empty seats. He knocked on Kathleen's door again, calling, "Lunch is ready." When she appeared in her dressing gown, he said, "Kathleen, can I tell you about a bad fix I'm in?"

"'*May*,' not '*can*,'" she scolded. "Don't sound so ignorant. You're picking up bad grammar from those bakery donkeys. I heard you say 'ain't' last week."

"I did not!" Frank protested, stung. "Owen, maybe, but not me."

"Don't get in the habit of blaming your faults on other people," she continued as they entered the kitchen. "Oh, God!" she exclaimed suddenly. "It's so awful in this house with my sister gone!"

That Monday morning Frank left the house as usual and walked the eight blocks to Diarmada's bakery, but instead of entering, he hesitated by the gate to the yard and then hurried on. He spent the morning wandering the streets, and by noon had found a new job mucking the horses at a livery stable on Franklin Avenue.

Mr. Diarmada shook his head sadly as he put his "boy wanted" sign in the window the next day. "I'm put out, really," he told his helper, "after I just gave him the tickets to *The Wizard of Oz*."

Dr. Kieffer examined Mrs. O'Brien's eyes and gave her drops. "Try to take a little rest in the day. You have big children now—let them do some of the work around the house. Put these in your eyes and a piece of ice in a rag on the bridge of your nose. Come back in a week if it isn't better." He escorted his patient to the consultation room door. "Have you heard from Anne?" he asked.

"Not a word," she said, searching his face anxiously.

"Ah, well," he replied. "No news is often the best in matters like this. Try not to worry," he added, wishing he had a better tonic for her ailing spirits. She thanked him, paid his nurse on her way out, and walked slowly down Grand Avenue, pulling her cloak around her against the chill morning air. She looked in the window of Mueller's Pharmacy at the display of hairbrushes. She stifled a sudden impulse to buy one. "Haven't you spent enough money today," she asked herself bitterly, "with your Dr. Kieffer nonsense, and Mamie still out of work, and no more free bakery goods?" She caught the reflection of Mrs. Mahoney in the glass on the other side of the street. She hurried down the sidewalk strewn with brown sycamore leaves and into her own gate.

November 1902

15

THE MESSAGE CAME from Chicago on a Wednesday in November, five weeks after Anne's departure. When Will walked into headquarters at nine in the morning, Sergeant McGuire on the desk looked up at him apprehensively.

"There was a telephone call for you from Foley in Chicago, Will," he told him. "Here's the number. Foley said he would wait by the telephone."

"For me?" said Will in surprise. "How come he didn't want to talk to the captain?"

"It's not about the investigation," said McGuire, discomfort written on his face. "It's personal."

A quip came to Will's mind, but he stopped himself before uttering it. He looked around and saw that the other policemen were not doing their usual work, but were watching him in arrested postures. The reporters from the *Post* and the *Republic* put down their playing cards, took out their pads, and looked at him expectantly.

He started to speak, made an uncommunicative noise, and tried again. "Is it about my sister?"

Captain Kieley came out of his office and stood silently by the signal board.

"I believe so," McGuire replied, head lowered.

Will looked at the telephone and then back at the desk sergeant.

"I don't know how to place a call to Chicago," he said after a pause.

"Oh, here, I'll do it," McGuire said hastily.

Mike Egan entered the room with a burst of greetings, which he cut short at a gesture from the captain. Will sat down on the bench in the little padded canvas cabinet and pulled the glass door shut. Foley answered the telephone the first time it rang.

"Is that you, Dan?" Will asked. A series of hollow thuds issued from the instrument, followed by an ear-splitting whistle. "It's me, Will—can you hear me, Dan?" he repeated. The interference abruptly ceased and he heard Foley's voice.

". . . a terrible thing to tell you on the telephone like this, but if it *is* her, I figure you ought to know as quick as possible," the voice from Chicago said.

"What happened?" Will asked, mouth and jaw tightening.

"I heard about it this morning, as soon as I reported, and when I saw the name Anne O'Brien, I thought to myself, Could that be Will's sister that ran away to Chicago while me and Cummings were working in St. Louis? So I went to Metropolitan Hospital to check the next of kin. Was your mother's name McArdle?"

"Yes," Will replied. "McArdle."

"Then it's her," Foley said.

"But what happened?" Will asked. "Is Anne hurt?"

"She's dead," Foley answered.

Will inhaled deeply, aware of the eyes watching him through the glass panes of the door. "Are you sure?"

"Will, she died in surgery last night. I . . ." Foley's voice trailed off for a moment. ". . . she was bleeding from losing the baby. I'm awful sorry, Will."

"Baby!" Will's voice sank to a whisper and he pulled the door of the booth more firmly closed, turning his back on the curious gazes of the policemen and newspaper reporters gathered around the desk. He leaned his forehead against the wall.

"Will?" said Foley.

"I'm here," Will replied, and then more loudly: "I'm here, Dan. I don't understand. She had a miscarriage? Is that it? And she died of it?"

"That's what the report says," Foley replied, an uncertain edge to his words.

"Where is the body now?" Will asked.

"That's another horrible thing," Foley replied, pausing to clear his throat. "She's being buried this morning. Right about now, I would guess. At Graceland Cemetery."

"What did you say?" Will cried.

"They arranged the transfer and the burial early this morning."

"Who's *they*? What about the burial permit? She can't be stuck in the ground like that—she's not just a . . ." Will broke off, feeling tears mount in his throat.

"All I can tell you is what's on the report," Foley replied, and then, lamely, "I'm sorry, Will, I wish I could do more, but . . ."

"But what, for Christ's sake? Who signed the report?"

"That's just it," Foley answered. "Desmond signed it, it's marked 'confidential,' and I had no business looking at it. I could get into trouble, Will."

"Desmond! Dan, why would the chief of detectives come out in the middle of the night for a death in surgery?"

"I don't know," Foley answered miserably.

"Why in the name of God are they burying her so fast?"

"I don't know," Foley repeated.

"Dan, I've got to talk to Desmond."

"Oh, no, Will—that's out. You can't do that. I shouldn't have called you, I guess. I should have just butted out. I don't know what went on, but whatever it is, it had Desmond and the Commissioner over at Metropolitan all night long. Rafferty, that covers the hospital, said twelve men—

---

you know, the knuckle squad—were sent over to keep the press away, and they roughed up a photographer taking a picture of some big politician who showed up around six this morning."

"But what's Anne got to do with politicians?"

"Listen, Will." The voice from Chicago sounded faintly in his ear. "I have to get off the telephone now. I had no business sticking my nose in, see, but I felt like I had to let you know. But whatever went on, it seems like some big people here want to keep it quiet."

"Dan, one more thing—does the report say whether or not she was married? Or anything about a man named Schneider?"

"I don't think so. No, it's a very short report—that's part of the funny business. I have to hang up now."

"Dan?" said Will.

"What?"

"Thanks for doing this."

"God bless you and your poor mother," said the detective from Chicago, and hung up the telephone. Will stood silently holding the crackling receiver, his eyes fixed on the radiator under the window.

"St. Louis?" the operator's voice said. "Are you still on the line?"

Will hung up the telephone, stepped out of the little cabinet, and headed through the knot of policemen and reporters toward the station house door. "I have to take the morning off, Captain," he said, and was down the steps and onto the street.

His mother was waiting for him when he came home, a telegram in her hand. She held it out to him and he read:

DEAREST PARENTS. REGRET TO INFORM YOU OF DISASTER. ANNE DEAD AND BURIED. LETTER TO FOLLOW. YOUR BROKEN-HEARTED SON, CHRIS.

By nightfall Will had repeated his conversation with Dan Foley so often that it had acquired the quality of a catechism in his mind: a series of stylized queries and responses delineating, without ever illuminating, a great mystery.

"But *why* did he say she was buried so fast?" Kathleen leaned across the table, her bosom threatening to spill out of her wrapper onto its surface, throwing the question in Will's face like a spitball.

"He didn't know," Will replied wearily, moving his chair away from the table to put a greater distance between her and him.

"I don't believe Anne was that way without being married," said Mamie, for the third time, through a stream of tears. "We always said we'd be each other's bridesmaids someday."

"What way?" Frank asked, his thin, freckled face paler than was usual. "What do you mean, she was 'that way'?"

"Never mind!" Margaret snarled, rounding on the boy. "You go to bed, Mr. Nosy Parker!"

"Leave Frank alone," said Will, standing up abruptly from the chair in which he had been slumped. "Just leave off, Margie. Your yapping is just making it worse for Mother."

Margaret, Kathleen, Frank, Mamie, Jim, Owen, and Will turned to look at their mother, who was sitting on a low stool next to Mr. O'Brien in his rocking chair. She was huddled forward, her face in her hands, when she felt their gaze upon her. She looked up at them, wearing an expression none of them had encountered before on her candid features: she was ashamed. The stern, probing blue eyes faltered and were veiled with misery.

"I don't know what to do, Will," she said.

Will paced across the kitchen, pausing before the stove to light the gas under the iron kettle, and then resumed his walking. "Do?" he said. "What do you mean, do?" He crouched beside the stove and poked at the ashes.

"We have to pray," said Mamie through her tears. "We've got to have masses said for her, and light all the candles we can, and pray that she might have repented at the last minute. You know, Will, she might have repented. God is good." She broke down in earnest, weeping quietly into her handkerchief.

Jim wandered across the room to the icebox, sliced a portion of meat from a joint on the shelf, and stuck it into his mouth. He stared angrily at his mother from under his beetling brows. "Don't blame me for the fights I'll have to get into," he said. "I can hear them wise guys at the brewery already."

Kathleen's voice suddenly rose like a siren. "She's ruined us! We'll never be able to hold up our heads in this parish again! She let a man do filthy things to her, and had no more shame than a dog, and was going to have a baby, a bastard!"

"Kathleen!" said Will sharply.

"A baby?" said Frank in wonder.

"She deserved to die—she was a dirty slut and she'll burn in hell for it!" Kathleen's body was heaving as she flung the words across the table.

"Oh, Kitty, don't say that," Mamie cried. "I don't care if she was bad—I want her alive! She's our own sister. *Please* don't say you're glad she's dead."

"A baby?" Frank repeated, thunderstruck. "Was she married?"

"No, you nincompoop—that's the whole point!" Kathleen screamed. "She was a whore!"

Will walked to Kathleen's side, put one hand on top of her head, the other under her chin, and squeezed. "Shut up," he said. Kathleen squirmed and rolled her eyes, but he only pressed her mouth more firmly closed.

"Are you going to shut up?" he asked.

She attempted to nod her head and he released her. She sank to her chair with a gasp, but said nothing more. Mr. O'Brien cleared his throat. "The newspapers will run it on page four, I would imagine. If they connect the story with Schneider, it might be page two. Of the *Reporter*, even the front page. Not the *Post*, though—it has more dignity. Although they spread that story about Julius Campbell's daughter all over page one for three days in a row. But he was a big Republican. On the other hand, the *Globe* is more likely to rake around than the *Post*. The *Globe* may have it by tomorrow morning."

"Will," said Mrs. O'Brien anxiously, "what are we going to tell people when they see it in the newspapers?"

"But it won't be in the papers," Will said. "Didn't I tell you that?" The kettle began to whistle and he turned off the gas. He poured the hot water into the teapot and took a canister down from the shelf.

"Not in the papers?" said Mr. O'Brien in surprise.

"No, they're hushing it up. I told you what Dan said." Will spooned the tea leaves into the water.

"But *why*?" Margaret asked. "Why do they care?"

"It's like I said, Foley doesn't know why," Will replied. They looked at one another, suddenly silent.

"Can I go down the block and tell Finnie Hogan?" asked Owen, excitedly jumping to his feet. They all told him at once to sit down and be quiet.

"Where's John?" asked Mr. O'Brien.

"He's at the races again," Jim replied. They stared at one another.

"So," said Mrs. O'Brien at last, "nobody knows about it but us."

"And Dan Foley," said Will.

"And Dan Foley," she repeated. "But he's in Chicago."

They fell silent once more. Mrs. O'Brien drew her breath and said, "We will say not a word of this to anyone."

"Mother! What do you mean?" Mamie exclaimed. "How can we not tell people that Anne's dead?"

"By shutting our mouths. It's nobody's business but ours. Do you understand, Owen?"

"Yes, Mother."

"And the rest of you?"

Mamie began to cry again. "How can I make believe I'm the same when Annie is dead and buried far from home?"

Mrs. O'Brien rose from her stool, briefly supporting her weight on the armrest of her husband's chair. She crossed the room and leaned over Mamie, cradling her bowed head against her breast. She stroked her thick black curls for a moment and then said, "Only amongst the outsiders do you have to make believe, Mamie—not here at home."

They agreed to keep Anne's death a secret within the family.

16

THE FOLLOWING SUNDAY MORNING Will rose before dawn, suddenly suffocated by bedclothes. He dressed, went downstairs, and made a fire in the kitchen stove. He sat huddled by it, wondering why he had felt either uncomfortably overheated or miserably chilled all week. He wished it were not a Sunday, so that he could go to work. The prospect of dealing with his family all day, of guarding his strangely defenseless mother from their extravagances seemed impossibly demanding. She entered the kitchen in a bathrobe, her hair in a braid down her back.

"I thought I heard your step," she said. "Why are you up so early? Are you going to the Fishermen's Mass? I was thinking on that myself, Will. We could go down to the cathedral for six o'clock and we wouldn't have to say 'how do' to all and sundry. I don't know a soul in that parish anymore, except maybe Edna McElroy, and I expect she's dead by now."

"The streetcar doesn't run on Sunday until eight," Will replied.

She made a pot of tea and brought it to the table. "To tell you the truth," she said, "I was lying there, waiting to hear you get up. I have a strange thing to tell you."

"What?" Will asked, in alarm. "Did something happen?"

"Yes," she replied. "I saw Anne in a dream. She was right there, Will, before my eyes. She was alive."

"I wish I could have seen her," Will said sadly. "It must have done you good."

"She was on like the porch of a boat, leaning over the rail, stretching out her hand to me."

"Then what happened?" Will asked.

"That was all. I woke up, and lay there, putting it together in my mind, realizing the meaning and understanding what we have to do and waiting for you to get up." She poured tea into his cup, her cheeks flushed and a kind of sparkle in her eye, which gave Will pause.

"I don't think I follow, Mother," he said cautiously. "What meaning are you talking about?"

"Will! Don't you see it? Haven't you had the thought this week? Haven't you said to yourself, what if Anne is *still alive* and *not really dead at all?*"

"What are you talking about?" Will cried indignantly. "Do you think you can be buried and still be alive? Mother, for the love of God, don't let anybody hear you say such a thing!" He stirred his tea, slopping it into the saucer.

"You don't grasp my meaning, Will," she replied softly. "I believe a woman died in a hospital and was buried in Chicago last week, but how do we know it was really Anne? Couldn't it have been someone else?"

"No, Mother, it could not," Will answered firmly. "There was a death certificate and a removal permit. Foley saw them and he wouldn't lie to me."

"But, Will, what we don't know is this: who gave out the name? Was it the same one who put her in the hospital? Was it Schneider?" She searched his face. "Is it Schneider's word we're taking that the girl in the coffin is Anne? Who brought her to the hospital? Who talked to the police? That unholy letter he wrote us, Will—God knows what barefaced lies he's telling! How do we know any of this is true? Did we *see* her? Did anyone belonging to us *see* her lying dead?"

"No," said Will after a pause, "no one who knew her

saw her dead. It's true. But that's incredible, Mother." He ran his hand through his hair. "Why would Schneider pretend she was dead if she wasn't? He's a scoundrel, but he isn't a maniac. Why would he do such a mad thing?"

"That's what the dream revealed to me, Will," his mother said excitedly. "When I saw her standing on the boat, I knew. He sold her."

"Sold her! White slavery, you mean! Is that what you think?"

"Yes, Will," his mother replied, her eyes fixed on his. "She never died at all—he sold her. Didn't you tell me his name was linked to one of those agencies? Didn't you tell me women with red hair fetched a premium? I'm sure of it! I know it, Will. Somewhere our Anne is alive and subject to God only knows what infamy. How can you sit there doubting it? Schneider has had his way again!" She took her son's arm and peered anxiously at his face. "He must be laughing at us now, for letting him lead us up the garden path again." She paused, gazing around the kitchen distractedly, then, turning once more to him, she said, "Will, I must know. My mind cannot rest as long as I am not certain."

"What do you want me to do?" he asked, a numb fear overtaking him. She pressed his hand and stared into his eyes imploringly.

"Dig her up and make sure," she said.

"Oh, God," he answered.

"Please, Will—it's the only way we'll ever be at peace. Please. Who else can I turn to but you? Please. You know what officials to talk to, and how to go about it, and how to satisfy the law."

"Mother," he said, "officials? Don't you see I *can't* get an exhumation order? And anyway, would you want reporters and photographers swarming around our house and her grave besides?"

"But if it's not her grave?" Mrs. O'Brien asked.

"But *if it is?*"

She walked away from him and looked out the window at the first gray light of morning on the snow-sprinkled back yard. "It doesn't matter anymore what people think. I have never begged anybody for anything in my whole life," she said, after a silence. "Will, I'm begging you to do this for me."

He contemplated his hands before him, wrapped around the teacup. At length, he rose and took her hand. "I will go," he said. "Let me talk to the captain—maybe I can have some time off at the end of the month."

"No," she said, "not the end of the month. *Today.* You must go now, before the ground freezes."

Will breathed deeply. It is time to act at last, he told himself. Now, when it is too late, I'm ready to break the law. He walked to the sink. "Go on to Mass without me," he said. "I have a great lot to do today, if I'm going to Chicago." He put his arm around her.

"Take someone with you," she said. "Take John—he's the strongest."

"I will take someone," Will replied, "but not John."

It was nearly eleven o'clock the next morning before Will and Frank had packed the new shovels, the crowbar, the dark lantern, the cans of gasoline, water, and oil, the crucifix wrapped in flannel, the chicken sandwiches, and the planks into the back of Mike Egan's automobile, and Mike was explaining the intricacies of its operation to Will.

"I don't see why you don't want me to come," he said. "I could drive and you could study the map. I could help dig too."

"Thanks, Mike," Will replied, "but this is a family misfortune. Frank here can read the map. Let me try this transmission business one more time and tell me what I'm doing wrong." He shuffled his feet, the automobile lurched backwards and died. Will climbed out grimly and reached for the crank.

"Aren't you going to disengage the motor?" Mike asked. "You're not going to Chicago at all. You'll be killed before you get to the Eads Bridge. How about if I went with you as far as Bloomington? Then I could take the train back."

"We'll manage, Mike," said Will shortly, "and if anything gets busted, you know I'm good for it."

"Is that a fact?" Mike said angrily. "And if you crack your skull, are you good for that too?"

"We'll be fine. Is it disengaged now?" Will asked.

"No, you have to push it a little sideways or it pops back into reverse. How about Decatur?"

"No," said Will.

"Granite City, then, and, Will, that's the limit. I'll take the train back to East St. Louis and then the trolley. At least I'll know if you can drive."

"All right, Mike, if you're so set on it. I think I got the hang of it now. What's the matter? It won't move!" Will was beginning to sweat, despite the chill autumn air.

"The bricks," said Mike. "I told you to move the bricks or you'll ruin the tires."

Frank, crouching behind the front seat on the suitcase, arranged the bricks under his feet as Will cautiously nosed the automobile out of the shed, up the dirt alley, and onto Jefferson Avenue.

"We can go straight down Washington and get on the bridge," Mike said, eyeing his partner nervously as the latter maneuvered the vehicle jerkily amidst the wagons, runabouts, and occasional automobiles of the narrow street.

Frank held on tightly to the seat before him, so paralyzed by assorted fears that he felt almost calm. The idea of leaving his home, his mother, his neighborhood to take a trip to Chicago nearly stunned him with apprehension all in and of itself, for he had never been farther away from his house than a trolley ride down to Carondelet Park. Illinois seemed a remote and hostile territory; the only references to what lay east of the Mississippi that he had heard from his elders conveyed to him a mixture of contempt and fear toward the ill-famed "bottoms" on the other side of the bridge. To traverse as alien a landscape as Illinois in an automobile driven by the shaky and perspiring Will seemed mainly a nightmare, compounded by his responsibility to follow the map. The ultimate anxiety, however, was not the trip itself, but the destination, for Frank was aware of the purpose toward which the shovels, the crowbar, and the lantern were to be put. He wished he could pray, but since Anne's death he had stopped addressing himself to God. At the approach to the bridge, he looked around him calculating that since he was unlikely to survive the journey, he should at least take advantage of it to satisfy the curiosity he had always felt about the world outside St. Louis before he perished.

The world outside St. Louis was not engaging. Their automobile wobbled erratically down rutted roads, crossing a bewildering maze of railroad tracks. At every grade crossing Frank was gripped with fear lest the motor stall. Will slowed down as he approached each stretch of track and then accelerated quickly, hoping to speed past the danger point as rapidly as possible.

"Are we going the right way?" Will asked, as they bounced over the poorly graded rails. "I can't drive this machine and look around both."

"The sign back there said this way to Granite City," Mike replied, "and it looks like we're following the river. Isn't that the new waterworks over there?"

"Don't distract me. I can't look," Will replied, steering

around what appeared to be a water-filled trench in the road.

"I was speaking to Frank," Mike answered.

"What is that terrible-looking place?" Frank cried. "Do we have to go through it?" The sprawling groups of immense, dust-covered wooden buildings lining both sides of the road seemed to converge before them.

"Will, please stop—let's go back," Frank implored his brother, panicked at the sight of the strange yard in which they found themselves. Huge vats towered over factory buildings and the air stank of an unknown chemical. A knot of gray-crusted workmen, gathered around the mouth of a chute, waved them away with a dull red flag.

"How do we get out of here?" Mike shouted at them. They pointed toward what appeared to be a vast tank, sunken into the ground, its brown surface broken by a large iron wheel.

"He means us to drown in it, surely," Frank whispered, vowing that if he were ever returned to the real world, he would go to Mass every morning for the rest of his life. Will steered the vehicle around the tank and found a road that led past a gate and out of the compound. "Massinhopf Chemical Company," Frank read, turning around in the seat.

Will stopped the car and climbed out. "I have to have a smoke," he said, gazing apprehensively at the rows of one-story gray buildings lining the road. Even the sparse vegetation was completely coated with gray powder. Frank saw his brother's hand tremble as he lighted the match.

"Who would live in a place like this?" he asked in wonder, noticing gray wash hanging from a line.

"Working people who need a job," Mike replied.

A woman appeared from the side of the house, carrying a basket. She moved toward the wash line and paused to gaze at them, pulling a colorless shawl over her shoulders.

Frank stared directly into her gaunt, ashen face, dismayed by her pallor and the bitterness of her regard. He felt as if she were blaming him for something.

"It's awful gray and scary here," he called to her suddenly.

"Come on, Frank," Will said, "let's get started. You mustn't stare at people and talk to them like that."

"There was a fellow I knew once," Mike said, turning back to the car, the woman's eyes still fixed upon them. "Do you remember Pat Downey, Phelim's brother, from the second district? He worked over here for a year, when he got fired from the force, and he was never the same afterwards. He told me he spits gray wool every morning of his life, and his food never tastes right anymore. Do you want me to drive a couple of miles, Will?"

Will agreed, in relief, and they climbed back into the automobile. The road continued a winding course across and through the railroad tracks. At one point it seemed to disappear completely, and they feared they were lost in a vast switching yard. A passing repairman waved them on and a few moments later they found themselves on a narrow dirt road, elevated some ten feet above the frozen mud fields. A sign told them that they had entered Granite City.

Mike looked bleakly at the blackened expanse of the American Steel and Foundry compound dominating the landscape ahead and said to his partner, "Now I'm supposed to find a train station in this folksome little place and go back to St. Louis, is that right?"

"I didn't say that," Will replied. "What's the next good-sized town on that map, Frank?"

Frank consulted the unfolded sheets, which rattled in the breeze of the moving automobile, further increasing the difficulties of navigation. "It looks to me like Decatur," he replied at length, picking a spot as near to Chicago as he dared.

"Decatur! Isn't there anyplace closer than that? Decatur is halfway to Chicago!" Will objected.

"Which way, Frank?" Mike asked. "Do we want Collinsville or Edwardsville?"

"Edwardsville, I think," Frank replied, "and from there the next place is Mount Olive. Hey, look! Is that a mountain over there? Look! There's another one!" The road wound among the slag heaps, gob piles, and tipples of the coal fields, its very surface composed of bituminous dust. "I wish we weren't here. I thought there were farms and cows in the country. What are those men doing?"

Mike pulled the brake of the automobile and halted it before a throng of men standing in the road.

"Turn around, boys," said one of the men, himself coated in fine grit, "if you don't want to get hurt."

"But we're going to Edwardsville," Mike protested.

"Sure you are, Edwardsville—for a picnic, I bet. Say, men, these fellows tell me they're going to Edwardsville. I say they're scabs." In a moment the automobile was surrounded by a mob of men with blackened skin and clothing. One of them pulled the shovels out from the back and waved them over his head. "Shovels!" he shouted, "I'm gonna break some necks." He swung the shovels and the crowd moved toward the car.

"Tell them you're policemen," Frank whispered hoarsely, terrified.

"I got a better idea," said Mike, and slipping the car into reverse gear, he lunged backward down the road at top speed, sending a striking miner who had been reaching for the lantern sprawling into the road. The miners shouted and ran after them.

"Oh, Mike! Look out! Here comes a wagon!" Frank

cried, and Mike braked, executed a precipitous U turn, and headed back the way they had come. "Our shovels!" Frank cried.

"We're well shut of that bunch for the price of shovels," said Will, still gazing apprehensively behind him.

It was after two o'clock in the afternoon when they stopped in the tidy little town of Highland, Illinois, parking the automobile before the square. An elderly woman wearing a strangely shaped white bonnet eyed them suspiciously as she swept the sidewalk.

"We have to let her cool off before we can add water," said Mike, tapping the radiator thermometer solicitously. "Why don't we eat our chicken?"

They sat huddled on a bench in the park, lunching from the basket Mrs. O'Brien had packed. Frank ventured to the edge of the square as the two men tinkered with the car's motor. "There's a candy store at the corner!" he exclaimed. "Can I get a drink? I've got money." He jingled the twenty cents of his savings that he had brought with him.

"We'll all go," said Will. "I could use a cup of coffee."

They seated themselves at a small table in the sweet-smelling store and drank the hot chocolate that the proprietor recommended.

"What does 'Luzern Zee' mean?" Frank asked, pointing to the sign in the window.

"From Switzerland, sonny, we come. You have seen the cows we got on your way into town? The finest cows in the whole United States."

Frank looked at Will and Mike, who shrugged. "Cows?" he said. "We didn't see any cows. All we saw were coal heaps and terrible-looking buildings, besides a bunch of miners that wanted to kill us for driving on their road."

"What way you come then?" the proprietor asked. "You

come the wrong way!" He eyed them curiously. "Where you from, anyway?"

"St. Louis, in an automobile that Mike and his cousin made from parts," Frank said.

"All the way from St. Louis to Highland in an automobile!" The candy maker shook his head in amazement.

"Is there a store around here where they sell shovels?" Mike asked, interrupting.

"Shovels!" The proprietor stopped wiping his glass case. "What do you want in Highland with shovels? They must sell such things in St. Louis." A look of suspicion crossed his blunt features. He glanced nervously at the window of his store and, spotting a passer-by, he went to the door and hailed him. "Mr. Koepfli!" he called. "Come help me tell these strangers where to buy shovels." They exchanged a few hasty words in German and Mr. Koepfli hurried down the street. "In a few minutes someone to help you about the shovels comes," the proprietor said.

"Time to go," Will said, tossing two nickels onto the table, "if we're going to get that manure loaded before dusk." They bade the candy store owner good day and walked back to the automobile, feeling his gaze upon their backs.

"This place is *too* neat," Frank said uneasily, as a pair of women leaned their white-bonneted heads through a window to regard them intently. "Let's go now."

Mike screwed back the radiator cap, replaced the water can, and cranked up the motor.

"I'll drive for a while," said Will, and soon they were leaving Highland, on the way toward Pocahontas, Mulberry Grove, and Vandalia. They fixed a flat tire near St. Elmo and filled the crankcase outside of Pana, where, to Frank's astonishment, roses were growing under glass roofs. Night was falling as they entered Decatur.

"If there's a Catholic church in this town, I'd like to light a candle for my kidneys," said Will, as he steered the automobile to the edge of the street, its hood level with the elevated wooden sidewalk. "Show me how to get these lanterns mounted."

"Will," said Mike, "how about if we spend the night here and get up early tomorrow?"

"Look!" Frank cried excitedly, pointing into the dusk. "Lake Michigan!"

"Every wet spot on the ground you think is Lake Michigan," his brother replied. "It's just another cow pond." He pulled off his cap and rubbed his head and eyes. "I'm covered with every kind of dirt," he said. "Still, the dreariest job is yet to come." He and Mike sat quietly, staring into the dark streets of Decatur.

17

THAT NIGHT they had their supper in the mess room of the jail and slept in a back room of the Decatur police station. Frank lay in a narrow cot, flanked by Will and Mike Egan. He watched the yellow glow of the coal fire through the isinglass of the stove and breathed the smell of the wooden room where men slept and changed their clothing. He felt safe within the confines of the jail, between the two sleeping policemen. He thought it was good to be on the force and to be able to drop in at the station in another town and be made welcome. It was like a club Mike and Will belonged to, or a secret society. He wondered drowsily why, with such a vast network of policemen in his club, Will hadn't stopped Anne from leaving. He saw her, amid a swarm of blue uniforms, protected against bad outsiders. As he watched, a red automobile drove into the crowd, and the policemen were knocked down. He turned his head restlessly on the pillow, picking up the little blue figures one by one, placing their shoulders against the fenders of the automobile, and willing them to shove. The Dion moved grudgingly backwards and then jerked sideways, knocking over more policemen and coming to rest at Anne's side.

When he awoke it was still dark, but he could see his brother pulling on his pants by the stove. He wanted to urinate and wished the room were warmer so that he could relinquish the comfort of the coarse but warm jail blanket.

"Did Foley tell you how to get to the lady's house that rents rooms?" Mike asked in a low voice.

"He told me Wentworth Avenue and Twenty-first Street," said Will. "I got the map McGuire gave me."

"Once my cousin Robert went to Paducah," Mike said. "He stopped at a lady's house that the husband was a towny of my uncle, Dan Hurley. Anyway, he got lost and had the devil of a time finding the place."

"Let's get moving then," said Will. "I want to drop you at the train station and get to Chicago while it's still light, so we can have a look at the grave before night falls."

"If I came with you," said Mike, "I could help you find Mrs. Walsh's and the grave. I told Kieley I wasn't coming in today."

"I got Frank—he can read a map."

Frank watched his brother buckle on his holster. "Will!" he exclaimed, "I can't exactly read the map perfectly yet. What about if Mike came with us a little more. Mother only said he couldn't help dig—she didn't say anything about Bloomington."

"When are you going to get out of that bed?" Will retorted angrily. "Move yourself, Frank—you're keeping us waiting."

Nothing more was said of dropping Mike in Decatur, but Frank felt that Will was annoyed with him.

After breakfast they went to Froelich's Hardware store for shovels.

"You're not from the salt house, are you?" the white-haired, heavy-lidded clerk asked.

A mist was rising from the stubbled fields as they made their way past the farms and through the small towns of central Illinois. Will was worried about the weather and stopped several times to ask farmers if they thought it was going to freeze. "They have a sixth sense about the weather, Frank," Will said, "the way Mike here can sniff a fan-tan three blocks away." The consensus of the farmers consulted on the road between Bloomington and Joliet was that there would probably be a frost that night, but not a hard one. Will and Mike were talking about how long it would take to dig six feet of dirt. Will thought it couldn't be very tightly packed and would probably yield to the spade quickly. Mike said he was sure gravediggers tamped it down hard, using rollers, which all but leveled the mound. They were arguing whether Chicago was colder than the rest of Illinois, and in consequence more susceptible to ground frost that night, when Frank, suddenly overcome with fatigue, cold, and general malaise, wrapped his head in the blanket, curled up among the implements, and fell asleep.

He awoke as the streets of Chicago began to emerge from the tangle of railroad tracks and factories on its edges and was taken with uneasiness. Fear of the city's notorious inhabitants temporarily superseded his apprehension of the task for which they had come. The unbroken straight lines of the streets they passed depressed him; they seemed to announce that a harder race of beings lived there than the people he knew in St. Louis. Feeling inadequate to the role of Will's only companion, he wished Will would let Mike Egan stay with them. Would Will be enough protection for him, even with his service revolver? On Twenty-first Street, where they parked the car, he expected the passersby to attack them and was surprised to find that they were ignored on the busy sidewalk. Only one child, a red-faced little boy in patched knickers, displayed an interest in the automobile. He pointed out Mrs. Walsh's house with moderate civility.

"They don't look any different from people in St. Louis," Frank whispered to Will as they carried their suitcases to the back bedroom behind the stiff back of their landlady.

"Foley said two of yiz, not three," she observed sharply, when they had deposited their belongings on the bed.

"I'm not staying," Mike replied. "Can you tell me where the Wabash station is?"

She consulted with her father, who sat wrapped in a blanket by the radiator in the kitchen. He marked the station on the map with an X.

"Do you know the way to the cemetery, now, Will?" Mike asked as they pulled up before the station to let him out.

"We'll manage, never fear," Will replied, the brusque tone returning to his voice.

"I'll be waiting for you on Thursday then," Mike said, still gazing intently at his partner, "unless you want me to stay."

"Go," said Will. "We'll be back tomorrow night." He put the vehicle into gear and drove away from the curb. Frank turned to wave at Mike and, when he was out of sight, climbed into the front seat next to his brother.

"Where do I turn now?" Will asked. Consulting his map of the city, Frank guided him through the streets to the entrance of Graceland Cemetery. "We have to hide these shovels under the seat," said Will. "The rest of the stuff we can leave in the trunk. Now, you're going to mark down the way in your notebook so we can find her grave tonight."

"But what should I write?" Frank asked apprehensively.

"I'll tell you," Will replied.

At the caretaker's office, there was confusion over the location of Anne's plot, and Will was afraid for a moment that they had come to the wrong cemetery. After a time, they were sent off down long series of paths and arrived at last at number 362, marked only by a clean-looking metal tag. Frank, white-faced, looked at the freshly turned mound of earth in terror. He wanted to tell Will that it was completely impossible for him to do as they had planned, that he would die of fear if he had to put a shovel into that dirt, and that Will would have to dig alone.

"Now this path runs right into that road ahead," Will was saying, "and the road curves over to the fence on the other side of that big white tomb with the two angels. So I'll count, Frank, and you write down what I say." They paced the distance from Anne's grave to the road and from the road to the fence.

"Are we going to have to climb over tonight?" Frank asked, pointing to the spiked iron fence.

"Let's see if there isn't a gate along here someplace," Will replied, tying a piece of string around a pike. They followed the fence past a pair of groundskeepers and an elderly, weeping woman dressed in black seated on a bench. They found a gate, and as Frank stared in fascination, Will fiddled with the lock.

"All right, Frank," he said at last. "We can go now." They walked back to the dust-covered automobile as the sun was beginning to set.

"What do we do now, Will?" Frank asked.

"We go back to Mrs. Walsh's and have something to eat, see. Then we go to bed. At three o'clock we get up and head for here again. I left the latch on the gate open. If the watchman locks it, I can loid it. Then, Frank, when we're finished, we'll start back to St. Louis."

"What if they catch us, though?"

"Foley will square it. Don't worry."

"Couldn't Foley square it *before* we get caught?" Frank asked nervously.

"I told you not to worry," Will said. "Nobody will notice a thing. I haven't been on the force for all these years for nothing, Frank. If I can't break into a lousy cemetery without getting nabbed I ought to turn in my badge."

Frank swallowed the additional questions that crowded his tongue, recognizing that Will felt his professional expertise was being impugned. He examined the map before them. "Will," he said, "we're only a few blocks from Lake Michigan. Could we drive over and see it—just for a minute?"

Will frowned. "This isn't a sight-seeing tour. Don't forget, we didn't come here to take in the attractions."

Frank, humiliated, stared at the row of stores they were passing and wished he had not risked such an ill-considered request. It was true that they had not come to see Lake Michigan, but, Frank recognized sadly, left to his own devices, he would surely have stolen a look at the thing.

Will pulled up to the curb behind a wagon marked EMERSON—MEN AND BOYS CLOTHING. "There's a fried-fish house across the street," he said. "What do you say to a bite here? I don't feel like eating Mother Walsh's corned beef and cabbage tonight."

"That house really smells, doesn't it, Will?" Frank said. "I wonder her old man doesn't mind it."

"He doesn't notice it, you see. We're all used to our own stink—it's only the other fellow's we take offense at." He climbed out of the automobile and, followed by Frank, crossed the street and entered the fish house. A waitress in a limp striped apron was turning on the lights when they came in. She brought them a menu, glanced at Will, and patted her pompadour.

"Now you can't be father and son—I just wouldn't buy that!" she said.

"No," Frank replied, "of course not. Will's my brother— he's only twenty-six."

"You don't say! Isn't that the world of coincidence? I'm twenty-one myself, but my brother Corny, he's twenty-six."

"I'll have the deluxe lake platter with a bowl of vegetable chowder to start off with," Will said briskly. "What about you, Frank?"

"Can I have fried fish and fried potatoes and ice cream?" Frank asked. "I never ate in a real restaurant before."

Will shrugged. "Don't go eating too much—it wouldn't do for you to have a bellyache tonight."

"Now, let me guess!" the waitress exclaimed. "I can tell you're not from Archer Avenue, but I'm not sure about the North Side."

"We're not from any side!" Frank said, delighted at being taken for a native. "We come all the way from St. Louis in an automobile!"

"All the way from St. Louis in an automobile!" Her broad face was illuminated with excitement. "Aren't you ever the sports! What does your wife think about that?"

As Frank started to explain that his brother was a bachelor, Will interrupted him. "She says I better have my supper fast and get started home. Bring me a beer with the fish."

The waitress's beaming face fell, and she turned sulkily toward the kitchen. "Frank," Will said, when she was out of earshot, "you've got to cut that out."

"What did I do?" he asked, hurt at his brother's tone.

"You answer every damn-fool question anybody asks you. When a chippy like that wants to know who you are, where you're from, all your business, you should turn it around so she's the one who has to answer, not you. Ask her if she's working for the newspapers. Instead, you trot out the whole tale, the trip to Chicago in the car Mike Egan made with Robert, you never ate in a restaurant, I'm twenty-six. The next thing you would have been telling her we're here to dig up Anne."

Frank's eyes filled with tears and he kept his gaze fixed on his cutlery. "I never would tell about that, Will," he said in a choking voice.

"Now don't start sniffing, for God's sake." Will leaned forward across the table. "You're too old altogether for crying."

Frank put his hand to his mouth and turned his head to the wall, willing himself to stop but unable to control the wave of grief that was engulfing him.

"Frank?" said Will after a moment. "How about a trip to the toilet and we blow our noses good. Mine feels like half the dust in Illinois got shoved up it."

When they returned from the bathroom, faces and hands washed, Frank was more composed. He recovered his self-esteem during the meal to such an extent that he risked asking his brother a question that had long occupied his mind. "There's something I don't understand, Will," he said. "I don't see why Anne would love a fellow that hit her. If he was nice to her and treated her grand, why then I'd be able to explain why she ran away."

"If he was nice to her all the time she'd call him a wet sock," Will replied as his soup was placed before him. "You've got to understand, Frank, how women are."

"Women? Do you mean just because she's a woman? Look at Margaret. She wouldn't let any fellow paste her— she'll hardly let anybody talk to her. And what about Mother? She's a woman, too." Frank eyed his brother eagerly, feeling for once that he was surely on his way toward getting the better of an adult in an argument. "Mother wouldn't care for being mistreated. I'm sure of that," he said.

Will stirred his soup, fatigue showing itself upon his face. "Mother is not to be taken for a model of women,

Frank. I should say, she *is* a model, but she's not what I would call an example. Not at all. Does she resemble Mrs. Mahoney or Bridey McBride?"

"No," Frank replied, "but why doesn't she?" Another grave conceptual gap was opening in his mind. "Why is it she'll never make up to a neighbor, Will? Mr. Macnamara asked me that and I answered him I didn't know. That's true. I don't know why."

"I'll tell you, Frank," said Will, moved by an unfamiliar impulse toward confidence, "but you have to keep it under your lid—agreed?"

"I won't tell a soul—I promise," the boy said. "It isn't something bad, is it?"

"Well, it is and it isn't. It has to do with long ago, on the other side. Most people we know, they came over during the famine, when the potato crops failed, and they could not have been poorer. But Mother lived in a big house, with servants, and her father held the lease on any number of farms. You must not speak of this to anyone," he said, crumbling crackers in his soup.

"But what's the harm in living in a big house?" Frank asked, floundering in his efforts to pull himself up to Will's level of understanding.

"It seems as if her father must have been friendly with the British authorities in some way—with a militia they had over there—and the poor Irish, they must have resented it. Why don't you eat your fish? Anyway, when her mother was stricken with cholera, and the servants, too, and they were dead in a few days, not one neighbor would lift a finger. In fact, the tenants burned the stables and killed the cattle and ate them. That's why poor Mother got shipped off to England in the middle of the night and never even found out who was dead and who was alive until she was over here for years. And she will not speak of it. She would not have told me, only once an old woman, back when we lived on Thirteen Hundred Biddle Street, cursed her in the street. She said, 'I know you, Catherine McArdle, a filthy rent racker hunted out of Galway City.' That was the only time I ever saw Mother look afraid or not have an answer. Right after that we moved and I never saw that old woman again."

Frank chewed his fish slowly, his eyes glued to his brother's face. "Poor Mama!" he said. "How scared she must have been! Do they still have the cholera?"

"Not anymore, and it seems as if the different hard times have gotten better. But some people remember the other side and what happened there. That's why when somebody says to Mother, 'Where are you from?' she says, 'Francis Xavier,' and not a word about the old country, the way the others do, with their 'Mayo, God save us,' and all that. Do you want a piece of pie?"

They drove back to Mrs. Walsh's house in silence, each wrapped in thoughts of what lay ahead for them that night. Will paid the landlady in advance and told her they would be leaving before dawn, so that she should not be alarmed if she heard them moving about. To their surprise she said she would fix them breakfast, since she had to be up anyway to get her Tommy off to the steel mills for the four o'clock shift. They bid her good night and retreated to the narrow back room with its slanting, linoleum-covered floor and its smell of vinegar. Frank did not bother to wash or brush his teeth, but dove under the covers as soon as his nightclothes were on, falling asleep a few minutes later. Will prepared himself for bed more deliberately, setting and winding his alarm clock, folding his trousers, and scrubbing himself thoroughly at the sink in the hall. He switched off the electric light, said a brief prayer, and closed his eyes. Visions of country roads rolled toward him with a dizzying intensity, so that he was forced to open his eyes and stare fixedly into the darkness several times. At last the onrushing landscape subsided and he slept.

On Washington Avenue in St. Louis, Mrs. O'Brien lay in bed next to her husband, her rosary twined around her fingers. She had lifted the shade and the room was bathed in moonlight. She prayed for clouds over Chicago and safe passage for travelers.

18

WILL AND FRANK arose as soon as the alarm sounded, Will silencing the clock with a swift gesture and groping for the chain that turned on the light bulb in the ceiling fixture. They looked at one another blankly, their eyes blinded by the glare of the unshielded bulb. They both felt strangely exposed by the noise that had signaled to the world that an illegal act was about to take place. They dressed hurriedly and went into the kitchen, where Mrs. Walsh was frying potatoes and sausages for the somnolent Tommy.

"Yiz is early risers, I should say," she remarked with no special curiosity in her voice.

Will shot a warning glance at Frank. "We're the fellows that get the worm—isn't that a fact?" he responded jovially, instantly regretting his choice of cliché, as Frank blanched visibly.

"Could I have just coffee?" Frank asked weakly. "I hate sausage."

"Eat whatever you want," said Will. "Only let's make it fast."

They departed Mrs. Walsh's and cranked up the motor of the automobile with a racket that echoed disturbingly in the silent street. It took an extraordinary amount of cranking before it started, and Will was sweating profusely when it finally coughed itself into mechanical life.

"She was cold and lonely from being out here in the dark," said Frank, patting the steering column.

"Now," said Will, "we turn left onto Ashland Avenue, is that it? You're my guide, remember."

"Will, shouldn't you mount those lanterns we got in the trunk?"

"I'm going to try it this way," his brother replied. "There is little stirring now and I can see where I'm going by the streetlights." They both glanced at the sky, where the moon was intermittently obscured by fast-moving clouds. They passed a baker's wagon and the aroma of hot bread suddenly reminded Frank of how far he was from home.

They drove slowly down the road next to the cemetery, peering at the fence. "I think we've gone too far," Frank whispered, and then, "No! There's the gate!" His heart began to beat wildly.

Will stopped the car. They looked around them at the deserted street, animated only by the branches of the trees along it moving restlessly in the wind. They took the shovels and dark lantern from the trunk and tried the gate. It refused to yield. Will took a bit of wire and a collar stay from his pocket. He fumbled with his tools as Frank's gaze swept anxiously up and down the dark street, behind the fence, and into the shadowy cemetery.

The words "Hurry, Will!" came to Frank's lips. He held them back. It stood to reason that his brother was picking the lock as rapidly as he could. They heard the sound of an approaching wagon. "Quick!" Will said. "Push those things through the fence." He knelt to the sidewalk, pretending to examine the rear tire of the automobile as Frank slipped the implements between the iron bars and into the bushes. The horse's hooves struck the stone pavement at an unhurried pace as with unutterable slowness the milk wagon drew abreast of them and passed on without pausing. The street was silent again. Will turned back to the gate and Frank sagged momentarily against the fence, as if his strength had departed with the wagon.

The full moon appeared briefly behind a bluish veil of cloud. A faint sprinkle of snowflakes whisked across Frank's upturned face and he felt a sting of coldness on his cheek.

"Will," he whispered, "it's starting to snow. Why don't we come back tomorrow night?"

"Damn it," said Will, "the shaft on this thing is so stiff I can't get it to budge. Stand over there, Frank, so you're not in my light."

Frank moved to the other side of the street lamp, his eyes glued on Will's fingers. He almost screamed when something cold hit his face. It was only a wet oak leaf, blown up from the gutter. He shut his eyes and spoke fervently, "Let it open now, God. I promise."

"Okay, we got it," Will said immediately as the gate swung open with a harsh, grating sound. He pushed the boy through ahead of him, locking the gate after them. They stood breathing heavily in the bushes when they heard a footstep on the board sidewalk. Looking out from the foliage, they saw a policeman approaching. He stopped to examine the automobile, and, raising his head, looked inquiringly about him. Noting the cemetery gate, he tried the lock.

"Somebody's at Elsie's place," he muttered to himself, glancing at a lighted window across the street. He continued his leisurely stroll, his footsteps dying slowly away.

"Let's go," Will whispered, and they retraced the path they had mapped out that afternoon to Anne's grave, Frank following his brother between the rows of gravestones and the swaying trees.

The Favor had worked again! The first time Frank had promised God in exchange for a Favor had been in the dentist's chair, when Dr. Kleinfelter couldn't get his impacted molar out. He had offered up the helpless prayer only as a last resort. No sooner had the words formulated themselves in his mind than the dentist had cried, "Eureka!" and proudly held up his trophy for Frank to see.

It was clear to him that the Favor would only work three times. Why God would bestow special consideration upon him was not mysterious in his mind—it was because he was starting not to believe in Him. The Favors were, he decided, like free samples at the baker's—a little something to get a fellow hooked. He had been planning to save the other two for some crucial moments in his life, turning points of his destiny, such as if he were about to drown, or, conversely, if he stood to make his fortune on the draw of a card. But now he had used up two, and there remained only the one. That might mean he would have his life *or* his fortune, but not both.

The snow had become a light shower of icy crystals, which struck his face in erratic gusts as he followed the black figure of his brother ahead of him on the path, shovel in one hand, lantern in the other.

"I think this is it," Will said at last, crouching beside a grave marker and lighting a match. He looked around apprehensively at the freshly dug mounds dusted with snow stretching on either side of them. "This must be the new part of the cemetery. I wish there was more cover." He stood up, replacing his woolen gloves on his hands and pulling his cap lower on his ears. He glanced about him once more and then lifted the shovel and swung it into the earth. "I'll start then."

"Can I help?" Frank asked.

"Here, light the lantern, but keep it covered until I say." Will tossed the boy a box of matches and began to dig. A wave of terror washed over Frank as he watched his brother. Surely they weren't really digging up a coffin with a dead body in it. With Anne! To penetrate her grave, to force open her last resting place, to look at what no one was ever supposed to see!

"No, Will, please—let's go home," Frank whispered, appalled at the words even as he uttered them.

"Point of no return," said his brother calmly. "Take the other spade. You can dig too. Only don't throw the dirt on me."

Frank picked up the other shovel and began to dig too. The thud of metal striking dirt mingled with the creak of the tree branches in the wind, the rustle of leaves, and the faint rattle of the frozen rain. It came to Frank's mind for the first time that they were exhuming the body for a purpose. It was not just some ghastly ritual to be gotten through; it was an effort to find something out. It might not be Anne! He felt suddenly bewildered.

"Will," he called softly, "who is it if it isn't Anne?"

Will, ankle deep in the grave, shrugged. "Just dig and don't worry," he replied.

Frank was sorry that he had asked that question. It did not exactly express what he wished to know, but he couldn't think of how to phrase an inquiry that would encompass his confusion. They had come to dig up Anne in case it wasn't she. It could be Anne, under his feet, or it could not be. He saw with dismay that Will was in almost up to his knees.

They would have to open it and look inside! He paused and leaned heavily on his shovel. Was it up to him to say? What if they couldn't tell? Would she be a skeleton? His heart began throbbing excitedly. I can't do it, he thought. I won't look. I'll say whatever Will says.

The mound of earth to the side of them grew as they excavated the grave. "Can you go faster down at your end?" said Will, pausing for breath. "This sleet feels like it's changing to rain. At least, maybe it'll keep the watchman indoors by the stove." He withdrew a bottle from his pocket, opened it, and took a gulp of its contents. He glanced at Frank, who was shivering as he dug.

"Are you cold?"

"I'm freezing."

"Here," said Will, "take just a little sip of this. It'll warm you."

Frank sucked eagerly at the whiskey only to spit it out in haste as it burned his mouth. After a moment, he wiped his nose on his sleeve and said, "Will? Can I try it again?"

Will passed him the bottle once more, saying, "Just a sip." This time the raw liquid slid down his throat and made a little glow in his chest. "Now dig!"

Will threw a shovelful of wet dirt over his shoulder. They dug, rhythmically bending and lifting their shovels, panting in the cold, wet night. After a time Will's shovel struck wood.

"I'll be damned," he said. "This isn't six feet. I'd be surprised if it's even five." He drew in his breath sharply and resumed his labor. A few minutes later they shone the lantern down upon the dark wood of the coffin.

"I'm going to have to dig out a place here so I can open it," said Will, turning to excavate a niche for his feet. He lifted Frank from the grave and said, "Now, pass me the crowbar and shine the lantern where I say. You don't have to look if you don't want. Maybe you had better not."

"I don't want to," Frank said, and as he handed his brother the tool: "But I'm going to anyhow."

Will shoved the crowbar under the lid. "Let it not be Anne! I promise!" Frank called suddenly in a hoarse voice, shutting his eyes as the lid popped open. The narrow band of light from the lantern illuminated a mass of reddish hair.

"Dear God," said Will. Frank opened his eyes and saw his sister's head lying sideways in the coffin at several inches remove from the rest of her body.

"Her head!" Will gasped. "It's cut off!"

Frank, uttering little cries of fear, hid his face in his brother's shoulder.

"She got her head cut off," Will repeated, staring into the coffin. "That's what they were trying to cover up." At length, he knelt awkwardly beside the coffin, took a pocket knife from his trousers, and carefully clipped a lock of her hair.

Frank got down on his knees in the mud beside the grave and stared into the open casket. He saw her face, bruised and distorted, at the peculiar angle to her body.

"Anne," he said. "Oh, Anne."

"They cut her head off," said Will, "and they tried to lie to us about it. They lied to me." He plunged the point of his knife into his fingertip and squeezed a drop of blood on the body. "Hand me the crucifix," he said. Frank pulled it from under his jacket, kissed it, and passed it to Will, who kissed it and lowered it onto the dead woman's bosom. They intoned a prayer for her soul and with infinite care they closed the lid once more. Many years later Frank tried to describe what he had seen in the coffin that night, but he could only recall the image of her gray silk dress with the dark spot of Will's blood and the coils of copper-colored hair.

They replaced the dirt in the hole, moving as if in a dream, tamping it down at last with the backs of their shovels. The dragged their gear wearily along the path toward the gate, indifferent to the noise they made.

"I'll tell you what, Frank," Will said as he scraped at the frozen rain on the windscreen of the automobile with the knife he had used in the old Irish ritual. "Let's find an all-night place and have a cup of coffee. Then there's a

fellow I've got to see before we start back to St. Louis."
The boy, huddled under a blanket in the front seat,
nodded his head in agreement, his face drained of emotion. He thought of Favors and twisted his mouth in pain.

As the automobile began to move down the street, he
turned around to see the cemetery gate once more.
"Goodbye, Annie," he said quietly.

19

AFTER THEY HAD DOWNED the scalding coffee, standing dumbly at the counter of the Corona All-Night Eats, they drove the automobile to police headquarters on Central Street. They parked up the block until it started to get light. Will did not speak. At eight o'clock, through the rain-streaked windscreen, they saw the night shift hurriedly leaving and the day men arriving.

"I think that's him," said Will suddenly. "You sit here until I get back."

He climbed out of the seat and Frank watched him in fear as he crossed the street. He had never seen Will really angry before, and the bottled-up rage in his brother's face made him seem like a stranger. Frank attempted to fasten the oiled-paper side flap more securely against the damp chill. He pulled the blanket around himself tightly and curled up in the seat, shivering still. Will wouldn't just go away and never come back, he thought. He wouldn't really shoot somebody with his gun and be arrested. He tried to comfort himself with the thought that Will had told him to wait. He watched the traffic and the people filling the street. They seemed to belong to another race.

The sergeant at the desk looked up at the man standing before him, noting his mud-soaked trousers and shoes and his air of scarcely concealed anger.

"Yes?" he said curtly.

"I want to talk to Desmond. Tell him it's Will O'Brien from St. Louis."

"The chief isn't around. Maybe I can help you. Sit down over there and I'll call you when I'm done here." He leaned back in his chair and resumed his conversation with a pair of men in street clothes and a reporter drinking coffee from tin cups.

"So I says to O'Gorman," the sergeant went on, " 'This time sheet is still filled out all wrong. I don't care *who* told you to do it that way—you got to do it over. So he says to me . . .'" To his astonishment, the mud-caked visitor reached across his desk, pulled the time sheet from his hand, crumpled it up, and threw it on the floor.

"Tell Desmond it's Will O'Brien from the St. Louis Police. Tell him I just dug up my sister that got her head cut off and I want to talk to him now. Go." The sergeant jumped from his chair. He stared at Will for a moment, started to speak, and then fled down the hall. He returned a few minutes later.

"Chief Desmond will see you," he said. "Follow me."

When Will entered his office, the chief of detectives was by the door, his ruddy countenance exuding warmth and hospitality. "Will O'Brien!" he said, clapping his hand to his forehead. "Holy Mother! How do you like that? Come in, sit down." He gestured across the figured carpet to a leather armchair, his shrewd eyes on his visitor. "Harry," he said, "go get Officer O'Brien some coffee and a piece of that cake you fellows were having. Isn't that something? Will O'Brien, for God's sake—imagine you coming all the way from St. Louis. Here, sit down."

"I'll stand," said Will. "I don't want any coffee, Desmond, and I don't want any more lies. Tell me how my sister got killed."

Desmond's beefy face sagged momentarily. "Oh, Will!" he said. "Lies! I wouldn't use that word. Not lies." His glance traversed Will's muddy clothing and he hastily closed the door behind the departing sergeant. "Did you really dig her up?" he asked nervously.

"Do you want me to tell you how she looked in the coffin?"

"No! No," said Desmond, backing around his desk and composing his features into an expression of kindly solicitude. "You must be undone, man. What a terrible thing! I want you to know how bad we all felt. For the love of Mike, if I had known she had a brother on the force! Why don't you sit down. I'll tell you all about it. The truth is, Will, I can't imagine how the hell it happened. What do you know about it, anyway?" he inquired suddenly. "I mean, what were you told? Who did you talk to?" He patted his blotter with an agitated hand.

"Desmond," said Will, fixing the chief of detectives with a malevolent eye, "shut that blather and tell me how Anne's head got cut off."

The chief assessed Will's demeanor with the practice of an old cop. He fiddled with a pencil for a moment, sighed deeply, and then began to speak.

"I guess that's the best way," he said. "There's no avoiding it now. Only you're going to have to keep it under your lid." Will nodded.

"She was being wheeled into the elevator of Metropolitan Hospital on a stretcher. The nurse pushed her part of the way in and then turned to talk to a doctor getting off the other elevator. It sounds like she was flirting with him. The next thing she knew, the overhead door came slamming down and decapitated her, clean as a guillotine." He paused and then added, "I'm sorry, O'Brien—it's really a hell of a thing. I know how you must be feeling. Why don't you sit down, have some whiskey—you've had a shock. The nurse had some kind of an attack herself, and then the elevator door opens up on the next floor and this old fellow, shuffling along with his cane, walks right in before he sees the body, and then, you can imagine, they had to put him to sleep finally to shut him up. Here, let me pour you a drink, for Chrissake."

Will stared at him. "Why did you lie?" he asked. "Why did you have to keep it out of the papers?"

Desmond ran his hands through his silver hair and abruptly laughed. He glanced at Will apologetically and took a deep breath. "The hospital spent $15,000 for safety stops on those elevators not six months ago," he said. "They were never installed. They were never even ordered. The director, Dr. Bob Whitely, he begged me to hush it up, Will. He told me a long tale about his money troubles and how he'd pay it back and how he never thought there would really be an accident. But I was going to blow the whistle on him anyhow, I swear to God I was, until the commissioner showed up, and then . . . another guy. This other guy throws a lot of weight around in Chicago, Will. He and Whitely, it turns out they go back a long time. Anyhow, after a while the commissioner told me to write the short form and get her buried by noon. And kill it with the papers. He didn't give me any choice." Desmond's eyes never quit Will's face. "I left the hospital while Whitely was working out his deal with her common-law husband."

"What!" Will exclaimed, startled. "Common-law husband?"

"Well, you knew she was in the family way, didn't you? This fellow who'd been with her came back. He wasn't the type you'd expect at a sewer like Metropolitan Hospital at all. He was slick as spit. He told Whitely he was a lawyer and he'd been in the elevator and witnessed the whole thing and he was going to sue the hospital and Whitely personally for triple damages under the common law. I think he was full of it, myself, but Doc was so rattled he was offering him money and begging him to take it and be quiet when I left. Common-law husband!" Desmond drew himself up and looked indignant. "If I hadn't had my hands tied, I'd have run him in."

"Schneider was in the elevator?" Will asked, white-faced.

"Was that his name?" Desmond frowned. "Yeah, that was it, Schneider. A lot of deals were made fast that night, O'Brien. I never pulled so many strings in such a short time."

Will stood staring stupidly at the floor, as if transfixed.

"Look, O'Brien," said Desmond, "the best thing is to forget it. Nothing's going to bring her back, is it? The son of a bitch is probably a hundred miles from here by now."

"Which son of a bitch? The doctor, you mean?" Will asked.

"No, not the doctor! The fellow she was living with— you know, Schneider. Will, you need some sleep. Why don't I have you put up at a good hotel here in town, at our expense, of course. You didn't talk to any reporters or anybody, did you?" He wiped his forehead, then pulled an oval cigarette from a tin box and lighted it, watching his visitor through the smoke.

Will started as from a dream and shook his head. "I have to go," he said. "Somebody's waiting for me."

He turned on his heel and left the office. The chief called after him. "What are you going to do?" but he did not reply. Desmond stepped to his window and thoughtfully watched Will cross the busy street, crank up the automobile motor, and drive away.

He told the commissioner that day at lunch that they probably would have no trouble from that quarter, seeing as how the girl's condition was a scandal. "It could have been worse," he said.

20

Two DAYS LATER, when the brothers had returned to St. Louis, Will went around to the *Post-Dispatch* and the *Republic* with obituary notices. They stated that Anne O'Brien, daughter of James and Catherine O'Brien of 3121 Washington Avenue, sister of William, Margaret, Kathleen, Mary, James, John, Owen, Thomas, and Francis, had been killed in an accident while visiting Chicago.

By the following evening the front door of the house on Washington Avenue was sheathed in black crepe, the shades were drawn, the shutters were bolted, and inside the mirrors were hung with black cloth. The family, clad in black, was assembled in the front room, which was lighted by devotional candles.

Margaret seated herself on the settee next to Mamie and Kathleen, who were weeping. "Monday is time enough to start dyeing the clothes," she announced firmly.

Father Degnan arrived and was admitted by Frank. He had the family kneel and led them in prayers for the repose of the dead. Only Mr. O'Brien remained seated, shuffling the newspaper clippings carrying the obituary on the round oak table, apparently oblivious to the devotional activity taking place around him.

A knock was heard at the door. Mrs. O'Brien motioned to Frank, who went to answer it. He returned to the front room and said, "It's Mr. and Mrs. Dolan. Should I bring them in here?" He looked dubiously at the dark room crowded with kneeling mourners.

"Tell them the wake is closed," his mother said.

When Frank entered the room again, he was carrying a wreath of red roses bearing a ribbon on which the words "Deepest Sympathy" had been sewn. He placed it on the stove and lowered himself again to his knees. After the priest left, Aunt Katie came to the door and was admitted. Frank showed her into the room and watched her embrace his father. The knocks at the door became more frequent, and the front room and the foyer quickly filled with floral pieces, the round oak table with Mass cards. Frank repeated, "The wake is closed" to Mrs. Mahoney, to James Cronin, the ward leader, to three nuns from St. Leo's, to Mr. Macnamara, to Pete Gentile, Mike Egan, and Frances Petrofsky, to Captain Kieley, to John Gilmore, and to Mueller, the pharmacist.

When he brought in the yellow gladioluses from the Kinloch operators he could bear it no more. He went to his mother in tears. "Why do I have to stay outside all by myself?" he asked. "I don't want to talk to any more people. I want to be with you."

She looked at him, expressionless, and made no reply.

"Mother?" he said.

"Come on, Frank," said Will. "I'll go outside with you." It was chilly and overcast on the stoop, but Will lighted a cigar and heaved a sigh of relief. "I hate that smell of flowers," he said. "At least there's no incense." They stood silent, thinking of the strangeness of the occasion.

A young woman came hurrying down the sidewalk, a dark hat pulled over one eye. She was carrying a cross made of white lilies. "I've come straight from the hospital. I'm sorry for your troubles, Will," she said, breathlessly pressing the flowers on him.

"It's good of you to come, Fanny," said Will, passing them to Frank who muttered, "The wake is closed," and pushed them into the doorway.

By eleven o'clock that evening the street lamp was illuminating an odd scene. Frank was letting the flowers pile up on the walk, too dispirited to drag any more into the house. There were wreaths from all ten of the police districts, and from Clayton, Carondelet, and the Mounted District as well. Will was deep in conversation with Mike Egan. Pete Gentile sat on the curb holding a spray of chrysanthemums.

"I know it's closed, Frank," he said, "but just remind your father Pete is here, if he wants to come out." Frank wearily dragged the flowers and dropped them in the dining room. He delivered Pete Gentile's message to his father, who did not respond. Jim had discovered the whiskey bottle behind the coal scuttle, and having quickly dispatched its contents, with the help of John, he fetched a new bottle from the store on the corner. Mrs. O'Brien paid no attention as Jim's voice grew louder and more argumentative. Tom was asleep on the floor, unnoticed under a blanket of assorted flowers from the A.O.H.

Mrs. Mahoney's window was open, and she passed out slices of cake and cups of tea to those who came to pay their respects. "It's the least a person can do for their best friend, ain't it?" she inquired of Frances Petrofsky, who thanked her for the refreshments. "Are you engaged to Mike Egan yet, honey?" she asked.

Four boys from the knacker, acquaintances of Owen's, started to become rowdy, protesting loudly that nobody had the right to close a wake. Will and Mike moved toward them and the boys scattered, shouting curses.

Sadie Bierman refused to go home, explaining she was Jewish and was used to discomfort when there was a death. She handed Frank a box of candy and, spreading out a sheet of newspaper, joined Pete Gentile on the curb. "The Irish are strange," she commented.

"You said it, lady," Pete replied.

Tim Goggins, whose house flanked the O'Briens' on the opposite side from Mrs. Mahoney, rested his elbows on his windowsill and talked with a small band of patrolmen who had stopped on their way downtown for the "last out" shift. "My father put me under an upside-down clothes basket," he told his listeners, passing them a bottle of whiskey and a tin cup, "and there I was, peering through the cracks, and I saw it with my own eyes, when the British soldier broke my father's back with the butt of his rifle, and it was the last day of my father's life." He paused for a turn at the cup. "And of my own as well, for I'm a walking dead man ever since, as you see me sitting here."

"Tim!" his wife's voice called. "Come to bed and stop your incessant blathering out the window."

"I'm conversing with the uniformed force," he replied in a tone of dignity, and to his guests: "She was born a Protestant and has no patience." The patrolmen nodded in understanding.

Joe Ward, who kept the saloon by Headquarters, greeted each of them by name as he pushed his way through the crowd, carrying a bottle of whiskey. "I came as soon as I could, Will," he said, and thrusting forth the bottle, added, "I'm sorry for your troubles. Muldoon's been out of flowers since nine o'clock, and he says there's not so much as a daisy left between the river and Kingshighway." Will looked around for Frank. "Maybe you ought to bring out some glasses," he said. "We could stand a drink, anyway."

Frank did as he was bid. Will opened the bottle, and as he poured a glassful for Mike Egan, awareness of Anne's disgrace and death washed over him afresh, and he felt sweat on his face. For a moment it seemed to him that none of it could have really taken place. It was the sort of horrible disorder to which families with no self-respect were subject. He arrested people who were led by their willfulness or animality into conflict with the rules of decent behavior, and he had little sympathy for them and their relations, despite their piteous complaints. He used to reason that in almost every case the person who found himself in demeaning troubles had failed to check some bestial impulse within himself, and that jail, in that sense, was like the zoo—a large cage containing those who fell below humanity.

How could the moral chaos have invaded him and his so rapidly? Anne ruined and dead, he and Frank marauding a cemetery in the middle of the night, and a Protestant one at that, he realized suddenly. Had his mother thought of that yet? For no real cemetery was named Graceland—real cemeteries were all called Calvary. Another woe, he thought, and poured himself an inch of whiskey. And a chief of detectives sounding like a madam with a fire violation! It made Will feel guilty himself, remembering Desmond's evasions. And worst of all, his mother, shamed.

Mike Egan's voice caught his attention. "Tell me, Will," he said in a low voice, as Joe Ward moved away to shake the hand of Phil Maher from the tenth district, "is anybody around here the wiser about Anne, do you think?"

"I don't know what they're saying. You can tell better than me."

"The captain and McGuire know she ran away with Schneider, but I don't think they knew she was in trouble." The two large men stood side by side, hands behind their backs, before the house of mourning, looking at the crowd spilling out into the street. "They wouldn't talk about it, and I don't feature Schneider spreading it around either," said Mike Egan. "How's your mother bearing up?"

"Like she's been chloroformed. And the old fellow's off

in some world of his own. I think we've all yet to take it in, Mike." He drank from his glass of whiskey.

Frances Petrofsky came to stand beside Frank. "It's getting awful late for you," she said gently. "Maybe you should go to bed." He leaned against her shoulder and she put one arm around him. "Do you want a piece of Mrs. Mahoney's cake?" she asked.

"My mother says not to take anything off of Mrs. Mahoney," he replied.

"Your mother is particular, isn't she, Frank?" Frances Petrofsky said admiringly.

"Oh, I should say. It takes her many a long day to rap to a neighbor, and we just moved in three years ago."

"I'm sorry about your sister," she said. "Mike told me that Will told *him* that you and Anne were real pals."

Frank began to cry. She was the first person to say anything to him as if he were entitled to bereavement the way a grown-up was. He felt humiliated by the tears pouring down his cheeks, and without answering her, he turned, went into the house, and climbed the stairs to his room. Owen was asleep on the bed, in his clothes, the bulb in the ceiling still lighted. Frank lay down next to him and fell asleep, too.

He was awakened from a lovely dream in which Anne and his mother were pulling shiny brown loaves of bread from an oven by a terrible noise. Both he and Owen jumped from the bed and hurried down the stairs. The sound—a high-pitched, prolonged wail—was coming from the front room.

Will entered the door of the house, a grim look on his face. "Who is doing that?" he called sharply. He pushed his way through the flowers and the people, Frank behind him. In the front room all eyes were on Mame, who presented a bizarre spectacle. She was crouching by the stove, her hands filled with ashes, her face soiled. She had unpinned her hair and it stood up like a lion's mane around her head. From her mouth came the peculiar sound, the archaic Celtic moan, imbedded deep in her mind by childhood wakes she had attended.

"Stop that this minute, Mamie," Margaret cried. "What do you think you're doing?" Mamie paid no heed. Eyes shut, rocking back and forth on her heels, she continued to produce incredibly protracted notes of pure anguish.

"Get up!" Margaret shouted.

"Mame," said Will, "nobody does that nowadays. Please stop—they can hear you all the way to Grand Avenue." To his horror, a second voice was added to the first, and turning his head, he saw the fine, modern, American face of his Aunt Katie contorted into a dirt-streaked mask of grief, as the ancient cry issued from her throat as well. Will looked in desperation to his parents, but they sat with their eyes shut. The movement of the beads was the only sign that his mother was alive.

"I need a drink," Jim announced, and shoving Frank aside, he lurched through the foyer and out onto the sidewalk, kicking over a basket of white carnations from Captain and Mrs. Joseph Kieley.

"You're another no-good louse," he said to John Gilmore, Kathleen's friend, and punched him in the nose. The ensuing brawl was tolerantly observed by more than a score of policemen.

Mr. and Mrs. Charles B. Orthwein and their two children, Charles, Jr., and Corinne, rode up Washington Avenue in their stately closed brougham, pulled by a pair of matching bays. They were returning to their home on Vandeventer Place from a performance of *The Wizard of Oz.*

"What do you suppose that's all about?" Mr. Orthwein

inquired, glancing curiously at the turbulent human panorama presenting itself on the sidewalk before the O'Brien house.

"And this block is where the so-called better class of Irish are living!" Mrs. Orthwein exclaimed. "Just listen! Look at them! It takes more than lace curtains to civilize people."

"Where, Mama?" said the little girl. "Let me see!"

"Never mind, Corinne," her mother replied, drawing the curtain.

"Ah, well, Beatrice," said Mr. Orthwein, patting his wife's hand fondly, "the world would be a dull place if everyone were *aussi sage que nous.*"

Will awoke late the next morning and felt sick to his stomach when he remembered the events of the preceding day. The prospect of the hours ahead held nothing to cheer him. As he shaved he tried to remember whether it was Wednesday or Thursday. When he came down the front stairs he was appalled at the disorder of the rooms. Flowers were piled on top of each other, the hall table had been overturned, and Tom was still asleep under a wreath. Will left him there. He found Jim sleeping it off on the kitchen floor, while his mother and father sat at the table, drinking tea in silence. He kissed his mother's cheek and held her roughly against him for a moment, then released her.

"Good morning, Father," he said. Mr. O'Brien gazed at him, an unfathomable expression in his faded blue eyes.

"Have a cup of tea, Will," his mother said. "We have time before we have to leave for Mass."

When they returned from the service at St. Francis Xavier, a wagon was parked before their door. To Mrs.

O'Brien's surprise, her son approached the passenger, an elderly black woman, and suddenly embraced her.

"I'm sorry I fooled you, Ollie," Will said. "I couldn't think of any other way."

"You didn't fool me for a minute, Officer O'Brien." Ollie had tears in her bleary old eyes. "And I hope you're not blaming yourself about what happened. Maurice and I, we've been crying all morning and wishing we could go live on the bottom of the sea and never come up for air."

Will shook hands soberly with Maurice. Ollie turned toward Mrs. O'Brien. "I brought you this here to make a meal off of." She held forth a dish covered with a towel. "It's called *Bunderfleisch* and you slice it real thin. It's tasty," she said timidly, as Mrs. O'Brien stared at the dish in silence.

"Mother," said Will, "this is Ollie, that I told you about."

"It's good of you to come," said Mrs. O'Brien, "but the wake is closed."

"Oh," said Ollie. "Maurice and I didn't *expect* to be invited in. We just wanted to bring you this little piece of *Bunderfleisch*. And say how bad we feel. Officer, if you'd fetch me a broom, I'd clean up this sidewalk a little for your visitors."

Mrs. O'Brien, startled, looked at the entrance to her home and saw the mounds of floral pieces, broken bottles, cigar butts, and trampled flowers around her door. "I'd be much obliged to you, Ollie," she said, "but first you and Maurice come in and have a cup of tea."

The household emerged from its stupor a little at a time. Will had to use a crowbar to open the locked bathroom door. He found John passed out, fully clothed, in the tub. Will turned on the cold water and left the room. Mamie appeared to be sleepwalking, her face still streaked with ashes, as was Aunt Katie's, who had spent the night in Anne's old bed.

Everyone stepped over Jim without seeming to notice him until Margaret came down, scrubbed and coiffed, her black gown sponged off, aired, and pressed. She pulled Jim up by the back of his collar and screamed in his ear. He came to, snarling. The rest of the family watched their struggle in silence. Maurice, having learned from experience that white people's quarrels frequently culminated in injury to black people, moved his chair back, preparing, if need be, to grab his godmother and bolt.

By noon the visitors were ringing the bell once more. Ollie had neatened the banks of flowers and was passing out sandwiches cut from the ham brought by Frances Petrofsky, a Swiss cheese and roast beef Dave Dwyer had sent over from his diner, two corned beefs—one from Macnamara and one from John Gilmore's mother, a salami presented by Mr. Yesner, and her own *Bunderfleisch*, which was the least popular. She had an enormous platter of pastries from Mr. Diarmada, which she was saving for later. The family was reassembled in the darkened front room, fresh devotional candles lighted and in place.

"I can't let anyone in, Will," his mother said. "We have no body to show."

"I know, Mother," he said, his hand on her beloved shoulder. "I'll be outside if you need me." As he left the room he heard a low growling noise being emitted from Mamie's throat. Here it comes again, he thought miserably.

That day and the next went by like a fever dream, as Will passed from the stifling atmosphere of the blackened room, with its heavy odor of flowers and whiskey and sweat, to the sidewalk, where it seemed to him that every human being he had ever known came by at least twice. The procession of policemen, old neighbors from North Jefferson, members of the Holy Name Society, the Mullanphy Emigrant Relief Society, nuns, school friends, boys from the brewery, the shoe factory, the slaughterhouse, telephone operators, girls from the Sodality, men from the bathhouse, people from the Altar Guild, and even the queen of madams, Mother Johnson herself, telling him it was a "damn shame," rolled past him like currents of the river. He closed his eyes and saw glaringly bright images of swirling brown water, black-clad women, and, abruptly, Anne's face. He opened his eyes in fear. He drank a little whiskey from time to time, careful not to let himself get drunk, using it to ease him through the vigil, to dull the panic Mamie's keening aroused in him. At one point he wished it wasn't ever going to end, that there would be no return to the regular order, but that he might stand at his mother's shrouded doorway forever, sealing off the inside from the outsiders, Mike Egan somewhere near him, but not too close.

By Saturday it had begun to taper off, and by Sunday it was definitely over, although with no funeral to climax it, it lacked a clear finale. The family went back to work on Monday morning. Even Mamie, face still stunned, went through the motions of looking for a new situation, moving her lips silently in prayer as she crossed the threshold of each prospective employer. They found her odd and did not hire her.

Mr. O'Brien took the photographs of Igorrotes, Moros, and Negritos pursuing their typical daily occupations and laboriously packed them into a cardboard box. He went down to Mac's himself for the brown paper and twine. He inserted a card bearing the words "Regards from James F. O'Brien," wrapped it, sealed it, wrote Pete Gentile's name and address upon it, and took it to the post office on Eighth Street.

"Are you sure it will be all right?" he asked the clerk anxiously.

"Don't worry, old-timer," said the clerk, tossing the package over his shoulder into a bin.

He slowly retraced his steps and, when he got home, climbed into bed. After he had a rest he would look for work painting houses.

Mrs. O'Brien and Vesta cleaned. They moved through the house as the angels of the Lord moved through Sodom, extirpating every last vestige of filth they encountered. The rooms reeked of antiseptic, the stoop shone like the high altar, and the tin ceilings dripped where they had been scrubbed with a brush. When Mrs. O'Brien felt satisfied, she and Vesta bought black powder and new tin tubs for dying the clothes. They worked their way systematically through every chifforobe and drawer of the house, except for Kathleen's. She wept and swore she would never wear black—only purple. In the end Mrs. O'Brien let her dye her clothing purple, but never forgave her for it.

June 1904

21

A FEW MONTHS after the wake for Anne the O'Briens moved to St. Aloysius parish, where they knew no one. They purchased the yellow brick house on Shenandoah Avenue cheap because it had been damaged by fire. When James O'Brien returned in the evening from his job as a union painter for the Board of Education, he carefully scraped, puttied, and painted the charred walls of the upstairs rooms. Covering the smell of burnt wood with that of fresh paint gave him satisfaction. He worked very carefully, and when he finished a room, it was as perfect as a little lacquered box from France. He said less and less as the months went by, and one morning Mrs. O'Brien confided to Will that she was afraid he was becoming a silent old fellow.

"It's in his family," she said. "He told me that his grandfather never spoke a word after his leg got crushed in the Gaels' rising outside of Limerick. I've always anticipated it, Will, and to tell you the truth, I've long been afraid he'd slip off on us this way." She stood at the sink cleaning a chicken.

"I wonder if he would go to the Fair," said Will, seizing the occasion to put forward a project he had been thinking about.

"Fair!" said Mrs. O'Brien. "Is it time for merrymaking then? Should we all wear colors and carouse?" She dislodged the gizzard with one stroke of her sharp knife, tossing it into the bowl.

"No, not carouse, but, Mother, it's been a year and a half," he began.

"Not until next week," she interrupted him, wrenching the liver from the bird and slapping it into the bowl.

"Almost a year and a half, then, and you've not left the house except for groceries and Mass. It's time for a little diversion, Mother—something to help the old fellow take an interest again." Will switched his argument smoothly from Mrs. O'Brien's needs to those of her husband, when he saw the cold veil fall over her eyes.

"And didn't we all have a glorious diversion at Kathleen's engagement party?" she asked scornfully, pulling another chicken from the brown paper and flopping it ferociously across her cutting board.

Will sighed. It was true. The party for Kathleen's engagement to a rich, Protestant businessman had been a disaster. As the betrothal toast was being downed, Kathleen, tremulous all evening in her lavender chiffon gown, had become hysterical. She burst into tears, threw the ring at her astounded fiancé's face, and ran upstairs to bed. She had not left the house since, and it was almost three months. She wept a great deal and ate very little. Her mother feared a decline. Dr. Kieffer recommended exercise, but his prescription had gone unheeded.

"And you must not overlook the social call I paid only last month," Mrs. O'Brien continued, splitting the chicken down the middle with a blow of her cleaver. Will was disturbed by his mother's irony and her virtuoso chicken butchering.

"Do you mean when you went to Virginia Morris's house?" he asked, knowing that was what she was referring to. Mr. O'Brien had found the announcement of Virginia Morris's engagement to Christian R. Schneider in the society page of the *Post-Dispatch* and put it in his wife's lap without a word. The photograph of Miss Morris took up a quarter page. She had been a maid of the Veiled Prophet in 1903. A few days later, after much prayer and self-interrogation, Mrs. O'Brien wrote Mrs. Morris a note, requesting an interview. The meeting took place in a morning room off the parlor of a fine house on Layfayette Square. Mrs. Morris and her daughter listened disdainfully as their visitor told how she felt obliged in conscience to warn them that Christian Schneider was a dangerous man and that, although she could provide no details, she had personal knowledge of his sinister and ruthless character. They heard her out coldly and then they told her that darling Chris had explained the whole dreadful affair to them—how he had married Annie O'Brien in secret, out of love, how she had met with a terrible accident—and that they were all so happy now that darling Chris, whose mother had been a Neidringer, was coming out of his grief and was preparing to start a new life with Ginnie and forget the misfortunes of the past. Mrs. O'Brien, clutching her purse as if it were a weapon, asked them if they knew about the previous Mrs. Schneiders and their accidents.

"Mrs. O'Brien," Mrs. Morris had said, rising from the wicker settee, "I don't consider it appropriate to discuss Virginia's future husband with you any further. Christian warned us that you were consumed with hatred toward him, and his lovely mother told us, the day she came to tea, that we might expect to hear outlandish tales about him from some quarters. I will say, however, that the insurance company paid right away, and the Armstrong Elevator Company awarded Christian twenty-five thousand dollars in damages. He told us about the check, didn't he, Virginia? Now, you know, big companies don't pay out money like that if there is even a hint of wrongdoing. So I thank you for coming, Mrs. O'Brien, but I think you would be well advised not to go around calumniating our darling boy, who has had so many troubles in his life up until now and who comes from such a good family. I'll walk you to the door. Ginnie, dear, you can go back to your room."

Mrs. O'Brien had turned at the door to address her hostess. "I will pray for your immortal soul," she said, and descended the marble steps.

She had told Mr. O'Brien of her meeting as he sat nodding. "I knew it," he said, after a pause, and putting his box of clippings on his knees, he searched through pieces of newspaper until he found the account of Schneider's out-of-court settlement with the elevator company according to the article, in compensation for the loss of his fiancée. He showed her another piece with a headline reading, "Bill to Require Safety Stops on Elevators in Illinois."

"You didn't show me these, James," she said.

"No." He shook his head. "No, no, I did not." He continued shaking his head, patting the arm of his chair absently from time to time. "I did not show them to you," he said.

"James," she said after a moment, "his mother, she must be a foul creature indeed, underneath her ladylike trappings, to countenance his behavior." He had not responded to her, but had restlessly run his fingers over his bits of paper, moving his lips silently.

Will knew he had undergone his own sort of decline since the trip to Chicago. When Captain Kieley called off the white-slavery investigation because prosecutor Folk was no longer willing to back it, Will had become incensed to an unprecedented degree and had spoken bitterly to his superior. Then, when Mike Egan had gotten married only a month later, his morale reached a low point. He spent his mornings off at the bathhouse, listening to the politicians, watching the card games, and letting Bones go over him.

He ran in a pair of society suffragettes for loitering with intent, and while the captain did not reprimand him, he gave him some very cool looks. He holed up with Jenny a few mornings, and then, disgusted with himself, spoke harshly to her and left, not to return. He was most at peace back on duty outside the houses on Chestnut Street, watching the customers come and go, greeting the proprietors and the girls, listening to the strains of piano music as they drifted out through an opened door, a part of the life and yet at a remove from its play of desire, want, and greed.

This day, however, Will was stirred on his parents' behalf. He reflected that people with common sense would view the family's retreat as exaggerated, perhaps even unwarranted. He felt that it was up to him to stand for the judgment of people with a middle-of-the-road outlook on life—one that he did not instinctively possess but that he could infer from the behavior of others and adopt as his own. In this way he had learned to harmonize with the world around him and to bring its sensibility to bear upon his family. His mother listened to him and would sometimes yield to the pressures he exerted, as when she gave Mrs. Mahoney's new grandson a crocheted cap, at Will's insistence. "Only a token," he had said, and she relented, grudgingly, sending Frank next door with the little box.

It was time now, a year and a half after Anne's death, for the family's paralysis to be finished. Will feared that, if his father entombed himself completely in his silence, and Kathleen permanently confined herself to her vaporous couch, and Mamie continued to frequent the disciples of Madame Blavatsky, the fragile mask of normality that the family had always maintained might be broken for good.

He felt strongly that the Fair was crucial, for to turn one's back on the extraordinary celebration of the new century was to reject the world indeed.

It would be enough to entice his parents, to begin with, he reflected. If they could be persuaded to pay a visit to the Fair, then Margaret's tyrannical piety would be undermined, and if the tide started to turn, he was sure, Kathleen would be off her chaise like a shot. It would give them all a new subject to discuss at dinner, for example, and then, after a bit, they would go back again, and perhaps take a meal at the Outside Inn or one of the other restaurants on the grounds. It would be expensive, and family finances had become worrisome since Mrs. O'Brien had insisted on a new house, and Mr. O'Brien had come down to painting for the Board of Education, and Mamie could not seem to hold a job, and Kathleen was declining. Jim, it was true, had been fired from Anheuser-Busch for drunkenness, but had immediately been hired by Lemp at a higher salary. The net, however, was distinctly less than before. Still, Will had some money put away, and surely if the family could be aroused from its torpor by spending it, the expenditure was more than warranted.

He pursued the subject further with his mother. "The Irish Village is supposed to be very fine," he offered hopefully. "There's a tenor there name of John McCormack, a young fellow who took the prize in all of Ireland for singing. They say he's a marvel and worth the price of admission."

"Caruso is better," Mrs. O'Brien said.

"But Caruso isn't going to come, and McCormack is already here, besides Lily Foley."

"Why should I spend my money to hear McCormack when Caruso is better?" Mrs. O'Brien asked, obstinate.

"And if Caruso came," Will countered, "would you go to hear him?"

"Indeed, I would not," she replied. "I have no time for that Continental business."

"Mother," said Will seriously, "you can see for yourself how the old fellow is falling away. I know you don't care for the entertainment, but will you combine with me to bring him out a little, and pull him from the newspapers, and then maybe he will talk sometimes, the way he used to. Or else, what?"

She hesitated, absently fondling the bowl of chicken entrails. "It's my eyes that are so scalded on me these days," she said, and after a pause: "It is true that he speaks almost not a word. And when I ask him a question, he seems to come back unwillingly, as from a great distance. It was a terrible pity and shame what Kathleen did that day at the trolley stop."

"Yes," Will agreed, "he was not himself after that, and whatever he finds in the newspapers, he doesn't share it anymore since that day."

He thought with bitterness of how his father had descended from the streetcar, wearing his painter's overalls and cap, to encounter the elegantly got up Kathleen and her fiancé. She had not returned her father's greeting, an omission that had forced her into a series of outrageous lies. Her intended seemed willing to believe that Mr. O'Brien had a black-sheep brother who accosted family members on the street, but it was unlikely that Mr. O'Brien accepted Kathleen's claim of temporary memory loss. At any rate, he seemed further diminished after that meeting, and further still when, at last, the Little Stigmatization of St. Francis was reassigned to Carlo Manouri. He continued to study his sketches of thumbs in his new third-story studio, but what purpose the drawings served was not clear, once the commission had been withdrawn.

"We could take the car to the end of the De Giverville line," Will said, "and we would be almost at the gate of the Irish Pavillion. We could just duck in for the John McCormack, and not wander around amongst the fountains and the lights and the different wonders at all." He observed her straining eyes and altered face cautiously, feeling her assent almost within his grasp.

Frank entered the room at that moment and said in an excited voice, "Are you talking about us going to the Fair?"

"Not you," Will said hastily, seeing his carefully laid trap sprung. "Why aren't you at work?"

"I got fired," the boy said guiltily. "A horse stepped on my foot. I hate horses and I'm glad I don't have to sweep anymore. Can I show you my foot? I hopped all the way home." He knelt and began unlacing his high shoe, as his mother wiped her hands on her apron and hurried to his side. Will shrugged, feeling that he had accomplished as much as he was going to that day. He left the house for an hour at the pistol range before his shift began.

The next evening after dinner Will wandered into the kitchen of their new home, where Mr. O'Brien sat in his old rocking chair, his reading lamp next to him, his stack of newspapers on the floor. The small kingdom he had thus created was in all respects identical to the one on Washington Avenue which he had quit. His appearance, however, had changed, and the faint color that had formerly enhanced his fine features was now completely gone. Will seated himself casually at the kitchen table, suddenly aware of his own muscular bulk and florid complexion. It's that I am a man, he thought to himself. And then instantly: He's a man too, the father of us all. He cleared his throat. Mr. O'Brien did not raise his eyes from the page.

"I was wondering," Will began abruptly, and as he perceived no response, he started again, softening his intonation. "I said to Mike, 'If there is anything in the newspapers about this fellow McCormack, my father will surely know all about him.' I said that to Mike. 'Mark my word,' I said, 'if there's so much as a line in any of the newspapers, you've only to ask my father—he'll have the story on the end of his tongue.' "

Mr. O'Brien looked up, his faint blue gaze encompassing Will without focusing on him. "Is it John McCormack from Athlone you're speaking of? Who won the Feis Ceoil competition along with Lily Foley, who's a great beauty, from Cashel. Is it? Is that the one? He's appearing at the Irish Village on the Pike, and is the toast of the Fair, and is fêted by every flannel-mouthed politician in St. Louis." He returned his attention to the *St. Louis Recorder*'s editorial on the New York City policemen who had been discovered to be millionaires. It crossed his mind that Will might be interested in the story, but the effort of conveying it seemed enormous, and he could not lend him the newspaper until he had read it all. He sank back into the welcoming pool of words and forgot Will's presence.

Will cleared his throat again. "It's just as I said to Mike! You've all the information at your disposal, and I wonder what you say to the dispute they're having."

His words hung in the kitchen, not having found access to Mr. O'Brien's attention. Will leaned forward and rattled his father's newspaper.

"What's that!" cried Mr. O'Brien, startled.

"I said, I wonder what you think about the dispute?"

"What dispute would that be?" asked Mr. O'Brien fearfully, flustered by his son's unprecedented onslaught of conversation.

"Do you think it's true, I mean, that McCormack is as good as Caruso?"

"Of course it's not true," Mr. O'Brien replied, to Will's surprise.

"How do you know?" Will asked. "Did the paper say so?"

"I heard him myself," his father replied, "and no human being could sing more beautiful than him."

Will thought for a moment that his father was mad. "Who did you hear?" he asked after a moment.

"Caruso! On a Zonophone recording that Mr. Emerson brought back from his trip to New York. He's the superintendent and is a man cultured in the Continental arts. He played it for me and Vincent McTeague that was painting the ceiling. There's no doubt about it, Caruso is the best. Now I would like to rest." He reached for the *Times*.

"I am thinking," Will said, plunging ahead desperately. "Wouldn't it be a grand thing to go to the Pike—yourself and myself and Mother—and hear McCormack sing, since you could compare him to Caruso and pronounce on their merits impartially."

"Go to the Fair?" Mr. O'Brien's eyebrows rose in astonishment. "Are you talking of an outing then?"

"I thought to myself, Wouldn't it do Mother a world of good to hear McCormack sing, since she's so quiet and bulgy around the eyes these days," said Will, recklessly abandoning the tenor-rivalry ploy and lunging after the Mother's welfare angle, all systematic development of strategy forgotten.

"You may have the right idea," said Mr. O'Brien unexpectedly. "Have you seen how like a goldfish her regard has become? An evening of McCormack and the Foley girl may put Mrs. O'Brien more at her ease." His face appeared infinitely weary, and for a moment Will regretted having aroused him to such emotional and conjectural heights. He firmed up his resolution, however, with the thought that a pleasant diversion might diminish his father's air of exhaustion rather than increase it.

"So then!" Will said. "It's settled. Friday evening, since I get off early, the three of us will set out after supper."

"Now I must rest," Mr. O'Brien said softly but firmly, and turned back to his newspapers.

When Will stepped into the dining room Frank was awaiting him. "Will!" he cried, "can I go with you? I would give anything, Will, for just a little look at it. Do you think they would let me come?"

"Not a chance, Frank," his brother replied. "But I'll tell you what. If this excursion goes well, see, and they both feel a little closer to the liveliness of life, as you might say, why then, later on I'll bring it up about taking the whole family. What do you say? It's only June—you've got until fall. It's just a matter of them getting warmed up to the gaiety and whatnot again." He patted Frank's arm absently and moved into the front room, where he seated himself upon the piano stool and addressed himself to the elusive rhythms of "Easy Winners."

Frank went out the back door to the shed in the yard and, looking around to be sure he was not observed, pulled a chicken skewer from his pocket and set about trying to pick the lock. He wanted to go to the Fair with single-minded intensity. It seemed to be the magnet of everyone's attention, and for weeks Frank had felt St. Louis all around him being pulled toward Forest Park. When he had asked his mother about it, however, she had dismissed the idea very curtly, and he felt he had offended her. Still, he could not let go of the wish. It seemed to him unimaginable that the whole world was coming to St. Louis, that twenty million people were expected to pour through those magical gates before the summer's end, that grown-ups were reported to be quitting their jobs and leaving their families all over the Midwest in order to spend the whole summer at the Fair, and that he should not partake of it at all. He thought of disobeying his mother and going alone but such an excursion was beset with difficulties, since he had only eight cents in his box and the trolley cost a nickel each way, to say nothing of the twenty-five cents to enter the Fair grounds.

When he worked at the bakery his mother used to give him a quarter a week back from his pay, and sometimes customers slipped him a few pennies besides. But since Anne's death his mother gave him no more money from her apron at all, and none of the men at the livery stable ever gave him anything. He looked back bitterly at the time when he had had more than two dollars in his box and wondered how he could have been so foolish as to fritter it away on frivolous things like candy and a book on locksmithing that proved worthless.

He put his skewer in his pocket and sat down on the step to unlace his shoe. As he examined the bruise on his foot, he thought about the Galveston Flood and the Magic Whirlpool and resolved that in one way or another he would have at least one day at the "Greatest Exposition of Them All."

22

THE FOLLOWING FRIDAY EVENING Will and his parents left their house on Shenandoah and walked to Tower Grove Avenue, where they stood waiting for the streetcar. It was still light, and the slanting rays of the sun struck the spring-flowering shrubs of the Missouri Botanical Gardens across the street in such a way that the bridal wreath and willow trees seemed almost to be illuminated from underneath, the glowing golden green masses cut into vertical segments by the iron bars of the fence. Mr. O'Brien, wearing his black suit with a straw hat and a blue tie rather than the beret and purple cravat he had sported when he was a professional artist, stood staring at one of the black-bordered rectangles, lost in wonder at the richness of the colors and shapes.

"It might be crowded," Will said nervously, pacing around so that he blocked his father's view of the botanical gardens. He feared his father's trancelike fixation on the fence was related to his own story of the cemetery fence in Chicago and the gate that Frank could not seem to stop talking about. He had resolved to keep his father engaged all evening and not let him slip away even for a moment, and yet here they were, only a block from home, and already the old fellow was stupefied. "We can transfer to the Scott Avenue line," Will said brightly, "and that will take us right to the Lindell Boulevard entrance. It's very convenient, really, because the Irish Pavillion is directly to the right of the entrance."

His father was staring as intently at Will's collar as he had at the fence and the sunlit shrubs. Will was relieved when the trolley hove into view. He and his parents seated themselves on the smart, honey-colored canvas seats. Will attempted to give the conductor a dime, but he refused it, saying that when Will O'Brien took the number eleven, his party were honored guests. "You should have brought the whole bunch," he added expansively. "You could bring your friends even, and their relations—never a fare for any of yiz!" Will was embarrassed by the conductor's loud, whiskey-laden effusions, which drew the attentions of the other passengers to him and to his parents.

"Well, Phil," he said with forced joviality, "there's no-body like the boys from the bathhouse for hospitality, and you're an example of the finest for being a sport when it comes to the fares."

A man seated in front of them turned around suddenly and sputtered with rage. "You are criminals!" he shouted, his bearded face only inches away from Mrs. O'Brien's. "Your corruption is ruining America! You steal the fares, you boodle the very tracks and the cars! I will call a po-liceman!" He rose from his seat, greatly agitated, and yanked the bell cord.

"What are you?" Phil Moran shouted, "an anarchist? A crazy man? This here is Will O'Brien—he *is* a police-man. Show him your gun, Will. He could shoot your whiskers off, you lunatic." Moran grabbed the man's arm. "Come out on the platform—I want to punch your mug for you."

"I'm getting off here. Come, James," said Mrs. O'Brien, and in a moment they had descended from the streetcar, Will in their wake. They stood in the late afternoon sun, watching the conductor and the incensed passenger grap-ple ineffectually on the receding platform. "Let's go home now," said Mrs. O'Brien, her lips pressed together into an ominous line.

"Look, Mother," said Will firmly, "there's no sense changing our plans all because of poor Phil having his snoot full. We're already on Papin Street. We've only two blocks to walk for the streetcar that goes right to the Lindell entrance. See the Goetz Lime and Cement Company there? Mamie has an interview with Charlie Goetz, that I know from the Mullanphy's, next week."

He took her by the arm and, maintaining a continuous stream of conversation, led her to the next trolley stop, Mr. O'Brien trailing behind.

The voyage out to the Fair grounds was marked by the gaiety of the passengers, all of whom were heading for an evening's entertainment on the Pike. The fine clear sky, the sense of pleasure in the outing, the spanking-new streetcar—all contributed to creating a festive atmosphere, marked by much friendly banter among the riders. When two young men mounted the car at Euclid Avenue in kilts, the hilarity became general. Will glanced uneasily at his parents, in their somber clothing, and at their remote faces, so unlike the hearty, ordinary visages surrounding them. He experienced a sudden surge of anger against them for their strangeness, for the air of grim distinction that clung to them like must from a prestigious crypt. He wished they had stayed at home, with their look from another century, and that he were going to the Fair with Mike and Frances Egan, and their friend Wanda. He wanted to belong to this lively, modern, purposeful car of revelers—or at least to appear to be a part of it. Mrs. O'Brien sat quite still, her stiff silvery hair all but hidden by her black hat, her hands folded over her pocketbook. When Will caught her eye, she smiled at him diffidently, as if to apologize for her dour presence amid the holiday crowd.

Everyone left the car together and crowded through the Lindell entrance in time to be rewarded by one of the great sights of the Exposition—the display of electric lights outlining the buildings when they were all turned on simultaneously at sundown. A sigh of pleasure issued from the crowd as the thousands of bulbs were illuminated. Before them stretched the Grand Basin, with its flotilla of gondolas, surmounted by the great domed Festival Hall, atop a high hill. On either side they were flanked by lagoons reflecting the glittering Palaces of Electricity and Machinery, of Education and Social Economy. Like a fairyland, the brilliantly lighted Exposition floated on its fountains and pools in the blue dusk.

Will and his parents paused in awe, despite their resolve to limit the excursion to the Irish Pavillion alone. Will checked his impulse to exclaim, content that his father and mother were willing to stand for a few moments with the crowd, permitting themselves to be enchanted with the rare scene before them.

"Never before," said Mr. O'Brien solemnly, "never before, on the face of this planet. A new world, Catherine." She nodded her head without replying and after a few moments asked Will to lead them to the Pavillion. They walked to the entrance to the Pike, stopping for a child who was riding in a saddle on the back of an enormous turtle. Inside they came immediately upon the Irish Village, to Will's relief, for he could glimpse a wild sort of Oriental dance taking place on a platform a few yards away, and he suspected the half-clad, writhing woman might be the celebrated "Little Egypt," a sight he felt his parents were far from capable of appreciating.

The evening's entertainment was being held in a replica of Blarney Castle which the Irish government had erected. stone by stone, within the Village. They seated themselves at the rear of the crowded auditorium just as the clog dancers were about to appear. Will sat back and watched them with pleasure. The immobility of the girls' faces and torsos contrasted strikingly with the rapid movements of their legs, and Will reflected that their eyes, too, showed the life that the rigid posture of the trunk denied. He liked their style and the music that accompanied them made him happy, too, for the peculiar monotony of its circular structure relaxed a part of him which had grown very tense. It was not like other music, he reflected, with a beginning, a middle, and an end. This stuff reminded him of the illuminated letters in the old Bible, where lines looped upon themselves and reemerged on the other side, like so many snakes sucking on their own tails. World without end, he thought, and was glad he had brought his parents out.

His mother clapped politely for Lily Foley's rendition of "Home in the Old County Down," along with the rest of the audience. The applause for John McCormack, however, began as soon as he stepped on stage, and many people stood up and had to be asked to sit down again before he could begin. The large, dark-haired young man with the unusually wide and expressive mouth seemed as delighted with his audience as they were with him, and the music that swelled from those sensual lips stirred the crowd to its depths. He and Lily Foley sang a comical Irish patter song, "Brian Og," with irresistible charm. When he finished "Sweetly She Sleeps, My Alice Fair," Will glanced at his mother to see how she was responding to the appeal of his voice. Her profile in the dim light revealed nothing of her feelings.

For McCormack's last offering he chose Tosti's "Venetian Song." When he reached the end he sang: "I am alone/The world's my own/I want to live or die," and then repeated the line with an effortlessly beautiful octave leap. Amid the enthusiastic applause of the crowd, Will heard a sound from his mother and turned to see her hunched over, her face hidden in her hands. She was weeping. Will turned away, embarrassed. He had never seen her cry before and had no idea of how to react to it. It had never bothered him to watch Kathleen in tears—it seemed to be a mere excretion on her part, without significance or consequence—and even Mamie's occasional wellings-up held no great challenge to his equanimity. The sudden crumbling of his stalwart mother, however, caught him unprepared. He looked toward his father, but Mr. O'Brien's gaze was fixed on the stage.

Mrs. O'Brien suddenly arose, pushed past Will, and hurried out of the auditorium. The two men followed her and saw her disappear into the ladies' lounge. They withdrew to a corner of the foyer of Blarney Castle and awaited developments.

"She didn't weep before," said Will.

"No," Mr. O'Brien replied. "Dr. Kieffer said she was suffering from the dry sockets. Maybe this will be a relief."

A new throng of spectators milled around them and then disappeared into the auditorium for the next performance. They stood alone in the vast ersatz-medieval hall except for a quaintly dressed woman seated behind a table, upon which was posed a large, cut-glass bowl filled with punch and a stack of cups.

"Do you think your mother is sick?" Mr. O'Brien asked Will after a quarter-hour of waiting for her to appear.

"Let's ask the lady to look in on her," Will replied, and a few minutes later the Irish woman reemerged from the lounge and spoke to them.

"She says to tell you she is not ill at all, but rather overcome with such tears and weeping as cannot properly be staunched, and she would be beholden for the borrow of your handkerchief, poor lady."

Both Will and his father hastened to offer their handkerchiefs, and the Irish woman accepted them with a curt thanks, returning to the ladies' room. They looked at one another almost guiltily.

"She must think we've injured Catherine," said Mr. O'Brien. "Indeed, appearances go against us here." They stood looking at a large map of Ireland showing its manufactures and agricultural products.

"Did you never think of killing him?" Mr. O'Brien inquired unexpectedly.

"Ah," said Will. "There was a time when I thought of little else."

"It was your constant preoccupation," said Mr. O'Brien thoughtfully, "although, by rights, the killing was up to me." Will looked at him in amazement. The idea of his father killing a man was ridiculous.

"I know what you're thinking," his father hastened to add. "No, no," he said, as Will attempted a denial. "I know how little use I have been in my life for the acts of courage. But I thought of a gun, you see. Even great cowards can be heroes with the modern weaponry they have nowadays."

Will withdrew two cigars from a case in his vest pocket and offered one to his father. "I haven't lighted up since two years ago," said Mr. O'Brien, accepting the cigar. The two men stood for a moment, smoking.

"At home, when I was a boy," Mr. O'Brien continued, "that's how the relations took care of family problems. Before the police became so officious as they are of late. A man would not dare come ravish a decent girl from her home, for the father and the brothers would find him, and then it would be all up with him. Of course it wasn't as civilized as here."

"She wasn't ravished," said Will.

"She wasn't?"

"No, she was not. Don't you remember how she tricked us, and lied to us, and went off in full knowledge and consent?" Will asked.

"It's a strange thing. Now that you mention it, I do remember, but these last months it seems to slip my mind. I had forgotten. I keep thinking one simple thought: If I were a man, I would have killed him." Mr. O'Brien drew on his cigar and regarded the ash sadly. "I hope you don't think it's yourself I'm reproaching, Will, because it is not."

"Let's have some punch," said Will, backing off from his father's unexpected confidences. He caught a glimpse of the two of them reflected in the glass of a showcase. He was moved by the image of his fragile, pale, stooped father, who barely came up to his chin. How could such a wisp of a fellow be expected to look out for a family of ten? But, dear God, if not the father then surely the brother! Then a wave of anger passed over Will. It was not he *or* his father that was to blame.

At last his mother emerged from the lounge, head lowered, eyes on the ground. "Find a cab and take me home," she said.

When they came back to the house on Shenandoah Avenue, Frank greeted them at the door. "How did you like the Fair? Was it as glorious as they say?"

His mother answered him sharply. "That will be enough prattle about Fairs! I don't want to hear another word about it in this house!" To his consternation, tears were running down her cheeks.

23

IN THE WEEKS that followed Mrs. O'Brien responded to her family with more acerbity than usual, frequently seeming agitated and tremulous. She did not allude to their outing until one day when she unexpectedly asked Will to find out if Zonophone or Gramophone had made a recording of John McCormack singing the "Venetian Song" and to please purchase it for her if they had.

One morning at the end of June Frank resolved to take the day off from the Cass Iron and Foundry Company, where he had been hired as a tender's helper, and go to the Fair. He decided that he would be sorry all his life if he missed it and that he would have at least one day of it, no matter what consequences he would have to face later. His decision was facilitated by a plan of two of his co-workers at the foundry, Johnnie and Joey Wincklemann. The brothers were as broke as Frank and equally smitten with the Fair. Their father, unlike Mr. O'Brien, spent nearly every evening wandering up and down the Pike with his cronies, but took a strap to his sons when they expressed their wish to do likewise.

"We only got fifteen cents between us," Joey said. "How much you got, Frank?"

"Twelve cents," he answered.

"Listen," said Johnnie, "I'll tell you what let's do. We can go like my cousin Allie goes—over the fence—and save twenty cents."

They discussed the comparative merits of climbing the

fence as opposed to picking the lock of the service gate and concluded they would leave it to the inspiration of the moment, but Frank would bring his chicken skewer and celluloid card just in case. They resolved to hitch a ride on the back of the trolley to save the fare, and if all went well, they would have a day at the Fair grounds with thirty-seven cents to spend among the three of them.

"Maybe we could swipe some change," Joey said. "Thirty-seven cents ain't going far, from what my old man says."

"I can't, because my brother is a cop," Frank said.

"Listen," Johnnie said, "there's a whole lot that's free, and what ain't free we can maybe sneak into."

"Or I can pick the locks of the back doors," Frank said.

They met at the corner of Scott Avenue and Sarah early on a muggy morning. They held onto the rails of the car's back platform as far as Taylor Avenue before the conductor came after them with his stick. Frank, whose gaze had been directed backward, had his knuckles rapped. Their second hitch netted them less than a block and, after waiting a long time for a third car, they decided to walk. They were hot and thirsty by the time they arrived at Kingshighway and stood looking at the edge of Forest Park.

"We can walk on the street or through the woods," said Joey. "I'm for the park—it's cooler and they got a river in there where I'm going to put my feet."

"But we could get lost," Frank objected, "and I heard they have animals in there. Let's walk on the street."

"Frank is scared of a bunny rabbit," said Joey, "or a robin redbreast maybe will make doo-doo on him." He grabbed Frank's cap and raced across the street, followed by his two companions. Frank's foot was still hurting where the horse had stepped on it, and his hand ached from the conductor's stick. As he followed the Wincklemanns into the wooded park, he began to dislike them and to wish he was with somebody else. He remembered Anne's promise to accompany him and unaccountably felt himself blush. The boys followed the winding dirt road into the forest. They were soon covered with a film of dust raised by the occasional passing vehicle.

"Where the heck do we go now?" Joey said, when they came to a meandering pond where several roads intersected in a confused pattern. "It's over there!" Frank shouted. "The Observation Wheel! I can see it already!" His heart raced with excitement. That much, at least, is true, he thought. They hurried on through the woods until at last, between the trees, they saw the fence surrounding the Louisiana Purchase Exposition. As they approached it they heard the voices and laughter of another group of boys.

"Chiggers!" cried Joey. "Hide—it's them Irish toughs." They scrambled into the bushes and peered out through the leaves as the menacing knot of poorly clad young men, carrying sticks, crowded around the fence.

"Where's that bunch of kugelheads we saw?" one of them shouted. "I want a fight before the Fair."

"You always want a fight, Nappy. Come on. I want to see some hootchie-kootchie dancers. Give me a leg up over the wall."

"Let's just bust up them kugelheads first," Nappy pleaded, but the rest of the gang, indifferent for the moment to his wishes, hurtled themselves across the road and were up and over the wall in a moment. Frank and the two Wincklemanns watched the gate anxiously, but no one appeared, and it seemed that the foray was successful.

"Me, too!" shouted Joey. "I'm going over the top!" He sprang from the bushes and sped across the road, narrowly avoiding a fast oncoming car.

"Wait for me!" his brother called, and then followed.

"But I can pick the lock!" Frank protested.

"Pick yourself, you dirty mick," shouted Johnnie over his shoulder, and was gone. Frank was alone.

He approached the gate cautiously and glanced around with feigned indifference. No one was in sight. He slipped the celluloid into the lock as Will had done, and a few seconds later, with a great surge of joy, he pulled the gate toward him and peeked into the Fair grounds. He just had time to glimpse a sign reading "Police Station Lavatory" when he felt his arm imprisoned in a viselike grip. "We got one of them, anyway!" he heard the policeman call.

A few moments later he found himself back outside the fence, his ear stinging from the clout the policeman had given it as well as from the admonition to stay away from the Fair grounds or be arrested. As he sat on the curb rubbing his cheek, the Mexican Brass band began to assemble at the nearby Parade Entrance, and Frank wondered how it could be that the whole world except him had access to the Fair. He pulled from his pocket the ham sandwich his mother had given him and ate it slowly, wishing he had something to drink. He sat there until a mounted policeman told him to move along, and then he limped over to Lindell Boulevard and took the streetcar home, figuring that he might as well spend the nickel.

24

It was a sultry morning in mid-July. Mrs. O'Brien was peeling potatoes in the kitchen when she heard a man's voice from the doorway say, "Mother? It's me. May I come in?" She looked up to see Chris Schneider standing at the screen door and she screamed. He entered the kitchen and moved impulsively toward her.

"Back off!" she cried, holding up her paring knife.

"My darling mother," he said, "I know you're angry with me, but please listen—I had to come and see you." He pulled a chair up next to her and leaned forward to gaze imploringly into her eyes.

"I'm not your mother, you consummate demon—I'm your enemy, as long as you live and in the world to come. Leave here at once or I'll cut your heart out!" She stood up and grasped the knife in her stout fist.

"Please, Mother, please, strike me! I deserve it, only just believe me, I loved her, and I never meant to do her any harm." Tears rolled down his cheeks as he started to unbutton his jacket.

"Stop that! Leave your clothes on!" she cried. "James! Vesta! Come at once!"

"I know you called on Virginia Morris and her mother to warn them about me, and you were right—I'm not good for women. But, Mother, I was *going* to marry Anne —I swear I was. Say you forgive me. Let me be your son, and I'll promise never to marry again. It wasn't true about the twenty-five thousand, Mother." He reached to clasp her hand. "Say just once, 'Chrissie, I forgive you.' Just one time, please, let me hear you say it."

She leaned, trembling, on the table. "Go!" she cried. "Marry, do what you please, only leave!" When he still did not move, she picked up the bucket of potato peelings and hurled it at his face. He fled through the door and was gone. When Mr. O'Brien came home for lunch, he found her leaning her head on the table.

February 1909

25

IT WAS EARLY in the morning when Will and Mike Egan came off their shift and pushed their way across the snowy street to the Perry-Neustadt automobile. After they had cleaned the windows and, with much effort, started the motor, they settled into the seats to let it warm up a bit.

"Look at this," said Mike, handing his partner a photograph of a small boy in a cowboy hat astride a pony. "The photographer came around a while ago with the pony," he said shyly, "and Billie was dying to get on his back, so Frances figured what the heck. It cost a quarter, but it makes a little souvenir."

They studied the likeness together. The little boy smiled out from the picture at them, waving his gun, his feet in their buttoned shoes protruding almost straight out from the sides of his sturdy mount.

Will regarded the child's likeness uneasily. Touched by the innocent face, he wished to compliment Mike, but at the same time he wondered if Mike were not just making believe that he cherished the tedium of domestic life in order to save his pride. He could not make up his mind, but at last felt impelled to offer some comment.

"Look at the way he holds his gun! You must have shown him that, Mike." He glanced dubiously at his partner's enraptured face and could hold his tongue no more. "Don't you get fed up with him sometimes? Running around and causing the racket and whatnot?" Will was thinking of the recent dinner he had taken at the Egans' flat and the child's noisy banging of a spoon on a pot that had irritated him finally to such an extent that he had seized the implements from little Billie's pudgy fingers and thrust them into the sink, to the astonishment of the parents and the howls of the child.

Mike's reply was interrupted by the sight of Sergeant McGuire, running down the sidewalk toward them.

"I'm glad I caught you," he said, pausing to get his breath. "I was afraid you'd be gone. Listen, Will, Schneider has been shot."

The story appeared in the *Post-Dispatch* that afternoon. Mr. O'Brien cut it out very carefully and pasted it to a piece of cardboard before he silently passed it to his wife.

LAWYER SHOT TO DEATH
BY LADY FRIEND
Christian R. Schneider Killed in Lovers' Quarrel

A dispute erupted last night between Christian Schneider and Marie Geissler, terpsichorean artist, at her flat on 5100 Cote-Brilliante Avenue, during which Schneider was shot with a small-caliber pistol and killed. Miss Geissler, who is reported to have suffered multiple injuries of the face and neck as a result of the altercation, was taken to the Female Hospital on Arsenal Street, where she has been placed under arrest awaiting charges.

According to Patrolman Leonard Steeger, the argument broke out around 3:00 A.M. when neighbors were awakened by screams, shouts, and sounds of breaking glass from Miss Geissler's flat. By the time Patrolman Steeger arrived on the scene, Schneider was dead, shot six times in the chest and head at close range. In answer to a reporter's question in the emergency room of the hospital, Miss Geissler remarked that she "wished the b* was still alive so she could fill him with lead all over again."

Mrs. Gerald Tanner, the woman's next-door neighbor, told police that Miss Geissler, who was billed as "Bootsie" in her specialty dance number at the Gayety Theatre, received frequent visits from Mr. Schneider at all hours of the day and night and from other men as well. The neighbor added that "the creature had a right to be arrested a long time ago."

Services for Schneider will be held at Armbruster Funeral Parlor on Clayton Road. Schneider's wife, the former Virginia Morris, whose father is vice-president of the Merchants-Laclede National Bank of St. Louis and a prominent benefactor of the city, was unavailable for comment.

The dead man's mother, Mrs. Augustus Neidringer Schneider, for many years a leader of society and a well-known philanthropist, could not be reached at her home in O'Fallon, Illinois.

The next morning the *Globe* carried a feature about Schneider's previous marriages and the unfortunate demise of his second wife, Emma. The *Star* quoted his first wife, Lucile, as saying that Schneider was a "brute," while the *Reporter* featured a two-column heart-shaped photograph of "Bootsie" Geissler in her abbreviated stage costume. The headline read: "Was it Self-Defense?"

The Mrs. Theobald Morris who sat at her daughter's side on a sofa in Armbruster's Funeral Parlor the next afternoon would scarcely have been recognizable as the same woman who had received Mrs. O'Brien's visit five years before. The spirit had been much altered and with it the entire cast of her face and body. The pride which had filled her during that interview had all drained out, and now she sat limply, a veil concealing her features. Mrs. Christian Schneider, her daughter, also wore a veil, but she had on an incongruous rose-colored dress, which she had donned at the last moment, for until then she had been determined not to come at all. She was leaning against her mother.

The photographers from the *Post*, the *Star*, and the *Republic* were swapping stories in the lobby, waiting for the room to fill, when Mrs. Augustus Neidringer Schneider, Christian's mother, entered the room on the arm of the family physician. Her cold, aloof gaze swept over the assembled mourners without pausing as she advanced toward the front of the room. She bore herself as imperiously as if she were on her way to see her son crowned, the rich gray velvet of her fur-trimmed mantle swaying behind her tall figure as she approached the casket. She left her escort and went to the coffin. Holding her wide, pale gray-veiled hat with one hand, she bent to kiss the lips of the dead man whose features so strikingly resembled her own. At length she stood erect and turned toward the room, offering no sign of recognition to her daughter-in-law or Mrs. Morris, who, hand in hand on the sofa, regarded the haughty apparition with a mixture of resentment and fear.

"She's got no right to blame me, Mimsey," Ginnie whispered in her mother's ear with a sob.

"Hush," Mrs. Morris whispered back.

Prominent St. Louisans arrived in groups of twos and threes, and soon the German banking, legal, and commercial families were crowding the main parlor. Mr. Armbruster opened up another room, and at the same time he told the photographers to clear out or his assistants would escort them. They left casually and slipped back in again behind Mr. and Mrs. Herman Hohencamp and party as they entered the thronged foyer.

The low murmur of conversation in the two rooms quieted slowly and then stopped when Mrs. O'Brien, flanked by her husand and Will, followed by Jim, John, Owen, Tom, and Frank, arrived. They stood framed in the doorway, regarding the opulent, discreetly lighted room with its assembly of well-dressed mourners. They moved slowly across the floor, the dead black woolen of their clothing forming an advancing pit of darkness in the mass of silks and satins which glowed somberly in the light from the eletric candelabras on the walls. Frank, appearing older than his eighteen years, walked alone behind his brothers and parents, mouth and eyes straight lines in a thin face.

They approached the coffin deliberately, ignoring the dead man's relatives. Mrs. O'Brien stood staring for a long silent time at the corpse's face. Mrs. Theobald Morris and her daughter Virginia lifted their veils and, clinging to one another, watched the visitors anxiously. The O'Briens' name was whispered around the funeral parlor, and all eyes were upon them. Mr. Morris, his fleshy lips oddly pinched, took a step forward and then stopped.

After a considerable interval Mrs. O'Brien turned from the casket toward Mrs. Augustus Neidringer Schneider. The two mothers saw one another face to face.

"At last," said Mrs. O'Brien in a voice which was not loud and yet was clearly audible to everyone in the room. "At last there is a body to be shown. The mills of the gods grind slow, but they grind exceeding fine." She did not seem to notice the photographers' flash or the faces of the bereaved as she walked slowly back to the door, followed by the men of her family.